Spatriati

T0281915

MARIO DESIATI

Translated from the Italian
by Michael F. Moore

Other Press
New York

Originally published in Italian as *Spatriati* in 2021 by
Giulio Einaudi editore s.p.a., Torino
Copyright © 2021, Giulio Einaudi editore
English translation copyright © 2024, Michael F. Moore

This work was translated with a grant from the
Center for Books and Reading of the Italian Ministry of Culture.

Production editor: Yvonne E. Cárdenas
Text designer: Patrice Sheridan
This book was set in Chapparal and Serifa
by Alpha Design & Composition of Pittsfield, NH
Circular art on title page and part-title pages
from Shutterstock/Omeris

1 3 5 7 9 10 8 6 4 2

Library of Congress Cataloging-in-Publication Data
Names: Desiati, Mario, 1977- author. | Moore, Michael,
1954 August 24- translator.
Title: Spatriati / Mario Desiati ; translated from the Italian
by Michael F. Moore.
Other titles: Spatriati. English
Description: New York : Other Press, 2024. | "Originally published in Italian
as Spatriati in 2021 by Giulio Einaudi editore s.p.a., Torino."
Identifiers: LCCN 2024006491 (print) | LCCN 2024006492 (ebook) |
ISBN 9781635424034 (paperback ; acid-free paper) |
ISBN 9781635424041 (ebook)
Subjects: LCGFT: Novels.
Classification: LCC PQ4904.E85 S6313 2024 (print) |
LCC PQ4904.E85 (ebook) | DDC 853/.92—dc23/eng/20240311
LC record available at https://lccn.loc.gov/2024006491
LC ebook record available at https://lccn.loc.gov/2024006492

Spatriati

. . . never content, never centered . . .

—GIACOMO LEOPARDI

Contents

Part One

Crestiene

(Noun. Masculine. In the dialect of Martina Franca, as in other southern Italian dialects, it refers to a person, a human being. "We're not Christians—they say—Christ stopped at Eboli—Christian, in their way of speaking means "human being" [Carlo Levi]. Also, a person who professes the Christian religion.)

When a cold-air front meets a warm-air mass on land, the warm air rises. Storms are generated. Rain and lightning, water and fire. I never understood, of the two of us, which one was warm and which cold, but I consider myself lucky to have met my opposite front in Claudia Fanelli, the *spatriata*, the name people around here use for the uncertain, the odd, the unclassifiable and sometimes the shiftless or orphans, as well as unmarried men or women, vagrants and vagabonds, or even, in the case that concerns us, the emancipated.

The first time I noticed her was in the school lobby, and I desired her red hair, her moon-white skin, her prominent nose. She seemed to have fallen from another world, a world more enlightened and evolved.

My name is Francesco Veleno. I am the only child of Elisa Fortuna and Vincenzo Veleno, two former amateur athletes who fell in love during an episode of *Games without Frontiers*, and for my entire childhood they raised me with the belief that I would redeem

3

them from the mysterious accident of having brought me into the world. Many years would go by before I realized that many relationships carry on, as Claudia would have said, for "official reasons." It is also thanks to her that I would realize that there are no official reasons so strict as to require three such different people to live under the same roof, unless they are serving a prison sentence. The court that had condemned Elisa and Vincenzo to remain together despite their obvious lack of love for each other complied with the cruel law of keeping up appearances, the harsh human code that demands rigor and absolute severity in even the smallest places.

Before Claudia, reality consisted of the things they told me rather than the things I saw. I belonged to the category of those who allow themselves to be driven by others, by events, by regulations, by prejudices. Signor and Signora Veleno drove me toward a life without upheaval, peaceful, the minimum necessary to avoid suffering. That is how things had worked out for them, in the end.

He was a phys ed teacher—he had also taken up fencing, briefly, with my mother—good-looking, open-minded and carrying around a legally registered Beretta M9 from which he would never be separated. I still hadn't understood that pistol-packing middle-aged white men were compensating for the loss of their sexual swagger.

4

My mother was a nurse at the Martina Franca hospital. During a brief period in my childhood, she used to call me "Uva Nera," black grape, because in Martina everyone cultivates the pale green grape, which is pungent, the one they use to make a dry wine that gets you tipsy after two sips. She, instead, had given birth to a boy with an olive complexion, dark haired, like the peasants in late summer or the Saracens of the ancient chronicles. The black grape is used to make Primitivo or Negroamaro wines. Wines that cloud your reason. This would prove good to remember later in life, when I made decisions on impulse.

No one in my family shared my features. No one was dark like me, no one had such a high hairline and broad forehead, or the burden of laziness that kept me flat on the sofa reading inane comic books. In the afternoon I was often alone, my mother practically lived in the hospital. Sometimes she would disappear for two or three days at a time. My father, after his day at school, would lose himself in the town bars, bragging about his exploits and reliving his athletic past, and come home with his clothes wrinkled and an allusive grin, like someone who'd had an adventure and couldn't wait to tell it. But he never did. Maybe because I was afraid to ask. Or maybe because he thought I wouldn't understand.

They were different, my mother and my father, and they were different even in the verb tenses they used to address me. Elisa was a woman of the present, often in the first-person plural: "We're going out." My father only knew the past tense, and the occasional future tense when he spoke about me. Holding on to his memories: a list of anecdotes that were glorious (to him); boring (to everyone else).

On one thing Vincenzo Veleno and Elisa Fortuna found themselves in miraculous convergence: they hadn't spent a single day at the classical high school, but they had the kind of respect for it that one reserves for something you can never achieve. It had shaped the minds of their bosses, chief physicians, principals, superintendents: all of whom were brains that had come out of the Martina Franca high school. My parents said that Latin would open doors for me, and that in those classrooms I would meet the children of important families. They considered it the most advantageous option. People well acquainted with the truths of others, but not their own.

For Claudia I didn't exist in the early days. She was the tallest girl in school, her red hair resplendent on her neck—the same shade as the cherries my grandparents used to harvest in the summer and transform into jars of purple and amaranth preserves. Her eyes were of two different colors, light brown and blue green, the kind of eyes that around here are called "di bosco," of the forest. She had a prominent bone structure, with sharp cheekbones and a long, narrow face.

During recess the lobby of Tito Livio would empty, the students racing to congregate against the wall and soak in some shade. The only person in the sun was her. If anyone had observed the quadrant of the playground from the sky, they would have seen an asphalt desert with a red dot in the middle. She had some of my same antisocial habits: she picked her nose and twisted a lock of hair around her index finger. Prominent among her books was the bright-colored cover of her Rumiko Takahashi manga. She came to school listening to music

7

with her headphones on, unconcerned about what any-one thought. Between classes I would sharpen my pen-cil near her, making small talk to dull classmates with square faces and tobacco breath. One day I overheard the nasty interrogation she was subjected to by guys who wanted to command her attention. "Why are you over there by yourself?" "Why are you like you and not like us?" they insisted with a smarmy attitude, breath-ing down her neck. Claudia replied, "It's hard enough liv-ing up to my own standards, much less other people's."

Unrequited love is an easy refuge for lonely and insecure adolescents, the ones who don't know who they are yet, and I knew almost nothing about myself. Every-thing that I'd been until that point I'd kept hidden, ter-rified that I might be considered a misfit. Mine was a childhood of the playground at the country church and ragtag soccer teams on the edge of town, with coaches who were too free with their hands and priests with wooden legs who wanted you to rub the stub in the sac-risty, while in the empty church the most mischievous kids played soccer, using the altar as the goalpost.

The Velenos didn't seem to care about the red marks drawn on my legs, they didn't care whether I prayed or sinned, not even when I came back from the play-ground covered with dirt, humiliation, and the stench of manure.

The school year had just ended, and the summer unfolded before me in fields of poppy and wheat. When

I got home, no one was there. I yielded to the silence, and then to the twilight that darkened the rooms, and sank into depression. All I had to eat was bread dipped in water with tomato and salt, my supper when my mother had the night shift and my father disappeared on his ambiguous errands. I fell asleep on the sofa. In the morning the house was still quiet, none of the commotion that usually woke me up when my mother came home from the hospital and my father filled the sink to shave and talked to himself in the mirror. Empty. With my eyes filled with gunk and my throat parched, I wandered about in a fog, until I came across on the Formica desk—a classroom desk my father had swiped from his technical institute so I would have a place to write—a white envelope. "To my uva nera." I had the feeling my mother had written it more for herself than for me.

> I had to leave but you weren't home. I want to talk to you about the days to come. I will be waiting for you at the hospital.

She was using the future tense, which was not reassuring.

I set foot in the hospital for the first time, and my nostrils filled with an odor like gasoline, the mostly empty corridors echoed with the squeaking of my footsteps on the floor, the huge plate glass windows slanted downward and inside the rooms with doors ajar motionless shadows kept vigil over bodies enveloped in white. My mother appeared with her shoulders erect, in uniform, a pair of clogs, and sheer socks. Her face luminous, her eyes bright and fiery, her hair confined in a blond bun on the top of her head. She hugged me tighter than usual, her embrace of my back was like an energetic massage, the transfer of a code from her to me, animals of the same species who recognize each other. She smelled of Sunday morning and held my hand, pushing me into the doctors' room, where we would have more privacy. She was whistling a melody from the song "Vacanze Romane" by Matia Bazar. She was happy, while I struggled to steady my nerves: What was there to be happy about in a place like this? She said various things that my brain elaborated and immediately repressed, the smile with which she had greeted me gradually turning into a more mechanical expression, severe.

"We will be apart, but only for a little while, we need some space." She got to the point: she had left my father.

"Later on you will understand," she concluded.

I went back home feeling gutted, focusing on the sound that rubber soles make on asphalt.

"Anyway, she'll come back, they all do," proclaimed the blowhard, my direct ancestor, seeing me at the door brimming with unshed tears and muted cries.

Our daily routine changed, he brought home plates of pasta wrapped in a warm rag prepared by my grandmother, or reheated canned soups, burning them every time and hurling insults at pans, gas flames, and soup manufacturers. It was never his fault, always someone else's, but I still didn't recognize scapegoat seekers and I didn't know how to deal with them. I harbored burning rage under the ashes of my mild appearance, not because my parents had separated, but because I hadn't realized it sooner.

Unhinged days followed. I tried to stay home as little as possible, the windows were never open, and in the kitchen dirty dishes started to pile up. I studied at the library or at a friend's house, but soon my classmates started to keep their distance because the black grape always has a few flaws: I didn't root for any soccer team, I didn't play *Street Fighter*, if someone slapped me I put up with it, and I fooled around with priests. I was looked at with the suspicion conceded to the different. I lived on the exact border between caution and secrecy: to avoid getting caught between the best and the worst.

One day a classmate of Claudia's stopped me at the exit to the school. Giada, who had been held back repeatedly, a miniature woman with her eyebrows turned downward, like the corners of her mouth. "Stay away from Claudia, she hates you." She didn't seem sincere, but rather than go to Claudia and ask why, I withdrew even more. I walked for hours in the old borgo with its smell of chimney smoke or through the pastures cleared by reapers, in the hot afternoons of September or on the windy days of October. I looked at the town through the tobacco smoke of the cheap domestic cigarettes or clay pipes of the old men gathered in front of the barbershop. I was mesmerized by how the barber softened the bristles of his brush, made of either pig or badger hair. As the shaving cream foamed beneath the circular strokes of the brush, the old men let their eyelids droop, and their whitened lips fall open, revealing their red gums. As boys they must have been like my playground friends: strong, skinny, nervous, broiled by the sun. The barber always used to say that badger is better than pig, it should be hunted in the fall and steeped in old wine. I gazed at myself in the mirror with my long hair and first growth of peach fuzz: I looked like a little black Jesus.

I took part in the procession of the Madonna of the Rosary, I wear a white cassock, in my hands an iron cross as tall as me, a wooden Christ attached to the top. Don Bastone prayed through a megaphone, gripping two altar boys who dragged him around like a bag of trash; a dozen rambunctious adolescents swung the censers back and forth. I prayed gripping the cross tight, its metal surface chilled my hands. They eventually tore their cassocks off and started hitting each other with the censers, enraging Don Bastone, who rolled around while everyone ignored him. They stole my giant cross and chased me to hit me over the head with it. I wanted to laugh, I wanted to pray, but all I did was observe the rebellion and think that no one in the universe would be as happy as Jesus Christ watching his angels beat each other up so they could bring a quick halt to the procession and get back to their games.

I didn't go back to my games: up the narrow road leading into town, on the hill between the ruins of a building and a chapel carved into the rock, I caught sight of her.

I had noticed many changes in the last few weeks: she wore her hair short and had on men's clothing, white shirt and black tie. That day she had on a felt hat and her tie was navy blue with red polka dots, a stern frown was on her face. From down the road, still enveloped in my cassock, I had the impression she was waiting for me. The seniors at school hit on her because she was tall, because her complexion was white, and because the sprinkle of red on her head was like seeing her thoughts aflame. But what I loved was her big nose and wide mouth.

"Ciao, Francesco."

Her voice awakened the chill that comes before goose bumps. In those few seconds between her saying hello and my response I suspected a miracle, because my hands were reddened by the cross: she had recognized my love and my silent courtship of her during the past few months.

"Claudia," I said timidly. In filling my mouth with her name, I felt a pleasure that was completely new.

"We have to talk."

"I think so, too." Do you really hate me? is what I would have asked her the next second.

But she preempted me.

"What are your mother's tits like?"

"What?"

"You heard what I said. Tell me what your mother's tits are like."

My eyesight clouded over.

"Don't you want to answer me?"

"I don't know." It took everything I had to say "I don't know," because somewhere deep inside I felt like I was disappointing her.

But her line of questioning had predicted my reticence by a wide margin, so she went back to her script to get to the heart of the truth, which I was slow to understand.

"So how is your father doing, then?" She took off her hat and shook her head.

"Why are you asking?"

"Because my mother isn't doing so well."

In my mind I started to compose a new picture in which I could see my parents portrayed in a way I had never seen them. Flesh, sex, humanity. I also perceived Claudia in a new guise: she was a kid like me, and I knew nothing about her parents.

"Veleno, do you know who my father is?" That sudden shift to my last name forced me into a more dignified silence.

"No."

"My father is a surgeon at the hospital where your mother works, and now they've gone off to live together."

There are no secrets in families, only the painful, sometimes miserable, sometimes inevitable pacts to leave certain things "unmentioned." And the unmentioned contains profound truths, the crises, the struggle between good and evil, the origin of relationships and of all traumas. With time I would understand that Claudia was sharing something with me like the winning ticket of the lottery. The unmentioned was right in front of us, exposed to our innocence. I became so upset that Claudia took on a puzzled expression: the nervous rage with which she had just confessed the secret of our families changed to an unexpected tenderness.

"Veleno, are you alright?"

"Yes," I said, but it wasn't true, and she noticed.

"You didn't know?"

"I didn't know anything," I blubbered, and my eyes welled up against my will.

"So I did the right thing."

"No, you did the wrong thing," I thought to myself, "now we'll become stepsiblings, and I wanted to go out with you, I wanted to love you."

Claudia's lips had disappeared into her mouth, she took a deep breath, and as she breathed her hair seemed to grow into a halo of light, sparks of agate and dogberry drew a line that divided and united us.

"Do you feel like coming home with me to talk about it a little?"

The town was buffeted by an annoying wind, the street signs creaked. We made our way through streets filled with people who had abandoned the procession broken up by the scuffle. Everyone stared at us: a girl dressed like a man, and a boy in a long cassock that brushed against the asphalt.

"Hey, kids, Carnival is over!" shouted one guy. Others gave us dirty looks.

"Everyone's staring at us," I said.

"What do you care, Veleno."

"I don't."

"Yes you do."

"But do you believe?" she asked me, point-blank.

"In what?"

"In God."

"Yes," I said, in a high-pitched voice. I had wanted to manifest pride, but what came out was an embarrassing squeak.

"And do you also believe in that stuff: the procession, the mass?"

"Can't you see how I'm dressed?"

"Appearances can be deceiving."

"Well you're dressed like a man, are you a man?" I pointed to her navy-blue tie with red polka dots knotted around her neck.

"These are my dad's clothes." She loosened the knot of the tie, saying it was thanks to him that she'd learned how to read manga, to listen to rock and Fabrizio De André. She gave a short oration of impressive intensity.

"I love my mother, but I don't go around dressed like a woman," I objected.

"What a pity. It would look good on you."

Now she was smiling, and she was smiling at me.

I pretended I didn't understand.

We continued walking in silence, taking the long way, skirting the old ring road, from where you could see the olive groves, the vineyards, the trulli.

Strong dislike, at age fifteen, sixteen, is a wall as high and solid as hatred.

"I had come here to smack you," said Claudia.

"Why didn't you?"

"As I was talking to you I realized we'd be better off as allies." And she added, with her blazing eyes inside mine, "We have to tell each other everything."

In that smattering of footsteps, I spilled my guts. I told her that my father had met my mother on *Games without Frontiers*, when Martina Franca played host to an episode. I told her about how during training in the gym they both went for the climbing rope, and that's where they fell in love.

"How do you know?"

"I don't. I just like to imagine it like that," I admitted immediately. There really wasn't much inside the guts that I'd spilled.

When we reached her house I noticed that her eyes had stopped shining, a gloomy shadow crossed her face. I felt uneasy as she scrutinized the window looking over the garden. She said, almost numbly, "My mother might be home, you should go."

The door opened that instant, as if her mother was spying on us. I noticed how with a gesture she ordered Claudia to wipe her shoes on the welcome mat, then the door swallowed her up. Through the window I could see the silhouette of Etta, her mother, turning toward me, still staring in disbelief.

When I was alone I realized the truth: my mother had left home like millions of parents all over the world who fall in love with the right person after marrying the wrong one. I was the child of the wrong one.

Claudia was raised in candor. White clothes, starched blouses buttoned all the way up to her neck. After doing somersaults in the living room, before the watchful eyes of her father, her sweat would be dried off with puffs of scented talcum powder. In her childhood everything smelled of talcum powder, white magnesium with hints of iris.

From her I learned a new way of talking about my parents, who until then had been untouchable or evanescent. Claudia was critical and affectionate, loved her folks and a second later seemed to despise them. Her mother, Etta Bianchi in Fanelli, was introduced to me as a compulsive cleaner, a woman of antiquated principles and contemporary neuroses, the second daughter of the Bianchi Caracciolese family, peasant nobility and owners of masserie and landed estates, who over the years had lost power, money and one of their two surnames. Etta had attended a country school and in her childhood pictures she was always in muslin dresses with collars that resembled lace doilies. Scrupulous in her inspections, she would clean Claudia's room like someone seeking hidden truths in dust motes. To her scrupulousness she added habits that her daughter considered tacky: she would take sneak peaks at her diary and on the day of her first menstruation, she gave Claudia a ring, calling it Rugiadina, little dew drop.

When we went for walks after school around the borgo vecchio, sometimes I would dare to hold out my elbow, keeping my wrist against my hip, hoping she would hook her arm inside mine. We reached the roof of an abandoned cloister and let our eyes be filled by the Itria Valley and the white craters of Ostuni and Locorotondo.

My mother had become more outgoing since she'd left, I didn't dare to admit it, but she and I were also getting along better.

Claudia spoke to me about the most minute details with the enthusiasm of someone sharing an essential secret. About how much she loved the scorched paper sleeve that enveloped LPs, and especially the exact moment when the needle on the record player started to vibrate in the black groove. Happiness for her was that second of hissing on an LP that comes before the music. Her father accompanied her to the record store. He knew his way around. He also took her to see the allegorical floats for Carnival being built inside large warehouses on the edge of town amid stones, nettles, and trash heaps. He let her taste the flour and water glue that the papier-mâché masters used to attach strips of paper to the steel armatures of the giant figures. In all her stories there was a subtext: her father was brilliant and he was the right man for any woman with great expectations.

The closer we grew, the further we became from the other kids. Claudia spoke better than anyone, she read Osamu Tezuka and Banana Yoshimoto but wasn't the best in class, she was flamboyant in her men's clothing but didn't befriend her female classmates who admired or detested her, she went to mass but didn't attend catechism class, was sensitive but impervious to teasing about her masculine nose or flat chest, participated in student assemblies by standing to the side and taking minority or extremist positions. One day she would be against the strike and the next week she'd be proposing that we occupy the school. They called her Papavero—poppy—and she laughed it off, in springtime the poppies colored the green fields to the south, they were the end of school, of summer, of our youth.

There was a light inside of her, while the others by comparison seemed extinguished, identical, same haircut, same sunglasses. During recess they would go up to the roof of the school and sit, turning their backs on the majestic horizon punctuated by the bell towers of the chapels and monasteries, by the green of the olive groves and the orange of the oaks. Their names were

Giuseppe, Luigi, Salvatore, Romina, Ilaria, and Valen-
tina, but they called each other "chicco" and "chicca,"
would date for a couple of weeks, then break up and
start dating each other again, playing at being adults.

And us two? No one would call us "chicca" or "chicco,"
and we wouldn't have let them anyway.

My parish playground Christianity also changed,
she experienced religion as transcendence, I watched
her during mass when she sang the Hosannah. The
flowers on the altar, the flickering of the electric candle
lights, the sign of the cross, and the "Now go in peace."
In Exodus God appears to Moses and says, "I am who I
am." Claudia would repeat it like a mantra, filling her
chest. The music of the electric organ, the chorus of the
children from Catholic Action, the Holy Scriptures that
spoke of justice, love and faith, the paper garlands, and
even the notes of the Hosannah that echoed between
the walls of the church. We attended the blessings of
white rose petals, wondering whether this was how
the Kingdom of Heaven was supposed to be: a crowded
assembly of prayers, songs and perfumes. After mass we
would look at the olive groves behind the iron bells of
the last church before the countryside.

In that expanse of time called youth, when every
second is an avoidance of the future, I dreamed of heading toward summer on nimble feet, of riding mopeds
down the gray roads between the Aleppo pines that
descended to the sea, exploring the secrets of the yellow

sand or of certain ruins abandoned in the azure coves of the harbor, where once upon a time the women would undress and go for a swim; of praying together to the sunset beneath the silver clouds that cross the narrow strip of sky over the Gulf of Taranto.

The adultery of our parents started to seem like a blessing. I was tempted to confess to Claudia a little germ of enthusiasm: in the end my mother was perfect for her father.

Our faithless parents returned home on Christmas Eve after the flight to a masseria built of Lecce stone. Christmas uprooted their adulterous passions and rearranged them on the riverbed of the Holy Family. To realign with the world of perfect, happy families who unwrap presents under the tree and migrate arm in arm to the midnight mass was pure, irresistible inertia.

Etta welcomed Enrico back like a returning war hero, hugging him and bathing him in tears. In a mystical delirium, before a handful of relatives who were preparing to consume the Christmas feast amid lit candles, red tablecloths and two large centerpieces filled with holly, she stood up holding a burgundy booklet in her hands to deliver the revenge she had hatched and plotted in the most minute details.

"Lo these many years have I been serving you; I never transgressed your commandment at any time..." Enrico immediately saw where she was headed and shook his head—"Etta, Etta, Etta"—but she continued her recitation. "But as soon as this son of yours came, who has devoured your livelihood with harlots, you killed the fatted calf for him...It was right that we should make merry, and be glad, for your brother was dead and is alive again; and was lost and is found."

Claudia stood up from the table, ran to her room, fumbled around for headphones, and played "Come as You Are" full blast, until she could feel the beat of Krist Novoselic's bass guitar pounding on her temples and Kurt Cobain's shrieks overpowering them. Her father chased after her and stood at the door like a stone, looking her in the eyes with an expression that professed innocence. "It's not my fault if I'm happy with Elisa," is what he probably wanted to say. When Claudia and I spoke that night on the telephone, she confided, in a drowsy, melancholic voice, that she had never been so embarrassed in her life.

My mother's return to the Veleno household had less theatrical flourishes. My father actually seemed annoyed, having organized a wild New Year's Eve at a shady villa outside the city with equally shady denizens of the local nightlife, and he was already talking about me spending more time with the grandparents, who weren't doing so great. His disappointment grew even more when he unwrapped the gift from my mother: a watch with a steel wristband and chronometer, something Vincenzo Veleno would never wear. We realized that the person who had picked it out wasn't her.

It was like every other Christmas in my life, we ate with the full Veleno and Fortuna clans, my father sarcastic and nervous, my mother feigning a superficial interest in our relatives' stories, a smile that resembled the kind mask with which one refuses an offer; she clearly couldn't wait to get back to the hospital, where she had signed up for the afternoon shift on the 25th.

Elisa and Enrico had not given up on loving each other. They would meet at a masseria with vaulted white ceilings in the middle of a dark field sown with oats, and a cypress-lined pathway at the entrance. They would leave the hospital from two different areas and meet in his car. Then they'd drive down the winding roads of Paretone listening to the latest album of Iggy Pop or a rare bootleg of Charlie Parker, whom my mother with golden modesty said she didn't understand but enjoyed nonetheless. They would pass vineyards and olive groves with the windows down, belting out "Sentimiento nuevo," by Franco Battiato, until they reached the cypress path, which swallowed them up and then expelled them at nightfall, enveloped in and overcome by their love.

Elisa painted her lips cherry red and highlighted her eyes with blue eyeliner, left home very early and came back very late, I caught her several times laughing to herself. Enrico had the same nose and the same silhouette as Claudia, softened by the veil of a wispy beard and shiny pate: to his daughter he always said that he had lost his hair because his ideas grew. To imagine them from a distance they seemed so colorful to me in comparison with the gray routine lives of the parents of everyone else I knew. To Vincenzo and Etta went the bonds to the earth, the children, the practical things; to the adulterers, a happiness that I found inexplicable, otherworldly. A happiness that I would seek all my life.

The person most dissatisfied with the new equilibrium that was supposed to protect me was me. This was the price to pay, lunches and dinners with a distracted and argumentative father, too focused on himself, and a sinful mother who had to compensate for a disadvantage. The victim/perpetrator and the perpetrator/victim. It was unbearable.

One day, while I was observing my mother untangle the blonde knot of her hair, I imagined that the hands of Enrico would have known how to do a better job than the rough fingers of my father. Turning to me she said, "I know that you're friends with Claudia..." I felt exposed and violated. "It's not healthy, Francesco," she added. Then she came to me and with her eyes on mine placed a hand on my shoulder. "But I can't forbid you," she clarified, as if she had been waiting for a long time to tell me. It was the meaning of everything that would come to be: no one could stop me from being who I wanted to be.

Claudia changed. Etta and Enrico's outward routine seemed to tame her, she dressed less imaginatively, and always had her head in the clouds, perhaps to escape the hypocrisy of keeping up appearances. I could read the change in her hands, her fingers, gnarled like twigs, were always wielding the pen she used to write in her diary. I was convinced that I was one of the protagonists of her notes, but when I snuck a peek one day after she left it unguarded, I was traumatized: not a single mention of me. Furious, I demanded an explanation, and she replied, "Do you talk to trees?" Seeing my quizzical expression, she added, "The things that matter in my life I tell the trees, I don't write them in my diary. Unfortunately the trees said that there's a problem between you and me."

"What problem?" I asked, dumbfounded.

"You're not a tree."

Claudia's surrealist period lasted as long as my revenge. I spoke to her about a mysterious female presence whom I loved but could not conquer. I saw her every day in church, I told her, she came from the countryside and we spent a lot of time together, having coffee, and she had even made me smoke a cigarette. Claudia didn't seem jealous when I asked her what I should do to win her over. She shrugged her shoulders, then said that it takes two to tango, and if the girl liked me she would have sent a more explicit signal than the ones I was describing. One Saturday afternoon in winter, when it gets dark early and the Martina sky is purple and steel, we took refuge in the Blessed Sacrament Chapel of the San Martino Basilica, a womb of polychrome marble, bronze and wood. It was one of our hideouts. Sheltered from the tramontana wind and nosy townspeople, I spoke to her about the mysterious girl with whom I was falling in love, but I mustn't have been very convincing. Claudia walked ahead of me, going around the altar to get a closer look at the *Last Supper* of Domenico Carella, and pointed to the fiery wound that opened over the heads of Jesus and the apostles: for me it was a skylight that transmitted warmth, but for Claudia that blaze was a flying saucer. Two ways of seeing the world. So I burst out: "Claudia, there is no other girl, I made her up, the one I've been talking about is you."

"I always knew." She narrowed her eyes. From surrealist to realist in three words.

"Want to go out with each other?" I wrote to her on a card that I left on her desk. We were in the middle of the class of the substitute math teacher. Claudia stood up and crossed the reflected sunlight that was blinding the students in the front row. On her feet, with her back to the blackboard, she cast me in the fresh column of her shadow.

"Don't you think the Velenos and the Fanellis have already caused enough grief on this planet?"

"Being your friend is not enough for me," I said, mortified, already prepared for her objection.

"I'll give you a hand job."

"Are you serious?"

"Of course not. I'm joking."

The teacher threw us out of class, shouting that he couldn't believe his ears and would report us to the principal. Claudia experienced his tirade without theatrics, and we continued our argument in the deserted halls of the school. The muffled voices of the teachers reached us through closed doors, together with the smell of chalk.

"Francesco, we can't be together."

"I'm the only person you talk to here, there are some things only I can understand." And out came the man, wounded and extortionate, telling the world that complicity is proof of love.

"My life here sucks, but the world is much bigger than the two of us." Her eyes tugged at my soul, as if what she was about to tell me took more out of her than it would to reject me as a boyfriend.

"I can't stay here," she continued.

"At this school?"

"No, in Italy."

The horizon clouded over and the sun through the windows became an unbearable spotlight, a flash before a sharp numbness.

"You're leaving Italy?" I stuttered as if I hadn't understood.

"Yes."

She was going to London. I thought it was just for vacation, but instead she would attend the fourth year of high school abroad, and then maybe return here for her last year. Maybe.

"Are you crazy, going away now?" I was hurt.

"You're the one who's crazy, no, worse, you're comatose. I can't breathe here. I want to be where things are happening, and here nothing happens, I'm learning nothing."

"But your parents are here!" What I wanted to say is that I was here, too.

"Exactly. My parents are here. And that's the reason why all of us should leave the place where we're born." For the first time I started to think the same thing. We said goodbye as the bell was ringing. She left school, forgetting her coat and backpack in the classroom: accessories, excess, objects she could do without.

I practiced the art of repression, a technique one toys with as a child when faced by trauma and ugliness, and perfects during adolescence. But the days of May slipped through our fingers and in June we bid farewell with a good cry as the rain beat against the windows and the ostro wind whistled in the chimneys.

"Don't do anything crazy while I'm away."

"I won't. All I'll do is wait for you," I said with atrocious devotion.

"Don't be pathetic, no one is dying."

"If you go out with someone, will you give me a call?" I asked her, looking like a lunatic.

"You'll get a lot of phone calls from London." She laughed. I smiled, too, but my heart felt like shredded silk.

Her empty desk was a black hole that I stared at every day. Rather than phone she wrote letters in which she told me about her host family, an oboe player and a sewing machine saleswoman who spoke to a dog as if it were human and shared minimal confidences with her in incomprehensible English, making Claudia feel in the middle of a perennial conspiracy.

My loneliness became so intense that even my father was worried. One day he proposed to take me hunting with him, but when I saw him carefully clean the barrels of his rifle in the bedroom while talking to himself, dressed up in camouflage that resembled the brown and green construction paper we use for the background of our Nativity sets ("I shoot at anything that moves, even the butterflies"), I pretended to be sick. I stayed home to read the cards that Claudia sent me, wallowing in the excruciating nostalgia which at that age leaves its own pleasant aftertaste.

For months I prayed to the Lord, to Jesus, to reveal himself through a small miracle. I asked for Claudia to arrive by surprise from the other side of the Channel through a sudden interruption of her London experience. One day my mother, with an excited voice and a conspiratorial expression, appeared at my door.

"It's her."

"Where?" And my heart fluttered.

"On the phone." Petrified, I stood up and raced the short distance to the receiver placed next to the telephone base. So, she had her first adventure to tell me. The lump in my throat made it hard to breathe.

"Is that you, my best friend?" I heard, in English, from the other end, with a faint buzzing in the background. My mother disappeared, leaving me with an allusive smile as if to say, "Only the two of us know how awesome the love for a Fanelli is."

I went straight to the point.

"Who did you do it with?" I didn't have time to waste, I had to know the truth immediately and initiate repression procedures as soon as possible.

"I'm in love," she said.

"I'm happy for you." I was dead.

"I'm in love with techno."

"I don't understand."

"Techno."

She told me rapturously that yes, she was in love, and it was an unconditional love. With electronic music. The lightning struck on a Sunday afternoon; the next day she had class at a campus with neoclassical architecture and vast green lawns on which no one dared to tread. She had tagged along with two girlfriends, one Indian and the other Chilean, and would have followed them all the way back to their home countries, eager to share an adventure with people who belonged to such distant worlds. She found herself on the far edge of the city, in Northwood, in a hangar. She had never seen anything like it: hundreds of kids dressed in black with rattails and shaved heads, colored sideburns; weird objects were scattered everywhere, things like spaceships, iron and aluminum capsules, rusty gears and old cars crushed like boxes; the few cars in the area were swallowed up by mud, and even her own bare legs, despite her heavy combat boots, were spattered with the loamy muck. Yet the sound coming through the wall of loudspeakers at the back of a run-down liquor factory had the same harmony as the song of the sirens, the amniotic allure of falling under the trance of a spiral. Claudia followed that sound, letting herself be transported up to a creaky platform of rotten wood. One of her girlfriends was dancing with her hair in her face, drinking beer from the bottle of a slightly older "friend" whom she'd met an hour earlier. It wasn't the usual music. This music seemed to hit a part of her brain that she didn't even know existed. No melody, only rhythm and bass lines that rattled your chest, and she realized that with alcohol the basses hit even better. The people around her had a lost, innocuous air. There were no men grabbing or jostling her like at our local discotheque. She was high, her face hot, her thoughts scattered, and a distilled happiness fermented in her blood. Smells she hadn't sensed in years returned: the hairy roots of a mushroom encrusted in dirt, the branches of a strawberry tree, the small joys of Sunday mornings when her father would take her to the Advent concerts and her tongue would become moist from the cheerful sparkle of red nonalcoholic drinks. She had the sensation that time was dilating. Music, and therefore art, made nature complete. It was like sinking into a time that came before everything, a time in which men drew on the walls of caves and listened to the burning of brushwood in the fire; rhythm, that was all she needed to feel at peace.

At the end of that long phone call punctuated by the sound of clicks, there were tears of happiness in my eyes. I didn't care at all whether or not she'd been with someone. I was happy because for the first time I had sensed the existence of another life, richer, more colorful, even immeasurable, and that life was within reach and being experienced by the person I cared about the most.

"This phone call must have cost me a hundred thousand liras."

"I love you," I said, trembling.

"Me, too, Little Frank."

"I have to take the test to get my driver's license," I said, triumphantly.

"So when I come back you'll pick me up?"

"When are you coming back?"

"Don't kiss too many girls while I'm away," she replied.

"Are you kidding?" I was happy but also shocked by that flash of ironic jealousy.

"Of course I am." The line dropped.

Rather than be soothed, my loneliness grew worse. I fled to the church playground even if I was too old to play with the children of my parish. As if at seventeen you couldn't be Christian anymore. But a fever was building in me. My horror vacui was filled with prayer, with hours spent behind the carboard windscreens where Don Bastone changed. I would go there, to the sacristy, and dress up in a long-sleeved cassock flared at the ankles, with a tight waist and a line of buttons in the front. I would steal a cardinal's rochet and the purple stole used during the Advent season, and promenade through the empty rooms while Don Bastone took his nap, and outside the church the town succumbed to the torpor of the afternoon hour, in summer the crickets and in winter the chugging of the kerosene train. I would look at myself in the mirror, swelling up like a toad. But the Lord's uniform was as heavy as armor, and I was chafed by the collar and the cold buttons of the cassock against my naked chest.

One day, while I played at saying mass in the sacristy, I heard through the window the shouts of a gang of boys younger than me, thirteen or fourteen years old. I went to the window and observed them with paternalistic benevolence, like a priest supervising from on high the orderly flow of the world. They were down there, bare-chested or in ripped T-shirts, running, jumping into the dirt with a nervous, feverish vitality, raising clouds of dust like animals freed after being penned in too long. They were just like I had been a few years earlier. When they saw me at the window they shouted, "Father Veleno, suck my dick!" and with their open hands pressed an invisible head to their execrable parts. I opened the window and blessed them, making the sign of the cross in the air.

While I was intent on impersonating the pope, a shadow dressed in a cassock appeared and in a powerful voice threatened that if they didn't stop, "quinces" would rain down upon them, and in our dialect quinces mean the punches country priests deliver to restore order. Don Bastone, livid and lame, did not notice me, while the boys scattered in an instant.

I tried to undress and escape, but next to the doorway of the entrance there was a bucket and a rag, a strong smell of camphor.

"Young man, don't go there, it's wet," shouted someone in a fluttering cassock. The smell of camphor became so strong that it burned my nostrils, I felt nauseous. It wasn't Don Bastone, but Domenico, a guy who served mass, about twenty years old, give or take, with high cheekbones. He was wearing a cassock even if he would never become a priest.

"You play this game, too?" I asked him candidly.

"It makes me feel more grown up." He had a sweet tone of voice.

"You look nice, Domenico," I told him, the way Claudia had told me our first time.

"Thank you, Francesco. You look nice, too. We should serve mass dressed like this."

Domenico was tall, he approached me with a steady, reassuring expression, he smelled like mint. I was not afraid of anything, even if it was already clear where we were headed.

"No," I said.

"No," he said.

We hugged. It was a regenerative hug, our nervous shoulders and hardened arms raised no opposition.

"We're not faggots," he asserted.

"I don't think so," I replied, but my lack of assertiveness hardened him even more.

"Just a hug, it's just a hug," I said to calm both him and me.

We kissed near our lips, keeping them sealed. The blood burned our temples.

I was so shaken that I stopped going to church. I began to read the Holy Scriptures on my own, after homework I would study the Gospel, supposedly the easiest book to read, but also the one that unsettled me the most. I stopped expressing minor desires, and went back to aiming high, went back to praying for eternal life. Every sentence of the Gospel I applied to my everyday life, with the underlying question, "Am I doing the right thing?"

So much time wasted in youth, so much time wasted in the search for an answer to that question, when it was better instead to not even answer.

Claudia returned from London that June. I could sense her arrival in the city, Martina smelled of wheat and figs, and like every summer the fields and the sea became closer to the city.

I kept my promise and went to pick her up in my mother's Fiat 600, I parked in front of the gate to her house, lemons glowed from the branches overhanging the road. Through the gate came a character from the silent film era, in black overalls and a bowler hat, round blue eyeglasses and a green rattail that descended down her neck. She got into the car and without saying hello started in on me.

"Are you crazy? Why did you park in front of my house?"

"So what."

"If my mother sees us she'll have a heart attack."

"If I hadn't known it was you I wouldn't have recognized you."

"You haven't seen anything." She turned her head around, showing me a sun and moon tattoo on the nape of her neck.

"What do you think?"

"Is it permanent?"

"Nothing is permanent in life." She saw that I didn't react. "I was joking, Francesco. It's a souvenir I'll have of that crazy city."

"So it's indelible."

"Forget about it. You're like my mother."

"I'm not like your mother," I grumbled.

"Did you know she stopped speaking to me because I have the tattoo and a piercing?" And she placed her finger on a thin ring shining on her right eyebrow.

"A piercing?" I was embarrassed a second after asking.

"I brought you a present," she interrupted.

It was an English edition of *Oliver Twist* with the dedication: "Friends are like good whiskey, they get better with age, but I detest whiskey, not you."

We spent the afternoon going down the few streets where I felt safe driving, but Claudia begged me to take her to the sea. At about twenty kilometers from the closest beaches, sunset was approaching and the air was cooling down. I tried to tell her that I'd never driven outside of the city, that I wasn't experienced enough, that I was afraid, but she ordered me to do it with the sweet determination she always adopted to throw a wrench into our conversations.

"We're going to do something together that we've never done."

Fear receded because she was next to me, stroking my hand as I shifted gears and whispering as if she were confessing a secret. "You're doing great."

The grapevines and rupestrian churches, the orchards of Cisternino, then the mountains dotted with oak trees, and finally the olive groves behind which you could see the horizon, two shades of blue in a kiss. "We'll be going back in the dark," I said, with a slight tremble.

"We're together, nothing's going to happen to us."

"You've changed."

"I'm bitchier and I discovered that I detest beer," and, laughing, "I also learned a ton of dirty words in English and how to sing 'Starman' by David Bowie."

I kept the windows down and breathed in the June air. Before the cliffs of Savelletri she took off her bowler hat and threw it on the dashboard, shaking her head to free her red hair and the green lock.

"Last night I went out with a guy."

"You saw someone else before me?" I said, disappointed.

"It was a guy I saw last year, too."

I sighed.

She sighed.

"He expected me to kiss him and if I didn't he'd tell the whole town that I'm a slut who had been with all his friends."

"Why are you telling me?"

"Because this place is filled with guys like that and I'm not used to it anymore."

"You mean that in London...you were with someone?"

"It's part of life, Francesco."

"Why didn't you tell me on the phone?"

"Because they weren't important."

"Are you in love?"

"No. I don't like anyone."

"I'm not like them."

"I know."

We returned home tired, I sensed a distant irritation, we spoke about our parents. Their daughter's year in London had changed the relationship between Etta and Enrico, forcing them to confront the absurdity of their charade. Etta started to file for separation, spending long afternoons at the law offices in town with attorneys who made big promises, while Enrico reinforced

43

the fiction by remaining under the same roof, but sleeping in a separate room.

When we got to her house the lemons in the dark looked like gold and the house lights like eyes of fire. Claudia fussed with the door handle. "Why are you lowering the window now that you're getting out?"

"I farted."

"Why are you telling me?"

"Because there are no secrets between us two, we're brother and sister."

"I didn't want to be your brother."

"It didn't depend on us."

"I don't like it."

"You're boring, Veleno, and besides, I just farted again."

"Enough, stop it!"

"You'll like it, you'll see."

"What, your farts?"

"No, London, Europe, the world, life outside of Martina."

When I got home I opened the Gospel with its leather cover on the bedside table. At night I often gave myself over to a sentence I'd pick out at random when I slipped under the cold sheets, and that night the book opened to Matthew, chapter 7, verse 13: "For wide is the gate and broad is the way that leads to destruction, and there are many who go in by it."

During the last year of school our relationship became even more intimate and desperate. I would confess to her how many times I had jacked off in the past week, how many times I had rubbed one out on the sofa while my parents were watching television. And she, serious, after observing me, with a theatrical shake of her head would burst out, "So did I!" I told her a lot but not everything, I didn't confide in her the half kiss with Domenico, so unsettling that it aroused certain fantasies along the same theme: the young priest shouting the words of the Passio Christi into a megaphone, the son of the picture framer and a crossing guard hanging from painted wooden crosses in the Cinema Nuovo piazza, the thighs of the centurions, the torso of Christ on the cross, impersonated by the son of an air force officer, the half-naked shoulder of Pontius Pilate, the ankles of Judas. I was discreet around the men who during the Passion ("No wonder it's called the Passion," I thought) marched with olive branches, torches and pointed poles. They pawed each other, jostled and betrayed with a kiss. Violent sensations that rose like a caress of the unconscious. I kept all of this far from Claudia, but also from myself.

We hated the fashions and the musical tastes of the other kids, wore acrylic tracksuits and necklaces of costume jewelry, and read the letters of Sibilla Aleramo and Dino Campana. But once again I had to step off her merry-go-round when Michele Duranti arrived on the scene.

They met at a party in a discotheque. Their relationship was announced to me through an obvious, innocuous question.

"You and I aren't going out tonight, do you mind?"

"Why are you asking?"

"I only feel right with you." For me this was love, I let it suffice for me, but she added, "His name is Michele, we want to see if it'll work."

"Who is he?" I pressed, maintaining my demeanor as best I could.

"A musician. He's thirty."

"Maybe a little too old," I commented, with a hint of annoyance.

"I kissed older guys in London," was her boastful reply, maybe it wasn't true.

"Now we're in Martina."

"I can take care of myself."

Michele Duranti was no head-turner, but he was solid and had sufficient experience. He always wore the same hoodie and when he played at pubs with his band of overgrown adolescents he flaunted a T-shirt that said, "My head is empty," a surprisingly sincere acknowledgment of who he was.

Claudia urged me to follow her to these concerts at bars with feral humidity and indecent acoustics: cellars, garages, dive bars. He spewed garbage into a microphone, saying *testing one two three*, then played an electric guitar accompanying the vocalist in rabid half-assed verses. Claudia was enraptured, and she helped him to cart around the instruments, wearing a hoodie like him and stuck her hands in her torn jeans while he brandished his guitar. On Saturday nights she waited for him all alone on a stone wall, rolling a joint. There was only one thing sadder than the concerts of Michele Duranti's band: the ends of the concerts of Michele Duranti's band, the moment when all that remained was the shouting of the musicians breaking down loudspeakers and the scraping of instrument cases being dragged toward the decrepit cars left on the unpaved surface of a parking lot.

When word got out that Claudia was dating him she became the most popular girl in school, because love is a passing fancy, as volatile and contagious as a virus.

Claudia dyed her red hair an austere mahogany, tied it back, wrapped a black scarf around her neck to cover the tattoo, and removed the piercing. She didn't talk to the other kids outside of school, and when she spoke to me, her anxiety about being seen made her voice shake. All her freedom was in the books she carried in her canvas tote bag, like *Caro Michele* by Natalia Ginzburg because in that title, perhaps, she was seeking a truth that could also speak to her.

Michele Duranti was an adult who treated her like an adult. He let her drive his car, let her watch the band's rehearsals, allowed her to work off the books at his clothing store on weekends. He wanted her with him when he met with suppliers or discussed a gig for a night. Claudia eased into him like a person seeking shelter from her own adolescence.

Unfortunately the people we like can be horribly different from what we expect. Michele Duranti, raised in the petri dish of patriarchy, was possessive, bulimic with tenderness, narcissistic, and bullying. He constantly pushed her to choose between him and the theater, between him and the school trip, between him and the senior party. Between him and me. Even if it hadn't happened yet, we could feel the moment approaching.

One Saturday night at the public garden, I was drawn by the shouts of a crowd of boys inciting two guys to fight.

Between the palm trees and a ruined trullo surrounded by gerbera daisies, two shadows were wearing each other down in a fight to the death until they blended into a single shape. One tried to throw the other to the ground. I had no love of brawls, but this one involved me. One of the two was Michele Duranti, who would soon get the better of the other. Claudia was crying on her knees between two girlfriends who held her back, shaking her head and trying to exonerate the boy at whom Michele was shouting to never do it again.

Word of that ugly scene reached the ears of Etta and Enrico. They reconciled the hope of separating Claudia from Duranti. They didn't know that this would instead persuade Claudia to give in to Michele. We were too young to understand that both foresight and detachment are useless when the passions rage, or when you are so disappointed and angry that you want to set fire to everything you don't like. Claudia aspired to set fire to the hypocrisy in which she had been raised, the feelings of shame and guilt. I didn't know how to understand her conflict, I only noticed that she was in danger, because I was a coward and a man (a man in love often has the armor of a savior and the substance of a preacher).

"Who did that to you?" I asked her one afternoon, pointing to the dark mark concealed beneath her sunglasses. I already knew the answer.

"You guys have to leave me alone," she replied. And there, in that plural, lay her truth.

———

I went back to beseeching the Trinity, going to all the churches in town praying that they would break up. At San Domenico I recited the Act of Contrition, at Madonna del Carmine the Salve Regina, at Sant'Antonio the Our Father, at Cristo Re the Glory Be to the Father, and finally at the Baita church, where on Sundays the Fanelli family washed away their sins, I beat my chest to the Hail Mary.

My prayers were answered.

Like all of the great turning points in Claudia's life, it arrived suddenly and unexpectedly. They were by the sea, no one was around for kilometers, and for no reason he pulled her hair. It was a gratuitous, arrogant gesture. She reacted and slapped him across the face; at that point his eyes lit up with an ominous glare. He pushed her down on the sand, then his hands reached her neck and started to squeeze. She couldn't breathe. The gray sky turned black. She remembered when she was a little girl and her mother would help her to pick cyclamens on the side of the road. From far, far away came a bright pink that faded, then another apparition: her father placing her on his shoulders so she could touch the big head of a papier-mâché puppet, and he was pink, too, pink everywhere, but always fading, Mamma and Papà farther and farther away, and from that pink a force was unleashed: she grabbed the wrists that were pressing against her throat and squeezed his veins and bones until she was loose and ran.

She confided that she had been saved by *Caro Michele*, when Natalia Ginzburg writes that the important thing in life is to walk away from the things that make us cry.

On the days after the end of her story with Michele Duranti, Claudia wandered around town with the martial solemnity of a spirt trying to get back up and regain its muscles, its tendons, its nerves.

"Why don't you like him anymore?"

It was a hot bright day in June, we were waiting to take our high school final exams with the awareness of a blade that cuts time in two.

"I don't know, he did too many drugs, had awful taste in music, didn't understand the things he was reading," she told me, and her eyes grew moist, then she started to walk, brushing the iron tips of the railing with her fingers, as if to count them, until we reached the gate to her house. "Anyway," she added, "I've learned a lot of things." She flashed a grimace meant to be a smile, but didn't quite make it.

With a handful of days left until graduation, Claudia changed again, dyed her rattail blue and cut the rest of her hair short. She had stopped studying what our teachers assigned—Pascoli and D'Annunzio—and started reading Elsa Morante and Dario Bellezza. In contorted poses she pored over tiny volumes of contemporary poets bought at the newsstand and gave me commentary on the verses that touched her. With a preamble like this our final exam could only end in defeat. The Greek translation—Zeus portrayed by Homer as a lazy libertine—seemed to harbor a threat, as if it were alluding to our future. Claudia passed me a crumpled sheet of paper with the translation and a note ("Lucian of Samosata was a guy like us") that I copied, interpreting it unfortunately as a sentence from the translation. Which raised suspicions.

During the oral exam they asked for an explanation, then told both of us that we had done a perfect translation but that our grade would be split in two. I bowed my head, speechless, Claudia, instead, stared right back at the commissioner's severe gaze. Life was enormous and waiting only to be devoured as soon as that annoying obligation had been fulfilled. The only one interested in grades was Etta with her lazy afternoons at the hairdresser's playing that ruthless board game where the townspeople trumpet the lives of their children like horses at the starting gate of a race. In the end they gave Claudia the same grade as me, eighty-five, which in the Neapolitan Smorfia stands for "souls in purgatory."

We couldn't decide whether to go home and communicate the not-exactly-thrilling news of the grade or get drunk and celebrate the end of that life of obligations. Our meeting did not last long because she interrupted every useless debate about the near future by looking me in the eyes with a sarcastic smile: she asked me why I still hadn't told her the big news that she had come to hear.

"I don't know what you're talking about."

"There's nothing to be ashamed of, I'm really happy for you."

"Huh?"

"Everyone says that you went with Domenico, the one that serves mass at your parish."

"I can't believe what you're saying!" I worried how rumors like that in town meant a death sentence, I could never set foot in the parish again without someone pushing me and tugging on my right ear shouting, "Faggot." "It's not what you think," I croaked.

"You shouldn't lie to me." She caressed me with the knuckles of her hand. "Don't be ashamed. Everyone has his own impulses. Me, too. Once, when I was a little girl, I fell in love with the girl sitting next to me in class." Her reassurance felt like the warmth of a cigarette lighter on a freezing cold night.

"We're many things during childhood," I replied bitterly. Finally, in a low voice, my mouth dry, I said, "In September I'm entering the seminary."

I saw her lips move, a slight puffing of her cheeks, as if she was gathering her breath.

"I'm going to become a priest!"

"Are you serious?" she insisted.

"I'm joking, of course."

Fog settled over the horizon of my future ambitions. So I pursed my lips and kissed her.

Part Two

Spatrièta

(Adj. Meandering, aimless, interrupted, it is used to describe interrupted sleep: *u sunnə spatrièta*. It can also mean foolish, unresolved, alienated, disordered, scattered and uncertain. The Martinese-Italian dictionary of Gaetano Marangi provides this example: *Lassə' apirtə u jaddənèrə e lə jaddi nə sə spatrajĕrənə int'a və́gnə*, "He left the chicken coop open and the hens scattered through the vineyard.")

Martina Franca is one of those towns that's big enough to shelter you from unpleasant situations, except for flagrant carelessness. One morning, in the vicinity of the parish, I ran into Michele Duranti, with gold chains around his neck and a tangle of snakes tattooed on his arms. I was going up the church steps and admiring the faces on the playground and the tirades of Don Bastone, getting ready for the days of June winds bearing sand and wheat. A part of me was already aware of what he was looking for, but another part buried that awareness beneath my sense of guilt and fear, I felt like an undeveloped creature: I still did not know that there are very different ways to desire someone, and had not considered the possibility of loving Claudia while at the same time craving the kiss of a seminarian wearing a cassock.

If you wait for something to happen the very worst thing will. Michele Duranti thought I was Claudia Fanelli's new boyfriend.

"Are you going to make Veleno her last name?" he asked, threatening, clicking his tongue.

I answered "Yes," without glancing at him, in observance of the rule to never contradict someone stronger and more desperate. I stared at the snakeheads on his biceps and ruminated on the bitter injustice he was about to mete out.

"You know what you are, Veleno?" he continued, with the allusive air of someone who knew my destiny better than me.

"I wouldn't know."

"You're a dickhead."

I stayed silent, he had bad breath.

"So," he pressed on, "you've got nothing to say, dickhead?"

"N'dd," I said, which in my dialect is a way of saying nothing. Answering with that guttural, bestial word gave me the time and strength to walk away. Dialect made Duranti miss the one second that separates decision from doubt. I moved slowly in the opposite direction, just as Claudia had done when she left him, with the backing of a novel. He hollered nasty sentences but didn't follow me, his many words did not have the same weight as my one.

"You weren't a coward, just wise," Claudia consoled me on the overlook that offered a panorama of Murgia. It was the longest summer of our lives, the one before university, a period of great expectations in the run-up to the new millennium. We exchanged ideas about poetry and music (do David Bowie and Iggy Pop have anything in common with Rimbaud and Verlaine?). We had superficial knowledge and high ideals, looking at a future filled with fear and possibility (me), hope and determination (her). Our lives hadn't changed after the first kiss, which was also the last. We had tried to like it, warm and dry, superficial, grazing the lips. We loved each other in a different way, but we did love each other.

At every sunset we went our separate ways home to our domestic charades. Etta bore down on feelings of guilt, the devoted wife and the cheating husband who sooner or later would have to pay for his disloyalty to the marital vows. In my eyes they were a couple as improbable as my parents. They had fallen in love on the train to Martina Franca in their university days. Enrico belonged to a family of lacemakers and embroiderers. On the train he noticed Etta with her lace collars and cuffs as she diligently wiped down the spot where she wanted to sit.

"In your opinion, is it possible to fall in love with somebody out of tenderness rather than passion?"

"No."

"Well I was born to two people who have tender feelings for each other, but have never really been in love."

I imagined him walking toward her with a silk handkerchief in his hand, his crown of hair still dirty blond. "My name is Enrico and you lost this," he says to her. "I couldn't figure out what I'd done with it," she brushes him off. "Yes, you lost it a while ago, I found it on the ground and had it laundered." This is how we portrayed them in the tireless game of reinventing the lives of our parents before they knew the love that would drive them to be wild and secretive.

After a summer storm, the kind that marks the ambiguous border after which the days grow shorter, we took shelter at my house. An upheaval in our routine of walks and secrets in the open air. The house was empty, Claudia scanned it with her eyes, her nose pointing toward the bedroom where we would change, furtive glances at photo albums and bookshelves. "My house is disappointing," I thought. There were no books, just knickknacks stacked here and there. But she was looking for traces of the woman who loved her father. Freezing, we took off our clothes, unabashed, naked except for the smell of rain, bare feet, and wet hair. Then she grabbed the hair dryer like a gun and shot a blast of hot air at me. She laughed, seeing me tousled by the scalding wind that blew on my hair and face. I felt a sense of fullness.

She confided that her father had opened a bank account in her name and deposited one million liras in it. One million! The amount seemed excessive to me, I couldn't even imagine it, and advised her to hide it in a wall. I turned off the hair dryer and a heavy silence pressed down on our shoulders.

"I'll take a trip," Claudia said.

I tried to dissuade her, on the basis of the most craven of scruples.

"Do you want to enjoy the money in the grave?"

"We have plenty of time ahead of us," I insisted.

"No, there is no time, Frank."

Claudia turned on the radio but only found the news: life imprisonment had been requested for Giulio Andreotti, the pope had fallen in love with Bono's glasses, some people had voted *yes* to sex between prisoners. She lowered the volume. "The crickets sound much better." The sky had cleared, we went out, leaving the house in turmoil.

"There is no time," kept humming in my head.

Dinners with my family after graduation were torture, because they had turned into celebrations of unsolicited advice. On every occasion there was an edifying speech from Veleno senior: one night he came up with the story that he had invested time and money in my studies. "The moment has come to settle the account and pay me back with an exemplary choice of university." What solemnity, what a surprisingly refined expression from the gunslinger of Martina, Texas.

61

I had always envied him, that air about him, so active, so dynamic, so unaffectedly practical. Often this led to petty attitudes that I didn't contest, tolerating them with that mix of passivity and resignation characteristic of only sons tormented by competitive fathers seeking confirmation of their genetic supremacy.

Cheerful, having had his fill, he changed the subject, my choice of university didn't really matter to him, and started to gloat about his exploits at school (a rubber lizard in the janitor's drawer). My mother, from the other end of the table, remained silent, her fork never approaching her mouth. On her white plate, green cucumber was in one corner, red tomatoes in the opposite, and then some onions and capers.

"While we're on the subject of investments, Claudia's father opened a bank account for her," I said to needle him. My father's glazed eyes crossed mine, filled with defiance. "And he deposited one million liras."

"Well fuck me," he commented with the bravado of the child crying out that the emperor is naked, "they're rich." He drank a sip of wine, beat himself on the chest, held his breath and snickered at having short-circuited a burp. The child wasn't a child, and we didn't need anyone to point out the naked emperor, whom we both could see.

I looked at my mother. "You're not Claudia, your father is not Enrico" was written on her face.

"You could open up a bank account yourself," she said. "But then tomorrow you have to get a job." She was mad at me.

"Yes. I'll get a job," I said half-heartedly.

"Francesco? Get a job?" my father intervened, scandalized. Through the window came a jingle: the ice-cream truck. "Gessyca Gelati, Gessyca qua, Gessyca là, Regali e Gelati, Gelati e Regali, Gelati, Gelati!" A cheerful, catchy melody, an irresistible invitation. My father stood up and improvised one of the performances that his students supposedly never tired of. He jiggled to the rhythm of the refrain, and with every burst of "Gelati" from the loudspeaker he shook his hips, until the music was swallowed up by the drone of the cars on the ring road. Then he reached out his hand and arm toward me, as if to pass me an object that I couldn't see.

"Go be a dancer."

"Let's hope he dances better than you," my mother said.

"I might not know how to dance, but at least I've never eaten from the plate of others."

"The plate?" my mother chuckled bitterly, "how can you stay married for twenty years with one plate? Wouldn't it have been better to marry, I don't know...an Oriental carpet...or a teaspoon, can you see yourself married to a teaspoon?"

"Always exaggerating, Elí." When my father called her Elí, it was a fake surrender, he wasn't taking her seriously.

"I'm a plate filled with cracks," my mother said, her eyes staring past her husband and her son, the four-ingredient deconstructed salad took on a new meaning.

"Let's not fight, Elí." My father wanted to stay calm, but his breathing became quicker. "That great man, your doctor, gave a million to a little girl and now he's the idol of you two, 1999 father of the year."

"Enzo." Pronouncing his name with a roundness that was a prelude to a harsh rebuke, my mother said, "I'm about to become unpleasant."

"Let's hear it."

"A father should discuss concretely..."

"...concretely..."

"...his son's future, talk to him about what to major in."

"You could do it yourself when you're not so busy at the hospital."

"You're the teacher, I'm just a nurse," she said, with an unnerving humility.

"Yes, a teacher of bullshit."

Stop it, I wanted to scream, but the Gessyca Gelati ice-cream truck erupted once again with its music.

RegaliGelatiRegaliGelati

My father didn't sit around to hear more. He danced his way to the living room, performing for a world of invisible spectators, which is why it was impossible to dislike him.

"When he was young he used to be fun," she said, sitting still as a stone, almost, inside a light blue suit that showed off her long neck. "Now he's become tragic."

But the eyes of Elisa Fortuna in Veleno were hyacinths that opened to the sunlight. For a brief period that sunlight had been my father, but now it was Enrico. Those hyacinths had seen the people of my town get sick, recover and sometimes die, they had tended to and embraced their grief. There was a world that my mother bore like a second skin, and she'd become callused. Elisa Fortuna had become hardened in character and discipline. A callus is a thickening of the skin, an attempt of the cells to defend themselves from the pressure that in medicine is defined as a "mechanical insult." There were many of us who were *mechanical insults* around my mother.

"Are you seeing her?" she asked.

"I don't understand." But I did.

"Are you going out with Claudia?" It was hard for her to utter the name of her lover's daughter.

"No," I replied, lowering my head but continuing to look at her face through the corner of my eye. "But I wish I was," I added.

"I thought so."

"I love her, even more than I love myself."

On her face I read the clear and serene expression of relief.

On the card she left me with the keys to her car, she simply wrote, "To Francesco."

She no longer called me "Uva Nera," and even if by now I was an adult, I minded. I dreamed that she would see me as a stranger or a foreigner who intrigued her, I dreamed that she would hold my hand the way she did when we went into the sea. But she had developed a new form of love: complicity.

Claudia and I ventured out, in fact, with the special permission of the adulterous parents but against the wishes of the ones betrayed. The warm air of a late summer afternoon a couple of miles from Taranto, the droning of *Artificial Intelligence* inside a dilapidated old factory, on our way to an underground party inspired by Spiral Tribe, loudspeakers two meters high and mud up to our ankles for three straight days.

We crossed the lunar plain of Orimini, a stretch of low Italian oaks between enormous white masses, flat stones broken up here and there by a wild blueberry bush poking out. The rubble of abandoned masserie and a grove of giant Macedonian oaks where clusters of freaks from every corner of the region would dance for days. The sky was filled with streaks of rust, and the steel mill announced its presence through the stench of rotten eggs. We drove as far as the line of cars on the side of a road marked by the jagged half-moons of a stone wall. Claudia had been quiet the whole ride, I softly patted her naked knee. She was wearing soccer shorts and combat boots, a sleeveless T-shirt and her hair down to her shoulders.

"My mother gave me a loculus in the cemetery as a present." She enjoyed breaking moments of silence with loud announcements like this.

"A gravestone?" I parked and looked into her eyes to see how much truth there was in what she was telling me.

"A gravestone, my name in gold letters is already there for all to see."

Pulling her hair back to rein it in with a white rubber band, she got out of the car with a leap.

"Are you sick?" I asked, fearing that a terrible revelation lurked behind that information.

"No."

"Then your mother is sick."

Claudia shook her head as if to say there was nothing she could do about it.

"Everyone gives what they feel."

"What does your father say?"

She sighed. "He gave me that money to wash his hands of me." We sat on the hot hood of the car, the rave music in the distance sounded like the scratching of an army of locusts.

"What did you want from him?"

"A trip."

"You were in London for a year."

"A trip for me and him."

"He can't?"

"He doesn't have any time. His free time is for your mother." A bitterness fell over her that embarrassed me, and I was ashamed of having put her in the position of having to repeat it to me.

We walked as far as the grove, crossed a bridge over a dry riverbed as the music began to bury the song of the locusts, the trees embraced us in their shade. I noticed a couple dozen half-naked bodies flinging themselves about, rubbing against the black loudspeakers, as if they offered oxygen for survival. A girl with a giant red poppy printed on her T-shirt came toward us, like an apparition, green hair, skinny wrists. "Everyone free!" she shouted, the breathless howl of a person running out of gas and drawing on their last reserves. Claudia obeyed in her own way, taking off her T-shirt and leaving her bra on. "Didn't you hear what I said? Everyone free," she repeated.

In the distance a gang of kids was running. They'd gotten wet and in their hands they were holding white and black stones.

"They're all nuts," escaped from my mouth.

"They're free." Clauda corrected me. The girl in the T-shirt took off her clothes, unhooked her bra, and her white breasts shone beneath the rays of filtered sunlight. Then from a bag she extracted an object as if she were handing us an illegal item: a yellow plastic whistle. "Blow into it. Join in our noisemaking, noise belongs to everyone." She had eyes that looked beyond, far beyond, toward a future where noise was the soundtrack on the road to ecstasy.

I spent the first hour looking around and trying to understand what I was hearing. The whistles kept savage time with the tribal rhythm of the loudspeakers, the saturated textures, the repetitive pace. Techno music distorts time, shrinking it to a continuous present, it was the music of prehistoric humans, of the hunters and warriors of a primordial world, of fires ignited with flint. I understood why revolts were fought to the rhythm of the drumroll.

There were about twenty of us, swaying with the same movements our grandmothers used to make so they would be allowed to dance by themselves, pretending they'd received a fatal bite from a tarantula. "Only drink from sealed bottles," Claudia warned me. I protested, but once inside I appreciated her concern.

She stripped again and again and put clothing back on at random, because her unguarded body felt exposed to the Scirocco breeze, to the breath of people like her. I ended up wearing the tight T-shirt of a much smaller boy, Claudia a Hawaiian shirt. I looked at her neck, her hands, her pink tan line.

Then I lost sight of her. My heart racing, my tongue dry, an invisible weight on my chest, my knees wobbly: a kind of panic attack that kept me from asking for help. I would learn as an adult that panic is a form of repressed libido, and neuroses are a bodily reflex in the face of danger. Was this my life without Claudia? A terrifying solitude from which not even asceticism would redeem me?

I ran through the woods for a long time, relying on the spirit of survival, and only when I was about to end my search did I find her, closer than I had thought, hidden inside a small ditch, supine, with her fingers intertwined.

"What are you doing?" I shouted at her.

"I'm testing my new grave."

"This isn't funny." I was tired and angry.

"Come below the earth with me, my dear friend. Come. Let's see how it feels playing dead together."

I would have followed her to the bottom of the sea, and in a flash I found myself looking at the sky, lying down in the ground, amid the pointed leaves of the oak tree and the dampness of its roots.

"They dig these holes as a resting place for their buddies who dance. They dance for days."

"For days . . ." By this time I expected anything, the music entered us the way the earth absorbs the rain.

"Don't you think that playing dead is one way not to be afraid of it?"

I didn't answer. It's only when you're young that you can talk so seriously and at the same time so heedlessly.

"I'm going to go to college in Milano."

"Why Milano?"

"Because it's far, but it doesn't seem far enough. I've decided to try and study business at Bocconi University."

"Why are you telling me now?" Claudia had spent the whole summer without telling me such an important thing.

"I filled out my applications in London, when I was managing the little money I had to live on . . ."

Golden blades of straw gleamed in her tousled hair.

"Did your father make you?" I asked, while she was lying there with her hands joined over her belly button and her eyes lost amid the oak branches that covered the sky.

"No. He and my mother are still convinced that I'm going to study Italian or medicine."

"I was convinced that you were interested in literature," I told her, with a pang of disappointment.

"It's not enough for me."

"Well, since when have you cared about business?"

"My father gave me money, he opened a bank account for me, he took me to the bank. I want to show him that I'm taking his present seriously."

I was confused. The music in my ears had turned into an annoying rumble.

"I want to understand why we have rich and poor. Philosophy isn't enough for me."

"A Marxist at Bocconi University! A cog in the giant wheel of the ruling class!"

I heard her laughing through her nose as if she was suppressing it.

"If that's what you think I won't try to change your mind. For me it's a question of self-defense. Studying business is like judo."

"Judo?"

"To defend yourself from the vicious. I don't want anyone to boss me around."

She was fleeing from her parents. The flight could last as long as a rainbow or forever. To study business in a city that we southerners see as the mecca of affluence and cosmopolitanism. She was enrolling at a prestigious, competitive university to prove to herself and others that she was destined to have a master, and that she was the master of that destiny.

The police sirens erupted before nightfall, the sky was magenta. The electric generators that powered the music were turned off, but the blowing of whistles continued for another hour or more while people scattered, pushed out by about a dozen police, although they seemed to be twice as many. "We're not hurting anyone," Claudia shouted. I also wanted to yell what was so bad about a hundred kids dancing half-naked in the woods, but once again Claudia had gone there first. I looked at the serious faces of the policemen IDing the partiers. To one side the pale, narrow faces of the dancers, to the other, the wrinkles of the men in uniform, forty-year-olds assigned to repress that gathering of deadbeats. The only woman had her ash-blonde hair tied back, a stern expression on her face, and the bored gaze of someone reciting a part.

Claudia and I, indifferent, allowed ourselves to be identified: to have a police record at age nineteen was a kind of adventurous debut, worthy of telling everyone when we got back to town.

But our car was gone.

Everyone had left and someone had gone home with my mother's automobile.

"Shit happens. Let's go to the city and call someone to come pick us up, then I'll file a police report, they can usually find cars like yours," said Claudia, exhibiting the same serenity as when she'd buried herself alive.

"From here it'll take a couple of hours but we'll get there in time to catch the last train." She wanted to reassure me, even if it was obvious that the trip wouldn't be easy. The light from the smokestacks started to rise beyond the last hill before the dark sea and a sudden mistral wind cleared the air. Claudia pulled out a flashlight and I noticed her pale, nervous arm. We started to walk.

"I've never been on a country road at night," I said, with a tinge of fear.

"This isn't the country," she reassured me.

"It's not the city, either," I rebutted, pointing at the indistinct darkness all around us.

"Maybe we're lost," she said nonchalantly.

"Are you joking?"

"Yes, Francesco, I always joke when I'm scared."

It was an unforgettable walk.

We put everything behind us: the stolen car, the lies, Milano and Bocconi. We marched on, using as our lodestar the steel mill and the clouds of reddish-orange smoke it expelled into the darkness. We got into a long debate about our separated parents at home. "All my girlfriends' parents are separated, it's just that they keep on living together," she told me. In that period Claudia's truths about love were already jaded. Eternal love didn't exist and I was still a dreamer who believed that it did.

On the border of Taranto the sky was filled with stars, and the red tooth of the Isola del Borgo jutted up on the horizon.

At the station we found out there were no trains until the next day.

"Now what do we do?" I asked in despair.

"We wait." Her sense of security had collapsed, too. Drug addicts, shadows of sailors sleeping on benches, homeless men tossing around empty wine boxes, seagulls shrieking as they fought with the early morning parking attendants.

A car with a metallic finish pulled up as our sense of adventure deflated. A voice from the driver's seat called out.

"Are you Enrico's daughter? Need a lift?"

An elegant man with a tan stuck his head out of the window and looked at us, or rather, ogled Claudia in a way that was both suggestive and reassuring.

"Who are you? And how do you know who I am?"

"Marco Curcio."

"Marco who?"

"I'm a friend of the family," said the man, without repeating the last name that we had heard loud and clear.

"I'm not alone and we don't accept candy from strangers." She laughed as she said this. "She's afraid," I thought.

"I don't have any candy to offer you, just a ride to Pergola."

Bingo. He knew where Claudia lived.

"Let's go with him." I was collapsing from despair and exhaustion.

But Claudia hesitated. She seemed to be more afraid of that man than of the shadows, threatening, that hovered around us.

"I don't trust him," she told me through the corner of her mouth.

"I'll take you and him," the stranger insisted as if he was asking for another hand of poker.

The seconds ticked by. After seeking approval in my eyes, Claudia squeezed the fingers of my hand and pushed me into the passenger seat.

"You in the front with him and me in the back," she said, without giving me time to protest.

"Your boyfriend will keep me awake till we get to town," said the man as the engine roared down the faded strip of asphalt that twisted its way through the countryside.

"He's not my boyfriend," Claudia specified. A hardened adult voice emerged from her, and in half a second she'd shattered me into a thousand pieces.

Marco Curcio.

Until that moment he'd only been a name. It appeared on the scoreboards of the town tennis tournament, or at the café next to Porta Santo Stefano, where I'd heard that the coffee "had been paid for" by him. He was a "signorino," which in Martina means a confirmed bachelor, but others considered him little more than a deadbeat with a fat wallet. Thirty years older than us, or maybe a hundred, counting all the lives he claimed to have lived. He said that he'd done the war in Lebanon, been the lawyer for one of the Ustica witnesses, passed the written part of the bar exam to become a judge but decided not to take the oral since it would take time away from his tennis.

At the age of twenty we all think not only that we're marching to a different drummer, but also that our drummer is a solemn high note standing out from the crowd. We contested the authority of adults, but without really challenging it: the moment you become aware of your own innocence, you're lost. When Claudia was little, her mother drew a rough chalk square on their driveway and told her not to move from there. Erecting the columns of Hercules—an expedient to keep her from running too much and therefore sweating, a limit that like every limit is planted first in the mind. For a few minutes Claudia thought the white lines were magic, and sat there waiting for permission to get out. She was freed by Enrico. "I'm locked in here," she said, pointing to the white lines that marked her border. Enrico smiled. Wrinkling his nose, he crouched down to erase a segment of one line with a thumb. "Now you're free."

Marco Curcio erased another imaginary chalk line, removing her from a spot of trouble on a summer night. To all appearances he was a man who was stable, ironic, suave, a pragmatic advisor for the little mishaps of everyday life, with old-fashioned accessories (cuff links, a brass tie clip, silver cigarette lighters).

Claudia agreed to a date.

Having a coffee with him was like climbing up to a trampoline suspended over a mystery, and she was curious to jump on and give him a chance.

To Claudia he looked smaller than she remembered, and she immediately noticed the uniformity typical of dyed hair, but blamed it on the artificial light at night that distorts the outlines of reality. They met at an anonymous café on the outskirts of town, the kind with glass showcases of liquor and metal trays of Sperlari candies, and where impertinent eyes understood immediately that they were too complicit and allusive to be father and daughter. Curcio was flattered. Claudia felt a shiver of transgression running up and down her spine.

"Are you crazy? Are you really going out with him?"

"I'm just curious. I'd never let myself be touched by someone old enough to be my father."

"If something happens will you tell me?"

"Nothing will happen."

"I don't trust a guy who goes out with someone thirty years younger."

"Don't treat me like some idiot. I know men. I know how to keep them in their place."

They went to a jazz concert in the countryside between Cisternino and Locorotondo. He looked for her hand and she let him hold it, his seemed big and warm, she felt safe from an unnamed danger. They walked through the dust of pomace and clay avenues, sprayed each other with Verdeca wine as they toasted to envious, judgmental eyes, then he accompanied her home. Claudia liked that he wasn't ashamed to be seen with such a young girl, she got a kick out of the self-confidence and irony she could see in his eyes when, while looking at her, he told the waiter that his niece was thirsty.

"Everyone looks at us, Frank. It's a weird feeling."

"You're a lot taller than he is."

"You think people see the difference?"

"Of height?"

"No, of age."

"Yes, a lot."

"Then I'll put on makeup and tease my hair, I can look ten years older."

"I'm jealous."

"There's no reason to be. For now it's just a friendship."

"Have you kissed?"

"Not yet."

"What do you mean, not yet?"

"I can't say that it won't happen."

"Curcio is a lot older, and sketchy. Not to mention his fake tan and gold bracelets. I don't like him. There's something not quite right about his style."

"Not quite what?"

"I think he's shallow, hanging out in the piazza with a bunch of lazy rich boys."

"What, are you following him?"

"I've happened to run into him..."

"Stop it, stop it right now."

"You can't make me."

"You're like my mother."

"No, I'm not."

"You are. Just like Etta the busybody."

"I'm going to keep my eye on him."

"I adore you when you're jealous, Frank."

And she laughed really loud. I didn't. I hated myself and couldn't admit it because in Claudia I had sensed a change, a spontaneity toward life that was always veering in unexpected directions. She seemed to be testing a limit: How far can I go, how much craziness can I get away with?

Curcio's car raced through the night with the windows down, Claudia felt a deep sense of satisfaction, outside the countryside was bleached by the moon. Marco and Claudia stopped in front of her front door, a lemon tree the only witness to their good night. Her hair was filled with salt from their day on the beach, she kept it like that in summer, and enjoyed sleeping with the smell of the sea on her head. He pulled her toward him to bring her lips close. She smelled the acrid breath of an adult male, and sensed nothing but that long-awaited kiss.

"So that's how it went?"

"More or less, but you can understand, you're like me."

"I wish I was like you, but I'm not."

"I'll confess something only if you promise not to pout."

"I won't. I promise."

"I don't know if I should live so far away from Marco."

Claudia would move to Milano wondering whether she should end this story that had just begun. She was saying that the person she would miss was him, not me. I wasn't levelheaded enough to tell her what was right, that some loves can survive distance and time, that on the contrary, in distance, in time, in separations, loves are inflamed. I was nineteen and I knew nothing about love, knew nothing about nothing, but I could grasp her happiness and could not help but indulge it.

In the early days she never really left Martina Franca. She spent hours and hours on the night buses that connect Puglia to Milano, as if she wasn't really convinced of her separation from home. She didn't like Milano, and had imagined it more lively and rich, a city where it was impossible to feel alone, and instead she felt more lonely than ever. She had hoped to see a new horizon, the Alps with their white peaks, but all she saw were houses and clouds, and they weren't our clouds, and they weren't our houses: most of all she missed Marco Curcio.

I didn't stop spying on him, not even after Claudia left. He gave the impression of being an emancipated man while maintaining a serene relationship with his hometown. On Sundays when the streets were empty and the dinner tables full, Curcio ate by himself at the only trattoria in town that remained open for tourists. He claimed that he had traveled the world and at the age of fifty professed to being liberated. Free. Without a wife, child, parent, or uncle. Free from certain infernal August holidays, Christmases, Easters, spent with people with whom you have nothing in common. In him I got an inkling of what independence was. He could travel, change houses and jobs whenever he wanted. He was the projection of our future aspirations.

Of that first year of university when Claudia was with Curcio, I still have the impression that it was an extension of the summer we had spent together after graduation. I can still see Claudia curled up between the seats of the bus. She painstakingly scheduled her trips home at the end of every exam. It was my job to cover for her, because she would tell her parents a different arrival in order to spend more time with Curcio, who would pick her up. The phone call would come when the bus was stopped at a gas station in Candela. I knew that stop well, on the border of the Pugliesi people: on one side was the immense plain of the Tavoliere; on the other, the foothills and mountains of the Apennines. She would sit on the guardrail and let herself be deceived by the landscape while waiting for the bus to turn the engine back on. Puglia, Martina, our skies have these sharp-ass nails that scratch, you can never leave unscathed.

It happened on one of those mild evenings in May, that fragile preview of summer, on a dark bay of the Salento coast. On a night like that Marco Curcio took her to dinner at a masseria near Lecce, and she felt flattered. She spoke to him about the university, about love. That is the exact word that she used: love. Curcio didn't flinch; with slow, studied gestures, he looked her in the eye without ever removing his hands from her naked, nervous legs. She was wearing a miniskirt, she felt beautiful and sure of herself. The candlelight lengthened the shadows of the two lovers and their voices were faint so no one could hear them.

Claudia asked him whether the time had come to speak with her father, Enrico. "I have a good relationship with him, he'll understand that I'm seeing an older man."

Curcio blanched. He removed his hand from her leg, shifted his gaze toward a distant point on the horizon, and finally exploded, in a tone that barely contained his irritation. "The Italian family. Everyone participates in this charade of useless marriages: sooner or later they cheat on each other anyway, but on Saturday and Sunday they pretend to be what they're not for the sake of the children, who dream of becoming like them."

"Are you talking about my parents?" Claudia interrupted him.

"No, in general. I can't tell you how annoying I find all that."

A singer in a fringed vest and white cowboy hat was warbling the refrain from a song on a platform. They hadn't known that the restaurant had pretensions to being a cabaret. Claudia joined in with the singer, but she had never attempted to sing a melody in public. She rocked her head from side to side while Marco Curcio looked on in astonishment. Her red lips, the edge of sadness in her eyes, the audacity of her expression. The customers turned toward her, forgetting the cowboy, who covered his face with his hat to shield himself from the unequal challenge of Claudia's spontaneous grace.

After that they headed slowly toward the car. The willows along the avenue trembled in the wind. When they reached the parking lot he grabbed her hips from behind and pushed her onto the hood of the car. She put up no resistance and let herself go, slipped off her panties and felt the heat. The indiscreet eyes of indistinct humans were watching them from a car. Claudia was filled with a powerful emotion. When he was done she felt intact, as if nothing had happened, but she was wet and cheerful, disheveled and reckless, and she started singing again. Marco Curcio could have been any man at all in that moment, Claudia's heart was too big, wasted on one man alone, there was room enough for a whole family, for a friendship, for a child, for humanity.

"Sometimes I experience certain emotions only because I have someone like you to tell them to," she said the moment she got back.

"Don't spare me a single detail," I said, knowing that only in this way could I feel pleasure in my pain.

I agonized over her reports, I compared the present Curcio to the feral Michele Duranti, feeling like I was looking at the final and first drafts of the same classroom composition.

Claudia was wild about Naomi Klein and her book *No Logo*, but Curcio responded that for every decade of the just-ended century there had been a book that explained how everything was wrong. Claudia disagreed and took pictures of herself with her face painted white at protests against multinationals just to make him mad, even if deep down he was one of those people who think they can make the world a better place.

Once while they were observing each other, sitting on the edge of the bed in a hotel, their heads turned toward each other, the warm breath that precedes a kiss, Claudia had a strange previously unknown desire that suddenly took hold of her from the tip of her toes to her tongue. Curcio's eyes were small, a bit drowsy, and deserved a better frame. "Can I put eyeliner on you?"

she asked, surprised by her own frankness. His shocked gaze filled the long silence that comes before a request for clarification. "A light kohl, it's soft, just a hint," she specified, as if he were familiar with women's makeup.

"I don't know if I'll like it," he replied, embarrassed.

"I'll make you two lines, we'll kiss a little, then I'll erase them with a cotton pad. It won't take long. I promise." Her voice was probably faint with excitement. He said no.

On one of the following days, Curcio took her to a pine grove where the tree roots were covered with a blanket of pine needles. A ruined trullo was there pockmarked with outgrowths of starflower and nettle, a place where couples had their pictures taken before the wedding reception.

Curcio was carrying a camera to take a few snapshots. But the camera was left on the car seat and they found themselves running down paths of pine needles and brambles. He trudged along with his shirt unbuttoned to his stomach and his sleeves rolled up, breathing heavily. She ran, skipping like a turtledove, teasing him, then she turned around and threatened him jokingly. "Last one there has to strip naked." He answered her with sarcasm. "Doesn't make any difference for a flat-chested girl like you." Claudia pretended she wasn't hurt, stooped to the ground, picked up two pine cones, stuck them in her bra, and then stood in front of him. "Look at these tits! Have you ever been with anyone who had tits like these?" Curcio laughed, then Claudia turned serious. Looking into his eyes, she asked him to stick the pine cones under his shirt just like she had.

"Stop kidding around."

"I want to see you with tits." And she shook the scaled and mossy pine cones.

"Are you crazy?"

"Come on."

"If I do I'll make you pay."

"Anything you want."

"I'll slip your pine cones under my shirt and play at being a busty woman."

"Yes, please."

"Claudia, I'm going to do it." And a sinister gleam shone from Curcio's eyes.

"I know, it's going to cost me," she repeated, overjoyed by her inspiration.

"Lesbian. You're a lesbian," he yelled at her, having shed his previous bravado.

Curcio didn't understand Claudia's sense of humor, which was anarchist and overtly pornographic. He remained distrustful, and distrust—the inability to appreciate the diversity of others—closes the door to everything that is human, everything that Claudia needed in that moment.

More out of pride than genuine conviction, I enrolled in political science at a university that had more marble than a cemetery. Every day I took the train to Bari, with its bicolored sea, a shade of green by the shore, cobalt beyond the jetties. I gazed at the fishing boats and tankers in miniature on the horizon, the blue curtain to the north blended in with the white streaks of airplanes. It was a city of clean horizons, and in its grandeur maintained the soul of a village. University meant being twenty years old, a never-ending party, all you had to do was exit the gloomy classroom building to bounce from one house to another, from a party of Greek students to one of Calabrians, drunken and light, vulgar and annoying. I threw eggs from balconies and danced to Ace of Base with female students, keeping my elbow firm with one hand and swirling the index finger of the other. In the evening I took the train and at night I slept over in an off-campus apartment bursting with provisions and hormones. But sleep meant having less time for fun, so you played cards or you called the professor of ancient history passing yourself off as Leonides or Julius Caesar. We kissed with the excuse that we were impetuous, drank cheap liquor, then kissed with the excuse that we were drunk, and went back to drinking, or we sang parodies of Oasis, in Barese dialect, and finally in the morning we went to the university, in a daze, hoping that something would happen, that a bomb would go off, that the Turks would liberate Öcalan, or that maybe a sparrow hawk would arrive with a kerchief on its head and beak open, ready to sing "La Cura" by Franco Battiato.

For a while I attended the sociology classes of Professor Franco Cassano: I was in love with his book *Southern Thought*, where he writes that you have to be slow like an old country train, like someone who's walking and sees the world magically opening up before his eyes, because walking is like browsing through a book rather than taking a quick look at its cover. Then I would call Claudia and always tell her the same thing. "We have to be slow like a train." She would laugh, because the trains in the north weren't slow like the ones in the south.

I never completed my coursework, I kissed a lot of girls, with some of them I even spent the night, we slowly touched and discovered each other. We lived in the same cloud of ambitions and prospects, their names were Clara, Mariangela, Mirella, they all came from provincial towns even more remote than mine, and like me had read two books, give or take, and we talked about them, then we swore we'd march for peace, for the Kurdish flag, but the next day we would put on our good clothes and attend the funeral of Giuseppe Tatarella, a former neofascist, because they called him the Minister of Harmony and he was from Puglia, or because a friend of ours had worked for him.

Claudia would call me and tell me about Curcio, who had sent her flowers or didn't answer the phone, who on the phone had seemed aloof, or who one weekend was supposed to go to Milano to take her to a Prodigy concert but then never showed up. It was always Claudia who was traveling to him, leaving behind her new girlfriends, the idea of applying for an Erasmus fellowship, or joining the world of the off-campus students.

"Tell me about you, Frank, what kind of damage are you doing in Bari?"

"Drinking and making out, university life is a piece of cake."

"It horrifies me, all books and equations."

It also horrified me, to summarize life in a couple of words, maybe because I didn't have the courage to tell her that nothing moved me as deeply as waiting for her call or for her trip home.

One morning at dawn my university life ended. It was still dark outside. I was on my way home from Bari on the bus that took the night-shift workers to the Italsider steel mill, surrounded by broken seats and dirty looks cast by the driver through the rearview mirror. I got off at the station, half-asleep. Behind an iron gate the bus fleet was in repose; the early trains broke the silence when they started to move toward the city. The cranes were towering shadows and the school's yellow lights retreated from the approaching day: Martina looked so beautiful. A car with fogged-up windows turned on its headlights, flickered the high beams in a demand for attention. I was the only human being around, the deserted city buffeted by our damn tramontana wind that makes people either crazy or as hollow as the stone hills on the road to Ceglie. I was afraid, worried about a mugging, but six in the morning is too early for delinquents. Still the car looked familiar, I had a hunch. The window on the passenger side lowered and two people appeared, a man in a beret staring at me and at the steering wheel a woman with big messy hair, but a happy mess, as happy as the smile that accompanied it. "Francesco, hop in," she invited me, as if it was the most normal thing in the world, and I was in such a daze that I really thought that it was.

With Enrico Fanelli my mother was a different person. She didn't even seem like my mother. She drove the car in a relaxed way, while Claudia's father asked me what kind of fun I was having in Bari. The car smelled of deodorant and sex.

At home we got out together. Enrico, with a hop from one seat to the other, got behind the wheel. My mother blew him a kiss leaning toward the window.

In the elevator that took us home, I observed her in the mirror, and struggled to recognize her.

"Did you make love in the car?" I asked out of nowhere. There was a secret harmony in that moment, and I was jeopardizing it.

"Things happen." In her eyes I saw the flitting of hyacinths.

"It's not uncomfortable?"

"At my age, yes. Not at yours."

How I envied the harmony in that car and how normal it seemed that these two lovers could only live their love in secret, with the blessing of the wrong lovers.

At home my mother turned on the hall lights, then disappeared into the bathroom. You could hear my father snoring. Examining myself in the mirror—two big bags under my eyes, my cheeks gaunt—I finally understood the distance that separated me from the allure of my mother, the way she'd appeared when I'd surprised her that night. When she came out of the bathroom she had on a wool bathrobe with a Christmas pattern. She was different again, belonging to the society of all the parents in the world who look at their grown children and can barely see them as adults. "Well, Francesco, we've done this, too. Now you've seen everything." And she said it with relief, as if she were lifting a huge weight from her chest.

"Maybe you're right, it'd be better for me to find a job," I replied.

Her tapered neck leaned toward mine and with her mouth half-closed she planted a kiss on the edge of my lips that was neither maternal nor erotic, and therefore disturbing, which sent me to bed with a complicated masturbation to rub out. I imagined Claudia in the car with another man, her legs enveloped in smoke-gray stockings, her ankles sleek, her body opening up to the mystery of a stranger's body, her breasts small and the patch of hair between her legs an unreachable goal since her legs never ended, I was a Lilliputian held down by strings and rocks, I was small and modest, while the features of Claudia's body swelled so much that my eyes grew blurry, the time gone by was a mineral, the future a scented glop, I came in a paper tissue howling into the pillow, "Claudia, I love you."

"How many times?"

"Once, but very painful."

In the small country church, with oak pews and a walnut confessional, the shadow of a hoarse voice assessed my own shadows, the ones I harbored inside. A different priest had been assigned to take my confession.

"It never happened before?"

"Never like that."

"Is she married?"

"No, but she's the girlfriend of a much older man."

"Does she live in sin with this man?"

"They only see each other on vacation when she comes home."

"How old is the woman you desire?"

"We went to school together."

"Have you told her you love her?"

"No, or maybe yes, but she never believed me."

"How many times have you desired her?"

"I already told you, just once."

"I didn't mean the impure act."

"For me it's not impure."

"I'm the one who decides what's pure and impure."

"I'm confused."

"By what?"

"By your questions."

"Have you ever desired a man?"

"Never."

"Dig deeper into your memories. The eighth commandment is do not bear false witness."

"It's not a sin to desire another man," I answered with pride. The confession had taken an unexpected twist.

"So you have done it."

"I stopped right before."

"Let me remind you again of the eighth commandment."

The voice had changed tone. It belonged to a scammer who seemed to know who I was and wanted to expose me.

I interrupted the confession. My adrenaline and chest going a thousand miles an hour. I crossed the nave, reached the cloister where the children used to play, but after a hole was dug in the middle where a tomb was found, they could no longer go because the dead take precedence over children.

"Veleno!" Someone shouted my name, which vibrated inside a somber echo.

Behind me a seminarian leaning against the entry to the vestibule gestured to me with his hand. "Veleno, come back here."

I trusted the voice because I recognized its tune.

"I fooled you," he said with a fresh look on his face. Domenico's expression and laughter were honey on which to lay my bitter lips. His head was smooth and white like a cuttlefish bone. He had continued to dress up like a priest and serve mass.

"So you're a faggot then?" he shouted, but holding his index finger to his nose as if to impose a lower tone on my answer.

"Why did you hide in the confessional?" I protested in a loud voice, disobeying him.

"I like to listen to the bullshit that people say."

"Does Don Bastone know?"

"Don Bastone lets me, as long as no one finds out."

"Now I've found out."

"Anyway, I'm going up north tomorrow, the air force accepted me. And I'm going to tell everyone that you're a faggot."

"Why did you trick me?"

"Why, why, so many whys. Claudia is too much for someone like you, can't you see who she's with now?"

"I don't care."

"I'm getting married to Mariella, and you don't have anyone."

"I don't envy you."

Come over here, Veleno. I have something to whisper in your ear."

He wanted to kiss me, and I only wanted to smell the scent of our first and only half kiss. I trusted him. I crossed the space that separated us without stepping on the grout between one tile and the next.

Domenico stretched out his neck, and I noticed the shorter gown, you could see his yellow socks and naked legs, waxed. When our lips were close, so close that not kissing each other had become unbearable, he opened his mouth and bit my cheek.

It lasted a second, his teeth sunken into my flesh, a cruel pain.

"Fucking faggot, you're a faggot, you shouldn't have come near me," he shouted.

I was frozen, holding my cheek without protesting while pulling myself together for a dignified farewell. He said that he loved his Mariella and that he would become a good soldier, he said other things, and that I should never have allowed myself to talk about him, or to even say that I knew him. When I looked up, I saw him as more of an adult than he was, the first wrinkles on his forehead and his lips turned violet from the effort to bite me. He said that I had to forget his name, that he would go away forever and would have a family.

Two hot round drops moistened my eyes and slid down my cheeks, scalding the wound on my face. I went home with a strange feeling that I couldn't really call actual pleasure, although it came very close. All this I could tell her. I waited for Claudia and the complicit life that was ours to spend together. I waited for the only homeland that could recognize me.

"Who gave you this hickey?"

"A girlfriend."

"Or a boyfriend?"

"Or a boyfriend, of course."

We were walking through town, so close together that I could hear her breath quicken as we went uphill, everyone looking at us as if we were two wolves, one white one dark, the red and the brown, the black and the green olives, the cherry tree and the blackberry bush.

In men Claudia was seeking unpredictability, mystery, and a tender ineptitude in life, like the literary figures she loved the most: Jay Gatsby, Holden Caulfield, Fitzwilliam Darcy or the greatest of them all, Atticus Finch in *To Kill a Mockingbird*, with his innate sense of justice. At night she dreamed of Marco Curcio's hands touching her, blue veins and reddish hairs on his back.

She stopped being so wary of the big city. In Milano she lived near Porta Romana, the traffic and the silver dawn resembled the smoke of summer bonfires in the countryside. A new and unknown frenzy made her euphoric, on the wooden benches of the number 15 tram she suddenly felt cheerful. Milano revealed itself to be a place full of opportunities, a hubbub of noises that made her feel that she was never alone. At night she opened the window and listened to the owls. With her head tucked into her shoulders from the breeze, her eyes drowsy and her palms sweaty, she felt like she dominated the empty streets while breathing slowly. She studied private law, business economics, threw herself into her work with the pride of someone who wants to prove they can handle the most punishing expectations. She never retreated from her passions, electronic music and poetry. She smuggled used books to me with dog-eared pages and underlined sentences, like Calvino's *The Cloven Viscount*. Like the protagonist of that book lacerated in two, my miserable half and my good half suggested a reckless option: either camphor or fumarole, sleeveless cassock or rainbow-colored T-shirt, ornate scented corridors or a threadbare sofa.

She in the north and me in the south, distant birds, the migratory and the stationary. I found comfort in the thought that once she returned I would prepare a nest where we could live. I remained just one step below her and always darker, more and more Uva Nera. A sensible student, she had added to the million liras in her bank account by working shifts at a fast-food restaurant where men in ties tried their luck with her. "They all have hands as small and soft as the paws of a teddy bear."

"Don't let anyone steal this," she warned me, laughing.

For months I'd been promising to take her to the trulli, where lepers used to be confined to keep them away from the city, and where the peasants hid their belongings for the long winter; now they had become vacation homes and the houses of grandparents. My own, Giuseppe and Assunta Veleno, had lived in a trullo for more than sixty years, they cultivated a tomolo of land and fed the walls with whitewash every change of season.

"What did they do to your face? Did a dog bite you?" my grandmother asked, worried, as she came toward me.

"In a certain sense, yes," Claudia cut in.

"Is she your girlfriend?" my grandmother asked, her face lighting up as we walked toward her along the path of starflower and radicchio.

"No, I'm a friend," she answered. I didn't mind, although when my grandmother asked her name it was with a tinge of disappointment.

"Veronica." Claudia surprised me with a smile.

When we were alone, she apologized for the little lie. "They're still your father's parents, and my father is the one who ran off with his wife..."

102

Improvisation was the new game we were playing during those hours in the countryside. We had gone there without being told to, contrary to our behavior as children. Visiting my grandparents used to bore me, but with Claudia it was different. There was a captivating light, not to mention the smells. In the vineyard you could pick out the scent of the wildflowers, the medicinal herbs, the weeds, the sivoni, the spurge and the bitter chicory, the sage and marjoram bushes. The grapes were almost ready and the first sparrows had already sampled the ripest ones, a pine tree wept with cones, needles and tiny blue berries shaped like lapis lazuli.

We crossed the whole vineyard, following a chanterelle pathway, going as far as the almond trees. Claudia climbed up to the most solid branch; she shook it, some gems fell on my head.

"What do you do while I'm in Milano?" she asked me from up there, where being higher gave her greater authority.

"You know, you know," I tried to explain, dodging her heavy and inaccurate tosses.

"You've never told me the whole truth." She had the air of an inquisitor, as if she knew things about me that even I didn't know.

"I told you everything," I swore, and looking at her from down below, I noticed that her pants had been torn, and you could see the divine fold between her buttocks and her thighs. "The tree is ripping your clothes."

"Don't change the subject, Veleno..."

I thought back to the girls of those months: a classmate at university, a high school girl who went out with university boys, and a girl with really short hair and chipped teeth. In the end they all resembled each other, they were girls who were alone and isolated, like me.

"You're lying, Frank. Like that story about the bite marks on your face."

So I finally gave in. "I saw Domenico again."

Claudia propped herself up on the branch with one arm, then she stood up like a gymnast on a balance beam and jumped down.

"But nothing major," I specified. Her expression, which had seemed benevolent, turned serious.

"Did you have sex with him?"

"No, what do you think I am?"

"Why are you turning red?"

"Because I'm mad. Because one day he dressed up like a priest and played a trick on me."

"A trick?"

"He tricked me into giving my confession, but inside the confessional it was him and not the priest."

"A psychopath."

"He threatened me."

"Why?"

"Because he's afraid of that rumor about him and me."

"What's wrong with it?" Claudia asked candidly.

"We never did anything."

"Do you know how many guys they say I fucked in Martina?"

"It's not the same thing," I protested.

"So, I can be the Martina whore but you can't be the town faggot?" She laughed with her sylvan eyes. Then she added, "Do you finally understand why you have to leave?"

"I don't want to leave." And I looked at the almond tree, smelled the air, and now that I had admitted it I felt free.

"Do you know how many guys I saw in London, in Milano? And do you know that I kissed a girl, too?"

"I like you, and I don't like anyone else." I declared my love for the thousandth time.

"Don't be such a baby. Take a trip, get away from here, wake up, you might discover things about yourself that you can't even imagine."

The roar of military planes erupted, preceded by a whistling. It made us look up to the sky, as if to give some breathing room to the things we'd just said. From the nearby military airport of Gioia del Colle, reconnaissance planes would occasionally take off on ear-splitting exercises that offended the peace.

She took my hand and we walked along the path that led back to my grandparents. In the distance donkeys brayed, the sky started to turn gray.

"I've stopped putting up with the abuse of others, even those who say they love me."

"What are you talking about?" I felt my heart stop.

"I want to break up with Marco."

"Really?"

"I've already cheated on him twice this year."

"Cheated?" I thought I knew everything, but instead, nothing.

"I had sex with a Spanish guy just so I could meet his best friend, a Frenchman. Handsome, but an asshole."

"You didn't tell me." I was disappointed.

She added explosive details.

"Who was an asshole, the Spanish guy?"

"The Frenchman."

"You did them both?"

"Yes, but not at the same time, even if I would have liked to."

"Does Marco have any clue?" I asked, stunned by that unexpected confession.

"He's fifty years old, he can deal with it, believe me. He's got his own little things on the side."

A thousand pieces of information fermented in my head. I had to strip myself of every residual conformity, stop being afraid of desiring a man. I was on the verge of understanding that my truth was the deeply masculine something in Claudia and the deeply feminine something in the men who awakened my desire.

————

My grandparents were waiting for us with a tray piled with toasted almonds, tarallini, and a bottle of green-colored water. "We only have mint," they apologized.

I was used to their formalities, they would complain that they had nothing to offer but then bring out the pride of the country, fruit preserves and syrups. A peasant humility of which no trace was left in the younger Veleno generation.

We sat with the vineyard in our eyes and the casedda or trullo to our backs.

"Milano? But don't they teach business in Bari?" my grandmother objected when she heard where Claudia lived.

"There are more opportunities," Claudia answered with the automatic reflex of someone used to hearing the question.

"What a shame, there's no sea there or even the sky."

"That's not true, you can see the mountains and they're beautiful, too."

Then they began to speak intensely and for the first time ever my grandfather asked me to do him a favor. It had never happened before, I had always been the one, since childhood, to ask him: for candy, for presents, for money. "Will you help us with the harvest this year?" He was serious, he wasn't speaking to me as a grandfather, but adult to adult. My father had never acted this way. I was flattered.

"There's still one month to go till harvest," I said.

"We're not as strong as we used to be, and then we'll also need someone to help us decant the wine, your father has forgotten us," he concluded on a vaguely quarrelsome note.

Claudia and my grandmother had disappeared. The twilight altered the substance of the colors, a silence broken only by the confabulation and ruckus coming from the rooms. Claudia and my grandmother, when they came back out to say goodbye, exchanged a warm hug, two kisses on the cheek and the complicit look of someone who's been told a secret.

"And my grandmother, what did she tell you?"

"Women's things."

"Am I not supposed to know?"

"She wouldn't want you to know, otherwise she would have said them in front of everybody."

The street was empty, with the windows down the countryside blew into the car and our mouths. The radio was saying that two airplanes had flown into the Twin Towers of New York and one into the Pentagon in Washington. We felt tiny and powerless compared to those tragedies so far away. I thought in a few seconds that I would never take a plane again, that Claudia would stay in Puglia for a while, and I immediately felt ashamed for having imagined it.

"There's going to be a war," said Claudia, sadly. I didn't dare contradict her.

On the asphalt the bright red of a triangle appeared. A little farther ahead, right on the curve before the descent that brings you back into town, we noticed a cream-colored car with a woman's head poking out, looking straight ahead, as if she were awaiting an answer from the horizon.

It was Etta.

I hit the brakes and pulled up to the grass. Claudia got out of the car, annoyed.

"Mamma, what are you doing here?"

"I have to talk to you. Now." Her indignant precision promised nothing good.

Her facial features had been caught by a storm, all you could see, if anything, were her eyes. She was a portrait of sorrow, rage and resentment.

"Papà, did something happen to Papà?"

She pointed at me, and I thought the worst. "I won't tell you anything while he's here."

We stood there, waiting, the southern countryside had turned into the blazing finale of fireworks at the celebration of the patron saint of the town.

"Get in the car," Etta said.

"I'm not going anywhere until you tell me what's going on."

"With so many men on the face of the earth, why him of all people?" Etta had arranged that dangerous scene with her car stopped on a back road to teach her a solemn lesson.

"Who are you talking about?"

"Marco."

"Marco?"

"Do you know who Marco is?"

Claudia blanched. I had played along with her so that her folks wouldn't find out for a long time, and it had been in vain. Every secret love is destined to be discovered, especially when the love ends and all that remains is the secret. In the end, the most mysterious relationship continued to be the one between the two of us, precisely because it was so unabashedly in the light of day.

"Marco. Marco Curcio."

In the months following Enrico's flight from home, Etta had sought advice from a lawyer, and with this lawyer she had become infatuated. She distrusted psychologists, so she entrusted her impetuous, volatile stream of consciousness to the country lawyer, good-looking and eccentric, who offered her a glass of tonic water and silk handkerchiefs with which to wipe her tears. It was the period when Etta was crying in the third person ("What's a mother to do?"). She had told him the things that mattered to her, confessing that the only joy in her life was her daughter, that her daughter would redeem all the pain that was being caused in those years by Enrico and my mother. Later the divorce application was suspended, but the infatuation was still not extinguished.

All this I would learn in the months to come. Marco had tricked us, with the arid pragmatism of men who see seduction and relationships as a tool for manipulation.

Three hours later I found Claudia outside my house. They had been three long hours, because the world had changed, the town seemed to be holding its breath, people had locked themselves in their homes, terrified as they watched on television the towers collapsing. It was a different world from when we had left each other on the country road. Her eyes were two dark gloomy wells, and she was wearing a man's oversized sweater. She'd put on her father's clothes the way she used to when Enrico had left home with my mother.

"How are you?" I asked.

"I broke up with him."

"I hate him," I said.

"There's no need to hate him," she said.

"How is your mother?"

"She's worse than me. She has no one. I have you." But I took no joy in that crumb of affection.

We spent the night walking around Martina. Claudia was crying and laughing at the same time. "What an idiot I was." She would slip her arm into mine, then break away, as if with the beat of a wing a thought had left her head and had to be reclaimed.

"I have to pee," she said, as the sky grew clearer.

"Let's find a café," I proposed.

"I want to piss like a dog," she said, decisive.

"Me, too."

We went to an area with giant pine trees, climbing over the rusty fence, she extravagant, me clumsy, we chose a flower bed, she squatted and I stood, my back to her, we laughed together as our streams squirted.

In our childhood photos, Claudia always looked like the exact continuation of her parents, from their exact same mold, the opposite of the frail dark baby who had nothing in common with the pale Elisa Fortuna and the solid Vincenzo Veleno. That night seemed closer, more similar to what we had always been. We were blending.

"Can I look?" I asked without malice, as her stream dug a hole in the ground.

I turned around without waiting for her answer and saw a shadow, just a shadow, and Claudia's white teeth, turned toward me.

"How is it that our teeth can be seen in the dark?"

"Because we're aliens," she answered in a low and very serious voice.

The foggy dawn concealed an unexpected morning of sunshine. "Tomorrow I'm leaving and I'm never coming back," she swore, and her smiling teeth turned into a grimace that to me conveyed the sweet melancholy of a farewell.

Part Three

Malenvirne

(Noun. Masculine. Someone who upsets the balance, a killjoy, bungler, member of a community who has lost his bearings. A loose cannon. An already bad winter that turns even worse.)

She would never have wanted anyone to say that she had been "a respectable person," a phrase repeated on the day of his funeral, while exchanging perfunctory expressions of remorse. "A respectable man, truly respectable," as if none of the other men were. Clusters of people in bespoke suits, appropriate for weddings, baptisms and funerals.

Respectable. Respectable.

It also appeared in the obituaries, as confirmed by a notary with a mustache who smiled at her with the air of someone who knew the truth and was putting up a front to conceal it. Which meant that there wasn't much more you could say about Enrico Fanelli.

She knew what the people who said "respectable" were really thinking: Enrico Fanelli was a man who had everything. Money, a devoted wife, a daughter with a good job in Milano and a lover that many could only dream of. The doctor and the nurse on his ward. Clichés are comforting because they make us believe that there's a design to destiny, fooling you into thinking you are immune from its treachery. And then your heart stops beating in your sleep.

The heart attack seized him at a hotel room during a conference. His colleagues were only able to find out he was dead after asking the staff to open the door, since he had not shown up at that morning's panel.

I went to the funeral with my father. My mother stepped out of her room with a face like a dry riverbed. She'd been crying for forty-eight hours, but maintained her composure, as if secret love had also tempered her secret grief: her most intense passions exploded far from everyone. She said that she wouldn't go to the funeral because she didn't feel well. We pretended to accept her lie. She wasn't wrong, the funeral was grotesque. Claudia and her mother held each other up in a corner of the basilica. The crowd overflowed—the sacristy, the stairs and the piazza were packed—and that damn mistral wind tormented us as usual. Two figures threw themselves at the casket that divided the crowd. "Enrico, Enrico, Enrico." I stuck my head out, leaning against my father's back, and recognized two young women, dressed in the same way, black veil, gloves, thick stockings. A tall thin man with a ruddy face tried to keep them away. The casket advanced over the heads of the crowd that pressed to reach it, as if it held a saint.

At the cemetery Claudia looked taller than usual, her chin pointed toward the sky, her lips sealed. She didn't give the impression that she was falling apart, but behind her dark glasses was a sea of black.

The casket holding Enrico was too big, they couldn't fit it into the loculus, so a carpenter was called to shorten it. Etta was transfigured, touched by a strange grace, as if her diffident nature had been detached from her body. The cypresses smelled of humidity, and a light rain started to fall on the ceremony. Claudia did not want to look at the ends of the casket being sawed off, she came toward me saying, "It'll be like the surprise you find inside a Kinder chocolate egg." I knew she was thinking of her father's soul, ready to be released from that heavy mahogany sarcophagus.

The next day our bodies felt lighter, as if Enrico had taken away a piece of us. We went to the country-side to pick flowers, as if to honor a ritual: fennel, wild asparagus, angelica, dandelion, chicory. We sucked on the violet petals of the starflower and tasted the mal-low buds, remaining for the most part in silence. Then Claudia asked me about my mother. She had a yellow clover flower in her hair. I didn't answer.

"She was right not to come," she continued, and bent down to tug furiously on a weed. I heard her breathing change.

I went to hug her.

She bent her head to my neck, her half-closed mouth next to my ear emitted a boiling-hot breath.

"Francesco, did you see how many people were there yesterday?"

"Yes."

"Today no one was in front of the house."

"I am here," I reassured her.

"But your mother was there..." I felt a dizzy spell coming over me, afraid of what she was about to say. "We looked at each other for a long time, and I told her."

"That she was right not to come?" I asked.

"That my father wasn't as respectable as everyone thought," she replied.

"And what did she say?"

"That's why she loved him."

We hugged even tighter, turning ourselves over to the warmth of our bodies.

It is the common destiny of many children not to know the professional life of their parents, to have a general idea but to ignore the basic details. My mother was a simple foot soldier of general medicine. She had to deal mainly with the elderly and the occasional desperate case of a youth, she spoke very little about her job. My mother and Claudia's father never really worked together. In the company of their coworkers they addressed each other in formal terms, letting a complicit smirk escape, as exciting as a stolen kiss in the parking lot.

My mother was leaning in front of the bathroom mirror with the door open, intent on rubbing her eyelashes with her fingertips to soften the mascara.

"Where were you?"

"I did the night shift."

"You put on makeup for the night?"

"Good manners and elegance, at night you have to give the impression that you're as alert and neat as you are during the day, Uva Nera." She said it. I felt a distant longing.

"How are you doing?" I wanted the truth. Enrico had just been buried, Claudia had stuffed grass in her hair and mouth to keep from crying, there was a fire in her head.

"I feel like a vein that's been punctured a thousand times."

She told me that she had gone to nursing school during the period when she was practicing fencing with my father. There's a connection between an épée and sticking a needle into veins. Then she lowered her voice, although my father had already gone out without saying goodbye.

"Do you agree?"

"To what?"

"To a sleepover."

"Who are you talking about?"

"Claudia."

"Claudia?"

"Yes, Claudia."

"Why are you the one who's telling me?"

"It was my initiative. Her house is full of relatives that she can't stand and Etta is a basket case." I felt a strange form of jealousy, they had confided in each other and already met without me.

Claudia showed up late, it was midnight, my mother allowed me to do the honors of the house, while she, moving stiffly, went to make the bed, something she only did at night and never during the day, out of super-stition, I suspected: it was better to do nothing until Claudia appeared. Destiny should never be provoked.

Between the walls of the Veleno home Claudia brought a secret message from the other side.

She stopped my mother from making a separate bed. "I can be alone with Francesco, we grew up together," she said.

"Aren't the two of you too big for a twin mattress?" Elisa asked, slightly puzzled, carrying on her forearm bedsheets with a floral pattern that seemed to belong to a distant era, when in this house they were still expect-ing daughters rather than sons. From the look they exchanged, I realized that Claudia was not here for me.

Claudia never came to my bed.

The two of them, she and my mother, spent the night in the kitchen talking, while I eavesdropped, try-ing to catch a few words. My father suddenly appeared in my room, half-naked with a flashlight in his hand and a slurry voice. "What the fuck is going on?"

"Claudia is here," I replied cryptically, my mouth gnawing on the pillowcase.

He grumbled and went back to bed.

I was almost offended that he had nothing more to say, a little attack of jealousy, a minimum of curiosity about what was going on. Did nothing really matter to him?

I ran to the bathroom and looked at myself in the mirror. There was my mother's wooden makeup kit. I opened it, as tense as someone cracking a treasure chest: many pencils in a row like little soldiers. I sniffed their colored tips, they had a nice smell that reminded me of art class in middle school. Standing out in the kit was a prism with a hexagonal base about ten centimeters long that reflected the light like little mirrors aimed at the sun. The vermillion lipstick had an irresistible allure, a shiver of pleasure went through my body, like the time I kissed Claudia, which must have been a century ago. And the barrier between appropriate and inappropriate revealed itself for what it had always been: an impalpable strip of fog. I placed the lipstick on my lower lip and to that wax kiss I surrendered completely.

While my lips were being painted red and my eyes encircled in a runny halo of black mascara, I felt another humanity, another way of being male, which was nothing other than being a person. Complete, realized, true. In ancient times the kings put on makeup, traces of dye have been found in Egyptian sarcophagi and on Sumerian stelae, the great Native American warriors painted themselves with bloodred pigment before their battles. With a courage mustered by these notions, I started toward the room where Claudia and my mother were conversing.

"Look at me, this is who I am." I would stand in the middle of the kitchen.

At the door I could hear soft voices, whispering so as not to disturb the sleep of us men. But I was there, I had nothing in common with my father, they were what mattered to me, what mattered to me was everything their hands and their words had touched.

I saw them close together like a mother consoling a child, about to embrace, alike in their grief and in how they expressed absence. Rather than declare myself, I retraced my footsteps as if I'd been facing a bridge that I didn't dare cross.

I washed with soap and water and went to sleep.

In the morning, the smell of bread and coffee came from the kitchen. They were right where I had left them, they had talked all night and fallen asleep with their heads on the table; they had woken up and prepared breakfast together. Pale as a sheet, with slight circles under their eyes, their foreheads bare, their hair framing their angular faces. At the front door they looked each other in the eyes and Elisa said goodbye with a kiss on the cheek. Claudia's shadow resembled a flamingo. She looked at me to wave goodbye, she seemed liberated.

"When you remove your makeup, you have to make an emulsion with soap, otherwise you're left with a messy blur," my mother said.

I liked the way she said "emulsion." The skin on her arms was cold, her fingers slipped away from mine without giving me the time to reply.

Before departing again, Claudia staged another one of her Claudia-esque scenes. In the garden she made a pile of record players, her marble collections, a swivel chair, a papier-mâché head of Gorbachev from a thousand Carnivals ago, starched shirts, ties arranged on a brass hanger, a stringless guitar, a large painting of the high relief of a horse on the walls of Martina Franca, hideous terra-cotta trulli, medals, a hippogriff, armillary spheres, and suits that had belonged to her father. She was planning to start a splendid bonfire of purification that would usher in a future whose pages were yet to be written. Etta threatened to call the firefighters. "Put everything back where you found it!" Meanwhile her daughter circled the garden wrapped in one of her father's bathrobes, from which her marble ankles and calves stuck out. She looked like the Big Lebowski, and like every time she started to lose her grip, I was on the threshold of that great fire.

Under the lemon tree that had borne witness to her childhood, she pushed her hair to the side. Passing her hand over her face, she extracted a book from the pocket of the bathrobe and climbed up on the old chair.

"Papà. Listen."

Etta shook her head and swatted an invisible fly away from her face, then went back indoors to phone someone.

Claudia read aloud some of Vittorio Bodini's poems, articulating the words like a drill sergeant. She stressed the *r*'s in a poem that talked about returns, and had the word *polsi*, pulses, so powerful, because pulses are like the steering wheel of the hands, and guide the direction in which they feel. It filled me with loneliness, with desolation, I felt like I was one of those things about to be burnt.

When we were alone, Claudia loosened the bathrobe, revealing the boxer shorts and T-shirt in which she had slept. She joked when she was afraid, in suffering she became histrionic. Some pains are easier to bear through theatricality, celebrations, the history of mourning is made up of wailers and laments, of songs. When grief becomes unbearable the music gets louder, the ancients used to say.

"I was afraid you really did want to burn everything," I said, directing my eyes at the pile.

"It would have been cruel."

"You're beautiful when you read poetry."

"I'm better when I masturbate."

She changed register without changing her expression. And I stuttered, or shut up.

"Let's leave, Francesco."

"But aren't you leaving tonight?"

"Now."

We went to the airport five hours before takeoff. We stopped by the sea, behind the monumental entrance to the old Fiera del Levante of Bari. From there we watched airplanes climbing the skies or approaching the earth.

"While I was going through Papà's things, I had an idea."

From her bag she pulled out a red silk tie; a small stain on the narrow end was the clue that it had belonged to someone.

"A gift," she said, holding her hands out to me. They were tapered, soft, in harmony with the fabric, a shiny strip, as if the daylight was focused on that spot. "It's my father's." She held it up to her nose to smell it. "I think that he must have worn it many times when he was with your mother." For a moment I remained in silence, shaken. "I think your mother should have it," she continued.

"Then it's not a gift for me," I protested unpersuasively.

"It is. You'll make Elisa happy, and you love making happy the people who love you."

We arrived at the airport coasting the lamina of the sea and long fields that were uncultivated yet blooming with wildflowers and invasive plants. The yellow-petaled sorrels opened up to the sun but at night closed into a fist.

Claudia and I had fun cataloging the panorama, trying to give meaning to that activity. She told me that in the days leading up to her father's death, she had dreamed of cyclamens, light pink, white, like the time Michele Duranti had attacked her, pressing his knees into her chest, when he was about to kill her. In Puglia you can tell how far away from the sea you are by looking at the flowers in the meadow, the yellow of the dandelion and the sorrel before the blue of the anemone means you are a stone's throw from the coast, but we were hill people, we came from a land of bindweed and poppy, chickweed and chamomile, and especially of cyclamen, flowers whose roots are poisonous but supposedly protect you from evil spells. "Maybe they warn you of changes," I said. We set aside those thoughts beneath the departure signs at the airport.

Inside me was a wind that for the first time urged me to follow her to Milano. I would miss all those flowers, the light blue horizon of the sky twenty minutes from my bed, but maybe I would finally understand who this Claudia was that was now fleeing.

A familiar voice broke through the general hubbub.

"I raised you and now you're running away like a thief, leaving me with all this pain." One meter away from the security controls that led to the gates, Etta was making an embarrassing scene.

"I don't belong to you. People don't belong to you," Claudia replied, her eyes swollen and red, before entering the waiting area. Etta pierced me with eyes filled with rage.

"The two of you killed him and ruined her for me," she said, then she turned around and left.

When I got back to the car I couldn't breathe, my throat was dry. I waited for the airplane to depart. I looked for Claudia in the rumble that shook my ears, the kiss that we hadn't exchanged.

I hadn't known how to answer Etta. I had ignored the complexity of the relationship between mother and daughter. For me everything was black and white, good or bad. Etta was an enemy, and I was defeated.

The cyclamen was the flower of Hecate, the goddess of the Afterlife, a divinity who practiced magic and transmitted knowledge. But to remember this without being able to share it with Claudia filled me with melancholy.

I reached her during the night shift, when hospitals seem more welcoming. The big plate windows of the ward overlooked the Valle d'Itria, speckled with white lights, the cones of the trulli like stalagmites in an icy grotto. I tripped on the dimly lit stairs, made my way down the corridor. At the shuffling of my footsteps the women whom families paid to keep vigil over the sick looked up. I appeared at the only room with the television on but the volume off. She was waiting for me, reading a novel with her knees pointed toward the door, the same way she had waited for Enrico in happier days. I was drawn to the glass-doored cabinets of the first-aid room, the aquamarine furniture whose drawers were stuffed with medicine and the thought of my mother's legs wrapped around the waist of Enrico, who was gone now but still hovered around us.

We remained in silence, letting the electrical buzzing of the neon light speak for us. She had her hair tied back, her ears free of the gold hoops she wore during the day. I thought back to the night I had run into her and Enrico at the station. I dozed off and was awakened by the sound of water running. I greeted my mother with a kiss on her cheek, it was freezing and the hair over her forehead was wet. She accompanied me to the exit of the ward.

"Why is your hair wet?"

"I splash water on my head to stay awake. While we're on the subject of revelations, I know you wear makeup."

"I don't know what you're talking about."

"Your pillowcase." She knew how to cut through my bullshit.

"I still don't understand."

"I don't like the way you make your bed, and yesterday while I was fixing it I saw your pillow."

To me this act of remaking the bed after I'd already made it was a sign of distrust, and distrust always contains a seed of violence.

"Yes, every now and then I put on makeup before going to bed," I admitted.

"And then?"

"The next day I look at the stains on the pillow and try to understand if my dreams spoke to me."

"Do they? What do they say?"

"That it's best not to ask myself too many questions."

"The time will come when you'll have to, and have to find an answer."

When it came to shining a light on my contradictions, she was persistent, and maybe this was why I needed her so much.

"For now, things are fine the way they are."

The dawn painted our faces blue. We continued to share confidences. At one point she said:

"Enrico was someone more like me than your father."

"On account of the hospital?"

"On account of the pain..."

"What pain?"

"The pain I could share with him, not everyone can bear the pain of the person they think they love."

"What do you mean?" I was alarmed. Confessions like this made me uneasy.

"That you have to be strong and bear the pain of the person you love. Let me give you an example: pain is never being able to be yourself your whole life long."

We hugged each other tight, I could feel her muscles and elbows, the scent of vanilla, the scent of Mamma. She had made a huge effort to tell me her truth and she hugged me to catch her breath as if she'd just evaded a danger.

Years later I read the only interview that Kafka ever gave. It was to a young writer, Gustav Janouch. He told him that the heart is a house with two bedrooms: one is for suffering, the other is for joy. You mustn't laugh too loud, otherwise the suffering will reawaken. The opposite isn't true, unfortunately, because joy is hard of hearing. Elisa Fortuna and Enrico Fanelli had found each other in the refuge of silence. A silent joy lasts longer than a loud one, but holding it in for too long does harm to the soul.

Claudia's decade in Milano should be divided into two major seasons. The first still bore the residue of the hometown: Marcio Curcio, who had the nerve to write her a letter that she never opened; and grudges and fights with Etta, consisting of insults and long recriminatory phone calls—"Do I deserve to end up with nobody?" "There's nobody I can be with," she would say or write, and that hammering on the word "nobody" rather than on her daughter's name may have contained one of the deep reasons for their discord.

At school Claudia established a severe regimen of rigor and self-discipline. Electronic music and travel were relegated to short hiatuses, a brief three-month Erasmus fellowship in Utrecht, where she learned how to make pierogis from her Polish roommate and went dancing at legendary local raves below the windmills and atop the clover hills. Poetry was still her only diversion: she once told me that for her, poetry was the window at her desk, there is no inspiration without a window, without light and air.

Her texts had the tone that southern Italians indulge in when they emigrate, a little sappy and a little smug. "Can you bring me the smell of the sea when you visit?" Every now and then she would brave a few lines of verse: "I've learned to burn the bad dreams / that leave their ashes to sleepless dawn." Her verse showed traces of whatever she was reading, ruminations on troubled nights. Throughout those years our distance was nourished by tacit understandings.

The first time I went to visit her was shortly after the death of Enrico. I had started working at a cooperative that assigned public housing, in an office where a friend of my father checked the paperwork of families who had applied for a municipal house. Every day some lowlife would walk in with a crooked smile, flexing his naked arms as a threat. He'd rail against the mayor, the president of the republic, against Italy, then he'd say he was at the end of his rope, and threaten to set fire to himself or to us. In the midst of that finagling, I'd look into the lives of the applicants, and I always found a snag, always a source of income that suddenly turned up, an undeclared house, a rich family member. Bureaucracy was a tightrope act that taught me a lesson which would prove useful in the years to come: in the city there were far more roofs than heads, nobody would ever end up homeless, the problem was how to reconcile the demand for housing with the supply.

I traveled north to Claudia with a suitcase crammed with books that she'd filled by emptying her father's bookshelves and asked me to hide, afraid that her mother would make them disappear once she'd left.

It felt like the longest trip I'd ever taken. I left on a double-decker bus under the sun of one day and reached my destination in the light of another.

I remember every second of that Milanese dawn: the streets, wide and empty; the long lines of plane trees, and massive, uniform blocks of houses. In the piazza behind the monumental train station with its white façade, Claudia came toward me in a black cape, wrapping her arms around me like a girlfriend. While the other passengers disappeared into cars parked near the bus, we held that embrace on the street forever, the cold air pinching our skin.

The morning was later flooded with sunlight and an unusual warm breeze. We walked at a brisk pace as if the weather were threatening us with its inevitable transience. Claudia copied the men and women running up the escalator, and I plodded along behind her.

"It's not so bad here after all," I said, panting, one of those sentences that seem to conclude a dialogue that you had been carrying on in your head.

Claudia answered with a smirk of agreement, the most honest way she knew to tell me that she still hadn't made up her mind about life there.

I remember like a mirage—even the outlines are blurred—how thirsty I was, the exhaustion in my legs, the spirited euphoria of the outings, the Castello Sforzesco, Piazza Cordusio, the tiny streets around the Galleria, the many routes into the metropolis, which felt immense, as tangled as intestines, crowded and frenetic, and finally there, in front of the Duomo, the rain that fell in big drops, and the children who ran around with colored umbrellas creating fantastic trajectories like marionettes in a puppet theater. It was our only stroll through the city and I could see clearly why she had decided to live there: the incredible human variety that stood out to my provincial eyes. The elegance of the streets in the center that contrasted with the heaps of cardboard under which men with wrinkled faces and glazed eyes were sleeping.

That night Claudia and I went back to her place, an apartment with a granite floor and scribbled-on walls that told you that the only people who had ever lived here were off-campus students. The moment we arrived I met her roommates, and sat with one of them and her boyfriend while Claudia disappeared into her room for a phone call that "I can't ignore."

Giulia and Matteo gave me the immediate impression that they wanted to extort some kind of information from me rather than engage in a polite conversation. He had broad shoulders; she, cheeks as red as a mountain sunburn. Both were originally from a small southern Italian village, and both were rich kids like Claudia, even if in the North the rich kids from the South, by comparison, aren't so rich after all. They spoke to me incessantly with annoying small talk like *What's your major, Why did you quit, What will you do, You're not Claudia's boyfriend? Really?* Almost scandalized that we could sleep in the same bed without an official relationship. Then Giulia said that she had fought and made peace with Claudia a thousand times. How the heck can she be reading all the time and never get tired?

"That's the way she is, she really believes in the books that she reads, she believes that poetry and music improve our lives."

"And do you?" asked Matteo, as if he were scandalized.

"The one person who has made my life better is Claudia." It's energizing to say out loud the name of the person you love.

"You really are in love," Giulia decreed, with a knowing glance at her boyfriend. "We thought that you were the one Claudia was always on the phone with," they said together, with a hint of sarcastic laughter.

I headed to Claudia's room thinking she had finished her phone call, but when I got there she was still talking, a whisper muffled by laughter and sighs. She said goodbye in a bossy, almost harsh tone of voice. "Francesca will be here till Wednesday." That's exactly what I heard her say, Francesca was obviously me.

I couldn't hide my indignation. "Who were you talking to?" I asked, when she turned her attention to me.

"One of the guys that I see."

"That you see?"

"I mean, for now I'm in touch with him, nothing more. I'll see him after my final, if we are still in touch."

"And he's jealous of me?"

"He wouldn't understand, I always end up with men who don't understand. I did what I had to do, I changed one vowel in your name." The expression on her face like someone withholding a burst of laughter.

We traded insights on our identity but still hadn't grasped their essence. We took the books out of the suitcase and arranged them in a corner of the room, it was a literary series that a few years earlier a local newspaper had distributed with copies of the newspaper, there were novels and poetry collections by some of the best writers from Puglia, Vittorio Bodini, Raffaele Carrieri, Maria Corti, Mariateresa Di Lascia, Rina Durante, Maria Marcone. As I organized them one by one, I read the titles on the spines, trying to understand. They were unread, still wrapped in the same cellophane they came in, because Enrico—in Claudia's words—"like many respectable people he owned many books, without ever reading them."

I leafed through some of them on the bed that would be ours for a few nights, even if we slept with our backs molded to each other. Every morning I would wake up early as the daylight filtered through the cheap blinds of the room, look at the mountain of blankets underneath which Claudia slept and feel happy to keep vigil over her huddled sleep. I observed her while she studied, leaning over her books, with the light turned on even during the day, her notes scribbled on her knees, whenever her eyes looked up and met mine and without breathing a word we passed to each other the lemon tree, the vineyards of Lamie di Olimpia, the cherry tree of my grandparents.

With Claudia I would gaze through the window at the milky light of the morning: as the day lingered on the sky of Milano transformed into a silver reflection. I would go out alone, smelling the metallic odor that you inhaled from the air, the same odor that I had smelled in Bari and Martina near the train stations. I liked Milano more than I could have imagined, the frenzy made me smile, there was something autumnal in things, the wood of the seats on the number 15 tram. It was a world filled with opportunities, a buzzing of noise that made you feel you were never alone. "People underrate the noise of the city," I thought.

When I got back home it was night. Claudia gave me a little felt pillow to make the nocturnal crossing more comfortable, at the bus station the branches of the plane trees were filled with joyful birds.

"They're robin redbreasts," Claudia said.

"How do you know?"

"They come to my windowsill."

"I haven't seen any in the past few days," I said, with the feeling this was another one of her jokes.

"Because you didn't notice them."

That Claudia had referred to my favorite fairy tale from childhood was probably not accidental. It was the one about the robin redbreast who gets stained with blood when he extracts a thorn from the crown of Christ. They used to say that the same bird had kept the embers alive in the Bethlehem manger by flapping its wings. The words of the Church had remained inside of us like the sediment of wine. When there was a reason to be happy, and therefore finally be yourself, they would surface, sounding the way they had sounded during the masses and liturgies all of my life.

I said goodbye to her with a kiss on her bony chin, her hands let me hold them.

"Milano is so beautiful," she said, and then, sniffling with a nose reddened by the cold, "but it has never been so beautiful as it is here with you tonight."

The second part of the Milanese decade was inaugurated with Claudia's degree and the colors of our relationship took on new, unexpected nuances. The day of her graduation I arrived late due to the breakdown of an infernal bus. I recognized her in the vast chaotic corridors of the university despite her costume. She was wearing a blue wig and oversized shoes, her face painted white and a ball on her nose, and she endured the ritual pictures. "It's a farce," she told everyone, although it wasn't clear whether she was referring to what she was doing or to the ceremony or to the entire course of study she had completed. There was a celebration at a dimly lit bar, a lot of people I had heard her mention in texts and phone calls, names and faces overlapped and disappeared into the fog, her relatives and Etta weren't there, but I did find her old roommates, Giulia and Matteo, with better color on their faces and in the words that we exchanged.

Despite her clown act, Claudia immediately found a job in the human resources department of a company, one of those professions that no one could really explain, and that I struggled to reconcile with her confession a few years earlier when she'd told me that she would study business because she wanted to be the master of her own destiny. She changed offices twice, but they were always in reinforced concrete boxes, and always on the edge of town. When she spoke to me about her work at the company she was ambiguous, dwelling on minor details, often using the expression "commercial partner" and dwelling on anecdotes about the shuttle or the quality of the cafeteria food: her colleagues were an indistinct mass of names and assignments.

"A boring job lets you concentrate on other things."

"Like what?" I struggled to believe there could be anything boring in her life.

"Travel, Francesco, I want to make money to travel, and in this company if you rise through the ranks you can end up at a branch in America or Australia."

"America, Australia? Are you nuts?" I said to her, bewildered at the idea of us being even farther apart.

From that moment things changed between us, without our wanting them to, our lives simply adjusted to the routine, the job, the limited number of vacation days, the new friendships. She stopped sending me postcards of lapis lazuli skies, replacing them with emails and an occasional phone call, then even those became scarcer.

We ended up fighting, and this time it wasn't over one of her tempestuous relationships: it was over how we perceived our roots. In Puglia for a little while now there had been a new climate, the ruined masserie were being transformed and restored to their former splendor, the high-speed train had arrived, budget airlines from all over Europe connected our airports to the great international metropolises, divas and artists came to live in the trulli and a ton of films were shot against the background of our white stones and cliffs rising from the sea.

These were the years of Nichi Vendola, the gay but Catholic governor of Puglia, a politician and a poet. Maybe we had become fabulists, and heedless of how ridiculous we sounded would speak of the Pugliese Spring, of Puglia as the new California. Many emigrants returned home and established small creative companies thanks to the incentives created by the new governor, who for many of us was the emblem of this Renaissance. Claudia, after some initial enthusiasm that made even her come home to vote, grew wary and reached the decision not to return, not even for the summer and Christmas holidays. She cut off all contact with Etta, once and for all, even though her mother was always bragging about her—"my daughter is a manager"—to the other mothers of emigrated children, all of whom were part of the brain drain, misunderstood geniuses, bosses, captains of industry, university professors, researchers, writers, artists, Formula 1 drivers, but in most cases as desperate as everyone else.

"It's an illusion. I'm happy where I am," she told me, during one of those angry phone calls we made to each other.

"But you're an artist, a free spirit, you can create your own business, a school, there's a lot of financing and opportunities now, we need people like you." I would encourage her by using the first person plural, even if on the inside I was saying, "I need you."

"I want my independence, I don't want to be held hostage by anything: family, landscapes, sea and food, or your hideous rhetoric." Claudia threw back in my face every argument I had used to sell her on the possibility of a triumphant return.

"Is this the life you wanted? An office routine in a glass edifice on the outskirts of Milano?" And I envisioned her sitting there primly, in her sterile open space with its muffled sounds and air-conditioning-tainted environment.

"No jobs are as boring as people."

The thread between us frayed, Claudia would disappear for months at a time, breaking her silence every so often with a torrent of emails that I would print out and read over and over again. Sometimes she even sent me pictures she had taken with the company's new

BlackBerry of herself in the mirror of one of the apartments that she was constantly changing.

She would make a call to the guy saved on her phone as "Kevin Mover," and he would help her with his van to move her things first from one room to another, and later from a studio to a one-bedroom.

In her emails I would sift through every sentence in search of the gold that would make me happy. There were opinions of books and future plans, movies she had seen, existential questions that she asked me, and always she would find an opportunity to leave me a verse by some poet, rarely, maybe only once, she sent me one of her own poems. In the postscript she would slip in a reference to her current relationships, as if they were a marginal note to her life. I would hope against hope that she was doing it because somehow the love that counted was our own.

In her very first profile pic she looked bonier, her face came out as square and white as the marble of Greek warriors on a sacrificial altar, her disheveled red hair instead made her look like Medusa. I imagined her going into the office in one of her three pantsuits—gray, midnight blue and black—fifty hours a week, she earned an excellent salary, and deposited it in the bank account her father had opened for her back when she graduated, the only time he had treated her like an adult.

————

"When I come to visit you I'll bring a suitcase full of books," I promised, with the hope perhaps of being invited back to Milano.

"I don't have any more room."

"For books?"

"I have too many, I don't know where to put them, I think I'll give some away."

"But how..."

"I've read them already."

"I want to read them, too, I want to know the things that you love."

"Crebbi foresta"—let the forest grow.

"You're more than a forest."

"I was quoting *A Woman and Her Family* by Maria Marcone, the story of a southern Italian woman surrounded by male family members who is educated, writes, believes in psychoanalysis, and everywhere she looks she sees rotted and atrophied umbilical cords, people who are so afraid of severing them that they keep them attached."

"What are you trying to tell me?"

"Nothing. There's no message in the bottle, but I don't want to come back."

"We used to be on the same level, now you're ahead of me," I told her with a pang of melancholy.

"No, Frank, you're the one who hasn't budged, holed up in that shell you're in."

"I'm fine where I am."

146

"I'm not coming back to save you, you're the one who'll have to come to me."

I did things my own way.

I started to read her writers, it was the easiest way to feel close to her, to trace something of her in those pages. Those were the years when I read the most, because I had synchronized myself, or was trying to, with the spirit of Claudia. Maria Marcone, Rina Durante, Maria Teresa di Lascia, names that would have never meant anything to me without her, and by reading them I found an affinity with the things she was saying, I tried to understand them better, they're harsh books, angry, each holds a kind of repressed truth. In *Malapianta* by Rina Durante, I was struck by the concept of "collapsing while standing still," a sensation that you feel when your body remains erect, without tremors and changes, but inside "you have left and said goodbye to everyone." Just as Claudia had.

I had a life of my own in the town, of course, I kept up the habit of visiting my mother during her notorious shifts to tell each other secrets, even if we often sat in silence. But I was waiting for Claudia, only with her could I walk down the lava rock streets between Piazza Plebiscito and the mansions with their Spanish window grilles on Via Cavour, only with her could I savor the bitter ashes from braziers smoking in the deepest, most hidden recesses of the tangle in the centro storico that we call Curdunniddo. I clung to the rituals, I dipped my fingers in the holy-water fonts of country churches, I rubbed a Saint Blaise candle against my neck to treat my strep throat, I consulted the dawn of Candelmas before planning the summer to come, I ate no meat or chocolate for the forty days of Lent, I participated in Holy Week wearing a white hood over my head and a yellow kerchief around my neck, awaiting Easter night, the peak of my metaphysical tension, when my skin would cover me with chills. The dark church, the naves traversed by the breathing of the faithful, the dampness of the walls sticking to our coats; the officiating priest who burst into the central nave, enveloped in smoke from a censer that was burning outside the church. The deacon carried a large candle covered with effigies and from the darkness the faithful lit their tiny candles from it, the church vibrated with the singing of Lumen Christi and the light, little by little, extinguished the darkness, creating the illusion that these people were better than they had appeared years ago at the funeral of Enrico. Was this perhaps my Christianity, to be so afraid of men that I had to love them?

"I think I'll get engaged to a donkey," was her opening remark on the telephone on New Year's morning, not even nine o'clock, the sound of the clogs of my mother just returned from the hospital and me still half-drunk from a listless party with my old classmates.

"I'm still hungover," I mumbled, although Claudia's voice had an electrifying effect.

"What do you know about hangovers?" Her voice had a suspicious liveliness, the tone of a big announcement.

"I just saw ten of our classmates, ten, I tell you, ten."

"Why do you inflict this torture on yourself?"

"Well there's not that much choice around here," was my feeble excuse, as I tried to get up in the penumbra of the newborn day.

"After all your talk about Puglia is better, California, creative types, in the end you spend New Year's Eve at a class reunion."

"Let's not talk about it."

"Here's my news, I just got back from Fabrizio's house and I've come to a decision."

"Fabri who?"

"No one, just some guy I used to see who I won't be seeing anymore."

"But weren't you going out with a guy named Antonio?"

"Giuseppe, his name was Giuseppe, Antonio is the guy from last summer." Claudia and her fleeting, intermittent lovers, no one man seemed to convince her.

"Last night I was a little tipsy and I admitted one of my fantasies to him."

"To who?"

"To Fabrizio!"

"And he?"

"He was shocked, and weirded out."

"I think I know what you suggested."

"I want to test them right away, I want to show who I am right away, and if I have a fantasy I throw it in their face. I asked Fabrizio to imagine us doing it with another guy."

"And it weirded him out."

"I don't want to hide my fantasies anymore. I took a long walk, there were still people coming back from New Year's Eve parties, and while I was walking along Corso di Porta Ticinese amid a silence that you never hear in this city, I thought of getting engaged to a donkey. After all, I come from the city of donkeys."

"A donkey?"

"A big donkey with a beige coat and shiny black eyes."

"The Martina Franca donkeys are renowned, they're taken to state fairs all over the world." And I launched into the list of all of our donkey's features, which I'd learned through years of going to the annual fairs held in honor of our patron saint.

"A donkey is definitely much less afraid to listen to me, and then it's a loyal animal, protective, it defends its foals by giving kicks that can crush the skull of a predator."

"And this donkey, you'll bring him here, to a reunion with our classmates? Would he find anyone to fraternize with?"

"More, much more, I'll parade him around in the piazza, introduce him to my mother, finally a use for the trousseau she's been saving for me all her life."

"I think Etta might have something to say."

"Finally an heir to the Bianchi Caracciolese lineage, and from our union a centaur will be born, and you will help me to give it a name."

It was our most surreal phone call since I'd met Claudia, maybe it was her way of telling me that these men she'd left in the dust, innocuous or cruel, appealing or disgusting, up in their years or very young, but always, inevitably, superficial, meant nothing to her.

In my eyes and in my heart Claudia had, in the end, expatriated from the context in which we'd met and loved

151

each other, to me she felt as Milanese as our most illustrious compatriot, Paolo Grassi, the son of immigrants, who had gone on to found the Piccolo Teatro of Milano.

Claudia, "the Milanese VIP," as our former classmates called her, punning on the fact that in our dialect *vip* means the world's worst actor; the local gossips had never forgotten that messiness with Curcio. "Who's gonna marry a girl as crazy as that?" "Do you remember when she went around with the tie and blue hair?" Not having the gumption to react, I wouldn't answer, but I would stand up and leave, hoping to convey at least some of the annoyance Claudia would have felt to hear that kind of talk.

Once she went to a conference in Bari and asked me to join her. I took the train and relived the exact atmosphere of my university days when I tried to impress people by majoring in political science. Bari had a high yellow sun, I crossed Piazza Umberto and Via Sparano with a feeling of profound happiness, and seeing how early I was, I went to sit at a spot in the city that seems to extend into the sea, a kind of narrow pier with fresh-fish stands on the sides and a cement rotunda that makes you feel like you're on a boat surrounded by waves.

I waited for her there, under the high sun that people around here call the *mano del dio Levante*, "hand of the Levantine god."

She ran toward me awkwardly, her face thin, angular, like a painting by Uccello or Picasso, carrying her bag on one arm, and wearing gray cigarette pants. I felt a chill, she looked like another person, then I perceived a familiar sensation, she hugged me like she had that time in Milano, like a girlfriend and boyfriend who haven't seen each other in a long time, and we gave each other a kiss that was powerful and explosive.

"Can't you see how sunny it is here?"

"Tonight I'm going back on the eight o'clock flight." She froze me in my tracks.

She was different in her way of doing things, not only in how she was dressed. She started talking to me about Milano, the city was one big construction site, in a few years it would host the biggest world's fair and they were building subways everywhere. So I admitted to her that I liked going by myself to the Martina station to watch the trains. I didn't say that I was doing it to feel closer to her, but she understood.

"If you come back to Milano I'll show you the Torre Velasca." She spoke enthusiastically, but giving me the impression of pushing me away rather than drawing me close to the place she said that she loved.

"If you want I can get on the plane with you now." I was almost begging her.

"No, you can't, you have a job and so do I, and you will be coming to see me anyway, I'm moving again."

"Again."

"A bigger apartment, as soon as I'm organized come and give me a hand, but not right now."

I spoke to her about my job, maybe I would open a real estate agency. She approved, in her opinion it was the best moment to do so, then when I asked about hers, about her job, a shadow seemed to descend over her, she said it was like Tetris. The expenses were the little bricks she had to move around in order to get the combination that would complete the revenue line on which they landed. She had an excellent salary, but she worked long hours without free time to do anything else.

She asked me what I was reading, recommended *Separate Rooms* by Tondelli. She turned on her cell phone and showed me a photo of a page, then she read it aloud: "I wanted everything, but I always had to settle for something." I told her the sentence was brilliant, it was about us, even if a veil of sadness had fallen over me.

We walked in the heart of the Murattiano neighborhood of Bari, looking at the colorful shop windows and exchanging glances as if to say, This is who we are now. We separated near the station beneath the portico of the hotel where the convention was taking place, I would take the train back to Martina with a deeper chill in my bones, the sun had hidden behind a dark cloud, or maybe the evening had simply started early the way it does in the winter.

While she was seeking meaningful signs in each of her men, I fled from meaning, and lingered in my relationships on the border between faded affection and impure friendship. Daniela, Flavia, Marianna, Loredana. Claudia called them the "screen women," or occasional girlfriends, without my ever protesting, only a slight feeling of guilt toward them. Young women who were intrigued by my weakness, my tenderness, my kindness: I complimented them on their earrings and hairstyle. On the weekends we went to the movies, and they didn't mind cheesy comedies, the only films they showed around here. They all seemed to feel that things were okay. But deep inside of me, Claudia was right, there was an aspiration, a seed: I am not what I seem, I can be better, I can go further, stop being an imposter.

These relationships always ended when the time came to meet the family. It was the first act of truth, but with none of them did my wounds bleed. And in a true connection you cannot hide your open wounds.

In Claudia's life, at one point, an adult male took advantage of her once again, her former professor of political economy, Eugenio Baroni, married with children. The relationship had begun without great prospects. For him a simple extramarital affair, for Claudia a diversion. But the relationship quickly took an unexpected turn, unexpected for anyone but Claudia.

She held nothing back in describing their arrangement to me, as if she felt her life expand and she relived it through the stories she told me.

"I've screwed up."

"Do you love him?"

"I'm crazy about him, I don't know if it's love."

"Does he love you?"

"He's not even capable of loving himself."

I wondered whether Claudia's emotional masochism had something to do with her first love, Enrico Fanelli, but I tried to avoid playing the armchair psychologist. I was in the shoes of someone who listens but never voices his own opinion, terrified that I might negate her happiness or increase her turmoil. But the men who circled around her started to bear an uncanny resemblance: carnivores sniffing around for blood and sinking their fangs into it. Yet to me Enrico had always seemed the most mild-mannered man in the world, the man who loved my mother.

———

We went back to hearing from each other more regularly, as if the void Baroni had left her when he returned to his wife could be filled by our light and airy conversations.

"I imagine what his life is like when he goes home, how he speaks to his children, what he does with his wife."

"I don't think he does a lot."

"I know everything about her."

"He tells you?"

"No, I lurk on her Facebook page and have made friends with her hairdresser."

"You're diabolical."

"No, Frank, I'm a basket case."

After our phone calls I would walk through the white streets of the borgo antico, as far as the train station. Only the whistle of the last express train to Taranto, packed with factory workers and night-school students, made me feel completely connected to Claudia. The rails gleamed beneath the yellow spotlights, and kerosene tickled my nostrils. Sometimes I would smoke a cigarette to immerse myself more deeply in the frenzy of the metropolis, I was no longer in Martina, I was in Milano, and Claudia was there, just getting off the tram, between the shiny rails, ready to open her arms to me.

"Frank, I had sex in the same bed where he sleeps with his wife."

To me Professor Eugenio Baroni sounded truly depraved. One day he made a date with her via text, writing that she should wear a short navy-blue skirt and white ankle socks. Claudia was thirty years old and felt ridiculous dressing up like a Japanese schoolgirl to have sex with a man thirty years older.

I became involved in the preparations through countless texts: Would he settle for a tight skirt and white Supergas? Would just a touch of makeup be alright? Did his wanting her to get dressed up like that make him a pedophile?

They were to spend a whole night together for the first time. Beneath the high branches of the ancient horse chestnut trees in the Guastalla Gardens, he told her that she resembled one of the women in Boldini's watercolors. Claudia thought it was a kind way of scolding her for not respecting their pact. Baroni spoke to her obliquely as men do when they don't want to take responsibility. The gist of it was that they could no longer see each other secretly, the time had come to give a status to their relationship.

"Are we together?" Claudia felt stupid in the very moment that she asked.

"We are us," he replied.

He was occasionally serious, occasionally complicit, almost encouraging, as if to convince her that the relationship would change, but without any need to give a name to that change. His words sounded like a lecture on the sentiments. That morning, after it had rained all night against the window blinds of the hotel, he gave her a gold bracelet saying that this is what used to be given to slave girls who had become the favorite. Then he started to complain about his wife's family and finally about one of his two children, whom he considered a quitter. Claudia, although she was blinded by passion, could see his cruelty in those words. But she was not able to be the self-aware and confident woman she was in the presence of the professor, who sometimes took her out to dinner with his colleagues just to show her off.

Without being really convinced she asked, "Why don't you leave your wife?"

"And how did he answer?"

"How do you think any fifty- to sixty-year-old married man with children would answer? Let sleeping dogs lie."

"That's what he said? 'Let sleeping dogs lie'?"

"Worse, he said that he renovated the house with his wife, she spent a lot of money on it and he can't repay her."

"And what did you say?"

"That the time had come to try to do things differently."

"Do what?"

"Love, even if I used language that was a little more explicit...I was angry, Frank, really angry."

I gulped.

"Frank, you know how I am."

"Yes. And he?"

"He freaked out. He said that certain words should never come out of my mouth. 'Oh, yeah? So what should come out of my mouth? Or rather, in my mouth?' I said."

"Claudia!"

"It's what he deserved, he didn't have the guts to tell me the truth."

"What truth?"

"That I'm a girl to fuck and that's all, since his wife won't."

"Did you leave him?"

"No."

"Why not?"

"Because I want to show him his responsibilities: every action has a reaction, I won't let him walk all over me."

In her first years at the office she kept her distance, which everyone attributed to shyness. But now her male colleagues considered her a "bitch." Claudia couldn't stand the questions that at the office were addressed to her not in words, but in looks: "Do you have a plan for your life?" "How many men are pursuing you?" "Do you have anyone who cares for you in Milano?" (a hypocritical way of asking whether she had someone capable of protecting her). She would go home from the office late at night, couldn't even open a book, and started to feel the first waves of a distant nausea.

She received a promotion, read the financial reports of the client companies, studied business plans to balance the books, collaborated with an intern and a manager, married, three children, a timid sprinkle of white hair, so thin that the bright skin of his skull shone through. The manager had tried to establish an immediate complicity in, according to Claudia, the worst possible way: "Such a pretty woman doesn't have a man by her side?"

"I don't believe information like that has any impact on the kind of work we will do." Even if she would have rather answered, "Not by my side, at my knees."

Once a commercial partner that was expanding asked for an analysis of its expenses. Claudia prepared it in two days, but the executive assigned the task of presenting it to the manager. This start-up which was opening up offices throughout Europe was run by two women who when they saw the report asked expressly who had prepared it. They were serious, and seemed to have a veiled air of menace. "I'm just the messenger," said the man to shrug off potential criticism. Claudia took the situation in hand. "We used cutting-edge software." The women looked at Claudia, told her that the report was very precise, much more than they had asked for, and complimented her by shaking her hand. One of the two gave her a kiss on the cheek when the time came to say goodbye: the freshness of that woman's skin filled her with joy.

I know why she liked the professor, she could tell him that she hadn't slept the night she finished *L'ora di tutti* by Maria Corti because in her nostrils she could smell blood and in her ears hear the cries of the Christians decapitated in Otranto. He wouldn't have considered her crazy, no man with whom she had spoken in the last few months even knew Maria Corti or Vittorio Bodini.

The older the man, the greater presumably was the life he had lived. And so someone like Baroni deserved a chance. One day the computer happened to chew up a report she had written and she had to rewrite it completely, plus she got into a fight with a shadow that had threatened her from inside a car after slamming on his brakes at the pedestrian crossing. At home she read random pages of her books, copied into a notebook sentences that had struck her, but for her that wasn't enough. She wanted to discuss them, to share. We spoke on the phone but I could understand clearly: she missed him.

That morning she wrote him a message, just "Good morning," but before sending it she stopped to think about the consequences. They hadn't heard from each other in a while, she thought she'd add a cheerful emoticon, a sun or a face, or a red heart, or maybe green would be more advisable, to signify hope; or a broken heart? The phone rang in her hands, she remembered the deadline on an invitation to tender that the company was supposed to compete for and she still hadn't checked the document. The haste spread inside her like the plague, she stopped worrying about what the right words would be, and wrote, "Good morning, I only wanted to know how you were doing." Not until late that night did her phone light up in the dark while Claudia was trying to fall asleep. "My wife isn't well, this is a difficult moment, we are particularly close. Leave me alone."

She walked through the streets until she got lost, then she phoned me to tell me what had happened, that she felt so stupid, that the only man who interested her was burnt out, and married, that he didn't deserve her and had questionable tastes in literature, not to mention a wife who checked his cell phone.

Then she got into the first taxi in a line of white cars. In the rearview mirror she noticed the driver staring at her naked legs and that persistent gaze made her feel a subtle pleasure. It lasted a couple of seconds, immediately after which she was ashamed. When they reached her apartment building the driver warned her, "Be careful running around with such a short skirt here, this area is full of Africans."

Claudia was left speechless, the memory came back to her, the bitter breath of Michele when he sat on her chest at the Torre Canne beach, and then the text from the professor's wife, and when her classmates would make fun of her because she was the tallest, the richest, when a kid at middle school asked her where she had left her breasts, since she was still the only girl on whom they hadn't formed. It all came back to her at once. "Bastard," she thought on the sidewalk, the main door open, through the lobby she could see clothes hung out to dry and the geraniums turning red. So she removed her skirt and was left in her underwear, a simple cotton bikini, black and French-cut. Her thighs were illuminated in the reflected light that flooded the lobby. She walked slowly and aggressively toward her apartment, feeling powerful. The freshness between her legs gave her goose bumps, as if she had just stepped out of the sea in summer. When she was behind the door of her apartment she heaved a sigh. She filled the washing machine with the clothes she had brought on her last business trip, the smell of the city had stuck to every fiber. From her backpack she removed her agenda, leafed through the pages filled with appointments and reminders. At the bottom of that day's page she wrote one word, making the letters bold with her pen, a single word: FREEDOM.

After the new municipal regulations on public housing, the cooperative where I worked had to close. The office was a prefab surrounded by houses that were being bulldozed, someone poured gasoline all over and set fire to it. But the experience I gained ranging from bookkeeping to land registers ended up being useful when I became an employee of a real estate agency—in that period everyone was looking for bargains in Puglia at rock-bottom prices, and I managed to insert into leases a clause that turned rentals into sales. It wasn't a scam, just a loophole in the law. I had learned that people paid only to avoid headaches; young people wanted to get rid of the country houses, the trulli, specchia and pajare they had inherited, and speculators wanted to buy them for as little as possible. My job was to match supply and demand. I didn't wear a jacket and tie like my coworkers, but I was always friendly, accommodating, and as neat as a student taking his first finals; I returned all phone calls, even after the contract had been signed. I'd buy a caffè sospeso at the café in the center, free for whoever asked, since it's a sign of magnanimity and power that costs next to nothing. "This one is on Veleno, Veleno junior, because if it were up to Veleno senior, all anyone would get is a kick in the ass."

My office in the centro storico was a *iuso*, which around here is what they call the basements dug out beneath the old mansions like burrows in the stone. Through the glass door I would stare at the colored fascist symbol on an iron streetlight, shaped like an upside-down bell, unaltered since its installation a century ago, and a part of me felt exactly like that aging piece of iron surrounding the light.

At night I always went home alone, my parents would be watching television with the volume low, falling asleep on opposite ends of the sofa. I didn't want to become like my father, with his sloth. At school he would mark the absences in his class register and then send everyone out to play a generic game of "ball." His students could do anything they wanted in the cement playground where they were released like prisoners, even get into fistfights. And he, with his round angelic face, would ignore them. The more my real estate business grew, the more he felt a threat looming over him: that he would die poor. He was convinced that I would rob him blind, and he wallowed in an archaic, undying well of southern Italian self-pity.

Some days, when I wasn't showing houses, I would hole up in my office and play Tetris, let myself be hypnotized by the movement of the colored pieces, think of Claudia and succumb to listlessness until the phone rang with a new client, a new trullo to sell, a well-lit specchia with a vineyard that needed to be posted on the bulletin board in the column for special bargains.

My life became a litany of constant haggling: sometimes I could barely catch my breath, but then I would emerge from the day with the petty glory of the salesman who sees his business succeeding, and his bank account more in the black than the red. Contracts, purchase offers, mortgages, bank guarantees, every nuance of the planet on which we live. In the meantime, fifty Somalis had arrived in Martina, twenty years old and male. I would have loved to become friends with them, but none of these young men, with round heads and emaciated faces, wiry black hair and skin as dark as coffee, would deign to look at me. A cloak of suspicion quickly descended over these men, who wandered through town and slept at an abandoned hotel. They didn't speak to anyone and the only people who approached them were children and the patients of the mental health center. This situation was not just local, it was all anyone talked about throughout Italy; you would have thought these dark men walking down the streets were the cause of the economic crisis, poverty, murders, famines and earthquakes. Words like that didn't bother me, as a child I had heard them applied to Albanians and as a teenager to Romanians. Now it was the Africans' turn. They played a part in a script performed by the most incompetent and the most cruel, who often just happened to be the most rich.

Together with hatred for Africans came hatred for gays. City Hall had sponsored an exhibit by a young artist who painted pictures of men kissing. The exhibit was visited by his family and hardly anyone else, but the presence of the town coat of arms on the brochure caused an uproar. A rally was quickly organized at which a young politician from Martina thundered against money going to gays rather than earthquake victims. The people applauded him although there had been no earthquake in Martina.

The next day three guys between the ages of twenty-five and thirty, well-dressed, appeared at the agency, and the word got around quickly. They had decided to return to Puglia after getting their degrees because they had the courage and the desire to change things and they were founding an association to unite all the local boys of goodwill.

"An apartment or an office?" I asked them, convinced they had come to look for a place for their association.

"We are actually here for you," said the youngest of the three. He had long brown hair, prominent cheek-bones and a black chain with a small ivory talisman around his neck. My gaze remained fixed on that one detail. "In one year there's going to be an election and we know that you are quite sensitive to certain issues."

I felt a chill. "I don't understand," I stammered, as if they were interrogating me.

"Your father, we know that he goes around with a pistol...and that you don't have a very good relationship."

"My father isn't violent, he's just..."

"...a fascist."

"No, not at all."

"I'm gay," the one with the ivory talisman cut in, "but in Martina I can't say that. To be blunt, my mother doesn't accept it, even if for ten years now I've been introducing her to each of my boyfriends."

All I could do was nod. I let them talk, then I invited them out for coffee, but said that I wasn't interested in politics. They still managed to make me promise I would think about it.

The meeting with them left me unsettled, as if they had given me for the first time a picture of what I looked like from the outside. A victim of a fascist patriarchy who did not even recognize it. Being unsettled, over time, gave way to an angry self-consciousness: it was unfair, I thought, that someone who didn't know me could express judgments like that. The idea of a reconciliation occurred to me: invite my father to lunch or dinner, and show others that, if not complicit, the two of us were connected and loyal to each other, or basically what we had always been, mutually innocuous.

The game of Tetris was lost. There's a moment when the combination of pieces, the tetrominos, do not let you clear the line because of their size and speed, usually after the thirteenth level. Claudia still hadn't reached that level, but the size and speed of the tetrominos were so off-balance that she could no longer maintain the same rhythm as she had in previous years. When I asked her how she was doing, she always answered with metaphors about feeling besieged. Lately she had changed several business partners, often working with companies that delegated their administrative duties to her consultancy company. Every month her responsibilities increased, until the worst one of all arrived, the one that Claudia suspected was an excuse to get rid of her: she was asked to lower the expenses of the large commercial branch of a company that had already fired thirty people. She was supposed to justify another thirty cuts and take care of it personally. She didn't say no right away. She went on vacation, then took a one-month leave of absence, and in the end she was the one who got cut. They proposed a severance package. She accepted.

Her last month in the office was the worst, she was forced to see that she had formed no friendships with her colleagues, not even with the interns she had trained. On her last day of work she dressed the way she used to when she went to raves, in combat boots and a long denim shirt over black shorts. They saw her walking down the corridor holding her arms out as if she were balancing on an invisible tightrope, wearing headphones to listen to music.

On her first days unemployed she dove into reading, and set the alarm clock for early in the morning so as not to lose control. She took two trips, one to London and a shorter one to Paris. Both cities seemed grim and repugnant, maybe because of her mood, the people seemed diffident. "I'm just getting old." She phoned me twice one day to announce that she had started taking lessons in piano, painting and German. Then, after one month, she quit everything except German. "I don't have an ear and I don't feel colors, but what I do want is to read *The Metamorphosis* in the original language."

She browsed through the few job offerings that fit her CV, until on her Facebook page she found a friend request from one of her interns. The girl wrote that a woman had looked for her in the office and taken her contact information. She added that she dreamed of one day dancing down that corridor of grès porcellanato and rubber the same way Claudia had.

The woman who had asked for her contact information was the business partner who a while back had kissed her on the cheek after a meeting. She was opening up a branch of her start-up in Germany and was looking for a brilliant accountant whom she could trust, and she had worked well with Claudia. Claudia was flabbergasted. She articulated in her head the three syllables of the city where the branch would be opened: *Ber-li-no*.

A few days later she received a strange phone call from her bank. It was the somewhat professional voice of a young man. "Signora Fanelli, could you please come to our office? The director would like to speak with you."

"I live in Milano, I do all my transactions online," Claudia answered. She was in a hurry.

The man asked her if she had recently opened up an account online. "I don't understand." She thought that maybe someone had hacked her account, that a thief had gotten her pin code and drained small amounts from it month after month until it was empty.

Much worse.

Claudia Fanelli discovered that she was still trapped in childhood and had never left. Everything that she had deposited in that account had disappeared, withdrawn by an authorized person.

"I didn't withdraw a thing," she protested.

"I know, but your mother did," said the man. "This account had a double signature: yours and your mother's."

"My mother?"

"The last withdrawal was three days ago. From the Martina Franca branch. Antonietta Bianchi came by together with her lawyer, Marco Curcio."

Claudia arrived at the bank's headquarters on the eighteenth floor of a skyscraper. It smelled of plastic and carpet, sounds were muffled. This was not a good moment: people had lost a lot of money, funds had collapsed all over the world. In that period bank officers were stressed out and under the gun, but with her they were friendly. They shook her hand. They advised her to get a lawyer. They said that they were available to open another account and give her a two-thousand-euro credit limit.

The woman with whom she spoke had blue eyes and little black moles on her face. She paused frequently. When the moment came to say goodbye, she smiled and said that on the top floor of the skyscraper there was a bar with a nice view, as if she were confiding a secret known only to a small circle of people to which Claudia had just been admitted. Claudia sensed an uncommon kindness and felt obliged not to ignore it.

When she entered the elevator, she dried her eyes and pressed the button for the twenty-third floor. There she found the promised bar, a dismal counter surrounded by four cocktail tables and thin plywood walls. They were closing, told her that the coffee machine had already been turned off. She must have looked pretty despondent because the waiter asked her if she was alright.

"Yes, but I'm very sad," and she turned as if to leave. While she was going back to the elevator she heard two, three times, "Signora." The waiter told her she could stay without ordering anything. "There's a nice view, and you're lucky because there are no clouds today." You could see the Gran Paradiso mountain.

She followed him to a table by a small window, an embrasure, but the panorama was beautiful. Claudia had lived in Milano for ten years and had never seen the white summit of a mountain. It felt like a true farewell, "Because Italy is a country that begins in the sea and ends in the mountains," she wrote to me before announcing that she would be leaving, for a north even farther north than the place she had been all these years, teeming with the new Italians seeking fortune: Berlin. And even if it had been Atlantis, the island of Phaeacia or Mars, I would never stop following her.

Part Four

Ruinenlust

(Noun. Masculine. The pleasure elicited by the allure of abandoned buildings in ruins: power plants, old insane asylums, sanatoriums and villages reduced to rubble. A feeling of nostalgia for a time that has inexorably passed. The word originated in neoclassical culture, when travelers admired the remains and vestiges of civilizations that had disappeared. It also alludes to gratification over one's own failures and joyfulness over absolute ruin.)

I couldn't stand most people my age who lived abroad, once they'd expatriated they discovered that for twenty or thirty years they'd been living among barbarians. It doesn't matter what city they were in: Paris, Barcelona, New York, Beijing, Osaka, and obviously the most cursed of them all, Berlin. It doesn't matter what job or deeper reason was hidden behind their new life. Their homeland was rife with thieves, bureaucrats, religious fanatics, cronies, and mafiosi. But what had they themselves done to improve things? They'd left.

That is what I thought at the time, but those who leave and those who stay both have their reasons. Now, these many years later, I can see that. The undying appeal of the road not taken.

Claudia did not see things that way. The past, including her mother, needed to be erased. She only ever talked to me about her new city. Berlin, Berlin, Berlin. There she was free, she loved and got lost, worked and ate, failed and started all over again, without ever feeling like a nobody. By now her distance was not just geometric: it was existential. She spoke another language, thought in another language, and was surrounded by people who spoke other languages.

During Claudia's first months in Berlin I felt something akin to the time she was in London, when I would stare at her empty desk for an answer to my own uncertainties, or the time I returned from Milano and sublimated my melancholy at the Martina train station. Nostalgia is nothing more than a persistent distilled pleasure.

I imagined her in perfect harmony with everything, getting off the airplane differently than all the other travelers, a beach bag as her carry-on so she could pack more stuff, head held high as she went toward the exit, confident. In Berlin there were always bridges on which you could stop to gaze at the river. There were enormous parks with towering oak trees, meadows so manicured that it was impossible to discern our herbs, the ones we had picked as children to pretty our hair or to smell their scent. Such were Claudia's stories, enhanced by her arrival in spring, when all big cities become brighter, and their colors more vivid. Long walks, the chiming of her bike and her strained voice as she spoke into her headset along the path between home and work, her first friends and even the word *friend* resonated in a different way, recurring more frequently in our conversations than in the past.

Then came winter and the chiming of her bike bell vanished, but in the background something exotic lingered, like the incomprehensible U-Bahn announcements that Claudia told me about almost with pride. She had never spoken to me about the subway in Milano.

Claudia's winter in Berlin was one long night from November to May. The cobblestone avenues beneath the great holly oaks, the florists' kiosks inside the subway stations, bursting with tulips and sunflowers. The cemeteries that disrupted the neighborhood grid, blending in with the parks.

My life had gone in the opposite direction. In a short time I had set up a very respectable real estate agency. On the straight road between Massafra and Martina I would clock two hundred kilometers an hour. I calculated the time it took me from one town to the next: eleven minutes for twenty-four kilometers. I had to deal with clients who wanted to sell, with a supply that was killing the market and money that dried up, while the banks were failing and taking people's savings with them. My advice was always the same: sell piece by piece. One-hundred-twenty-square-meter apartments became three mini apartments, baroque mansions in the centro storico I sold by the floor, agricultural land was discounted since the taxes would have cost an arm and a leg and you were better off giving, donating, abandoning or removing your name from the stones you had inherited from your ancestors.

The highway I took was filled for long stretches with twists and turns, it climbed up a hill of holly oaks that concealed the old radar base, then came hairpin turns, one after the other, which became a flat and narrow tongue like the roads in the immense American West, with lunar rocks, ravines, and a violet horizon. I pored through the real estate registry in search of abandoned trulli in the countryside: I'd buy them for next to nothing and immediately after try to resell them at higher prices. Many owners left behind their possessions, in what seemed to be an ailment of my countrymen: roots grew between the gray stones of the specchie and stone cones, like carnivorous plants. And I took pictures, published announcements, hunted for buyers and reassured sellers. Grottoes, holes in the stone where with a little luck you could install electricity and running water: Massafra was the future because it was comparable to Matera but less expensive.

I would dress like an employee of a funeral parlor, dark ties, custom-made jackets, and eco-leather shoes. I was dealing with the property of people who had died or were leaving. Buyers wanted empty houses, the previous inhabitants' furniture brought bad luck; I arranged for the homes to be emptied. The companies that provided this service, after filling their trucks with stuff, would make the rounds of flea markets reselling it and making money off the forgotten memories of others. I would take a cut of the fee and sometimes, if there was a piece of furniture that interested me, I would set it aside. A family's possessions have a soul and the Japanese say that after fifty years a spirit grows inside them.

All the while I lost weight, feeling pleased with myself whenever someone would say, "What's happening to you, Veleno, are you eating flies?" Every day I would boil two eggs and hide them in my pocket. That would be enough for me until evening, peeling them only when my head started to nod and the asphalt on the road where I was driving seemed to disappear. The bridges in Massafra stitched together the flesh of a city scarred with ravines. It was like looking at the center of the earth, a place where I was possessed by the urge to howl. At night I would return home, tired and defeated, my eyes itchy, my throat dry.

My mother left one Saturday when the sunlight was flooding the living room. A shoulder bag and sunglasses to hide her blue eyes, which at home were always sad. "Don't make too much of a mess." She kissed me on the tip of my nose. She was going on a trip to Vietnam. At the front door my father had a forlorn look on his face. His wife and his son were an arm's reach from him but their hearts were far away. I immediately felt a powerful knot in the pit of my stomach. "Anyway, she'll be back," my father said, with a wavering voice. "Where have I heard that before?" I thought.

I found myself imagining how the story between my mother and Claudia's father began, the first time they locked eyes at the hospital, the first kiss, the moment of truth when they realized they could do it. I remember when one day, angry with my father, my mother had told me not to fall in love with your fencing partner because after he strikes you he retreats and she was sick of people who retreated.

I always hung out with the same classmates, even if as the years went by the group considered me a charity case, I never introduced girlfriends and I showed no interest in having a family, I was all work and no play, we got together because we had stayed in Martina, at bars on the edge of town, going toward Taranto with its burgundy sky.

I did kiss an older woman, a teacher who acted like me, when I talked she seemed absent. In our encounters we found a pause from the rest of our lives. Maybe all we wanted was tenderness, we breathed a sigh of relief when we went our separate ways without having sex. She returned home to her husband and in bed I remembered a scene from thirty years earlier: the lullaby my mother sang to me with a turban on her head.

Claudia told me, amazed, about the quantity of trees and vegetation and canals there were in Berlin. On the street where she lived she noticed a mulberry tree like the ones in the Martina countryside. The leaves of the Berlin mulberries were smaller, she said, the tip and the curves made them resemble a valentine. The resin melted into your hair. Etta came back to her like a ghost of childhood, when in the summer she used to place a white handkerchief on her head so the pine trees in the Fabbrica Rossa playground wouldn't get her dirty. A battle to recover the money wouldn't help anyone. That was another reason why Claudia was in Berlin.

She lived in a cold and empty attic apartment, the shipment of her books from Milano had been arranged through a service that every day, for twenty-one days, delivered a single box. It was the staggered move offered by a company that used the postal network, so for one month Claudia opened a box at six p.m. sharp the moment she returned from work. On the day that she signed the agreement with the company she had a pleasant sensation, imagining her arrival in a new city where time would little by little release pieces of her. Then a thought occurred to her: the temptation to lose the twenty-one boxes arriving from Italy as a balm for her wounds.

Her office was on a street filled with Turkish stores, spice stands, cell-phone shops, florists. She worked in the same room as two architects, a graphic designer and two colleagues with whom she shared the start-up, a small and quiet Armenian woman and an Indian woman recently arrived from London who opened her mouth only to say that in Berlin they spoke terrible English. Claudia was convinced that the Indian woman detested her. The woman who had hired her was no longer there, she'd sold her shares, the other partner was never present. Claudia had avidly studied Eric Ries's manual on start-ups and the development of business plans. The job was more focused on administration and bookkeeping than finance, tracking the growth plans of franchisees. More monotonous than she had imagined. Her two colleagues, cordial in a perfunctory way, fled from their shared space at five o'clock sharp. She spent her working days on the telephone speaking an English that had steadily become more fluent. The workday was more concentrated than at the Milanese Tetris, the lunch break lasting just long enough to nibble on a sandwich or a salad brought from home. Her interlocutors were cold but professional. No male voice ever shifted the conversation in an unsavory way. Usually she had to teach someone how to use software, or they discussed the results of the algorithm, other times she had to organize in different files the authorizations from various government agencies to open new branches. Claudia diligently cataloged names and positions, her only diversion a blue vase where every week she put scarlet roses or white tulips.

"I feel welcome, even if I still don't know anyone."

"Maybe it's just your frame of mind, the city doesn't matter," I replied.

"It matters, Francesco, the air that you breathe, the gazes of the people, they matter."

"The people? People are the same everywhere."

"I have the impression that here everyone is my accomplice."

Her reports resembled those of an infatuated tourist, and nothing is more boring than the stories of a tourist. She said that the sky seemed higher than in Italy. I answered that it was the latitude, and she replied that I was turning into a curmudgeon.

She was always walking, following the wave of green traffic lights. Under the Jannowitz Bridge she could hear the clanking of the S-Bahn trains. Despite the noise, there was harmony in that commotion of rails, bridges and streets which rested on the authority of the Spree, a friendly river with a silvery glare that smelled like cold air and was the color of a stray cat.

At night swarms of homeless people emerged pushing shopping carts and dragging bags full of empty bottles that the supermarkets converted into coupons. She gave them empty bottles just to get a smile in exchange. It was gratifying to receive kindness for such a simple gesture. Then she would return home to read a poet who was lately her favorite, Raffaele Carrieri. One night on the phone she gave me a long speech to explain that Carrieri had left Puglia to embark on unknown ships, a little like her. Sometimes you read books only to find out that someone has already been there.

And what about my reading? In the past I had relied on novels and poems to locate Claudia's absence as well as a method to dismantle the prison I had built around myself. The rustic metaphors of Carrieri summoned his origins and seemed to have been written for us: "I am the one / who is always wrong. / The worm, the fruit. / I'm wrong in love, / wrong where it's wide / wrong where it's narrow, / I'm wrong to die / in a place where I do not live..."

Even from a distance Claudia gave meaning to my life, she was white gas, every email or message, every phone call, every word of hers was like the flame of fire-breathers on summer nights dedicated to the patron saint of Martina. I traveled for kilometers and kilometers, conducted visits to apartments and the countryside, spoke with many people to whom I had nothing to say, and her flame was always present to illuminate the darkness that had settled over me ever since she left.

"I've spent the last two hours looking at the window of your house," I told her during one of our phone conversations.

"You're certainly not short of imagination."

"It's not that. I downloaded Google Earth only to see the place where you live."

"You'll never understand the pleasure I feel by the window with these sunsets."

"We have sunsets here, too," I protested while that damn tramontana wind of Martina almost kept me from talking.

"I grew up down there and they screwed me over and over again, those sunsets that look like finger paintings, now I need a sky that's drawn with diamonds."

This lyrical commentary was not wholly convincing, as if Claudia was trying to share only beauty with me, since she did not consider me ready for the contradictions.

"The anger is gone from your voice."

"Anger is a waste of energy." Seraphic.

"Sometimes waste is helpful," I rebutted.

"You talk about waste and you've never taken an airplane to come visit me."

"You never invited me." I made childish remarks and was ashamed yet incapable of repressing them.

"Why are you being so formal?"

"I'm afraid of the moment when we have to separate again," I admitted.

"So is that why you're missing out on the best part of your life?" For me the fear that pleasure would end outweighed any desire.

"If I don't go dancing, I'll go crazy," she added. She hadn't had time, or maybe wasn't in the mood, to explore the Berlin nightclubs. Now this natural need was coming back to her full force. For us dancing was something sacred, we came from a land where dance is a ritual more ancient than religion. Without either of us realizing it, Claudia's new life was about to begin only now.

Berghain, a former power plant, still had the severe aspect of Communist factories. It was known as "the temple" or "the church."

In the rain Claudia walked down a long avenue between skyscrapers, past the Ostbahnhof station, mud and the smell of wet vegetation. A long line of silent people dressed in black. "They look like they're here to offer condolences," she thought. Some tall guys with shaved heads wearing black latex and combat boots turned around to look at her, puzzled. She was wearing cutoff jeans, a long white shirt and ankle boots.

After she had waited in line for two hours, the bouncer, a tall man with white hair and a tattooed face, shook his head. "Sorry, heute nicht." He had examined her from head to toe for at least a couple of minutes.

"Why not?" she protested.

The bouncer repeated his gesture of refusal.

Claudia found herself going for a nocturnal stroll over the brightly lit bridge of Warschauer Straße. On one side she admired the glittering Ostkreuz station in the distance, and on the other the cranes, arms of light that entranced her. She wandered amid swarms of young people, the powerful bass from discotheques made the asphalt shake. She was alone and burned by the rejection. She drank at the Sanremo, a little bar with red lights and the stench of a kitchen, chatted with a couple of guys long enough to be bored. She danced at the Lux, a small club, but she didn't like the music, waited in line at the Ava, near the East Side, but turned on her heels when the bouncer told her to wait. The sky started to lighten. It was six o'clock in the morning, a new day. Out came the dark shadows, casualties of the night, pale faces and purple circles around their eyes.

Berghain by day has a more prosaic look, a factory surrounded by ten-story-high cement boxes. Claudia gathered her hair in a ponytail, exposing the tattoo on the nape of her neck. There was no line, the cement box vibrated, dark windows were illuminated by blue and white lights. Nearby a couple of thugs were dealing ketamine, a girl with no underwear and runny black makeup was squatting, defecating under a tree and moving her body to the rhythm of a music that had stayed in her ears. Faded little imps traipsed in and out with a stamp on their arm. Claudia gained entrance with a lazy nod. Being admitted, a few hours after the rejection, injected her body with a jolt of adrenaline. She followed a path of dim lights that led her to a staircase, the steps ended in a white cloud way up on the main floor, where a dense mass of half-naked bodies sweated and rejoiced. An enigmatic harmony prevented any turmoil. Claudia noticed another iron staircase and started to climb up to catch some air. From up there she contemplated the crowded multitude, lined up like an army, which followed a single musical trajectory coming from the back of the room: elbows at sternum height, chests tucked in, heads lowered and swaying, feet firmly planted on the floor. At the far end, in a brightly lit nook, a short girl with a helmet of curly black hair, that morning's shaman, played her instrument. She radiated a music that was hard and violent, but elegant. She reminded Claudia of the responsorial psalms and a frame of the only film of Salvador Dalí that she had seen, in which through a crack in an egg the man with a pencil-thin mustache appears.

"It gave me the sensation of the world waking up."

"You're more than a little burnt out if Berghain reminded you of Dali."

"Frank, the time has come to shine and I felt like I was shining in all that darkness."

Claudia continued to climb until she reached a room that was less crowded, surrounded by nooks full of muscular men in tank tops, belts and studded harnesses, tightly wrapped around each other. She found a little air pocket where she could dance, started to thrust with her elbows at shoulder height, her fists parallel to her breasts, eyes half-closed. A woman with a lasso appeared. She was the only colorful figure, a silver crown that held in place the thick jet-black hair that tumbled to her shoulders; a red bustier and blue hot pants showcased legs as muscular as an ice skater's. A man with a tight smooth chest slipped into the loop of her lasso. They were beautiful, thought Claudia.

The girl came up to her.

"I'm Wonder Woman."

"I'm Claudia, du bist schön!!!" she shouted, the bass shook the walls.

"Ciao, Claudia, I'm Italian, too, you have a horrible accent!" and she laughed. The man on the leash looked at them, uncomprehending.

"He's a cool guy, too," said Claudia.

"I met him five minutes ago. Want to do a bump with me?" A bright light emanated from her square, harmonious face.

Claudia shook her head no. Wonder Woman kept on dancing, squeezing Claudia's hips, then hooked one leg in the air around Claudia's torso, while her boot kicked at Claudia's ass and pressed her toward her lips. The man looked at them, amused, and his mouth joined in that kiss. Laurie Anderson's "O Superman" rained down on them in a version Claudia had never heard. Wonder Woman disappeared into the crowd, and Claudia found herself with the man in the lasso surrounded by human beings who looked like fish out of water. Mascara dripped from his eyes. He wasn't the only man in the place wearing makeup. Claudia liked him, he was kind. With his tense sweaty chest he looked like the angels at the Augustinian monastery of Martina. Statues carved like muscular ephebes to stimulate the fantasies of the monks and offer them serenity. She wanted to tell him that she was from a land of wind, chickens and olive trees, but he said goodbye, leaving her slightly confused. "I have to go. I work tonight."

Wonder Woman reappeared with her eyes bulging, her face ashen, her hands free, the lasso gone. "They stole the rope, now no one will tell me the truth! Nessuno, nobody, niemand!" Claudia looked at her quizzically. "I'm no longer Wonder Woman without my lasso, I'm Erika, I've gone back to being Erika." And she started to cry and laugh at the same time.

"When Wonder Woman ropes a man with her lasso he admits everything. Do you remember the TV show? The creator of Wonder Woman is the same man who invented the lie detector."

"Was she so high that she really believed she was her?"

"Erika wasn't high, she was just Wonder Woman, you should have seen her, Francesco, she really was her."

Erika took Claudia by the hand, pulling her along behind her, her eyes fixed on an invisible horizon. Clauda entrusted her feelings to her, they became reflections of each other, playing mirror the way children do. Claudia laughed. There was a sour infusion in the air, sweat and cannabis, violent surges of smoke descended from above, everyone danced by themselves, everyone was looking for their own world, one girl executed precise military movements facing the wall, as if she wanted to grab her own shadow. They seemed happy. It wasn't the synthetic drugs, the pervasive sex, the violent bass, the beauty of the DJ dancing in front of his console. It was something else. She realized this as she left Berghain, after more than fifteen hours of uninterrupted music in her brain, her muscles and her eyes. She had descended into the Underworld like Euridice, and met Persephone, queen of the Afterlife.

"How can you trust people that you met at a place like that?"

"I have the impression that someone lit a match in my dark room."

"Tomorrow you'll have forgotten her."

"I feel like I've been thunderstruck."

———

Erika lived in a house with two guys and a girl, in that phase of life when you scrape by because you're short on resources. The room was covered with posters like a little bedroom in the 1980s, on a bare wall there were scribbles of random sentences, dates, tic-tac-toe, snatches of songs.

Claudia let herself be taken, guided by an instinctive trust. Erika fell fast asleep still dressed as Wonder Woman. Claudia read the words on the wall, letting them cascade, as if her mind were a shoreline washed by the ebb and flow of the sea. She dwelled especially on the capital letters at the beginning of stanzas, letters written with a child's round and shaky calligraphy.

She remained in the twin bed of Erika's cubbyhole, while the roommates on the other side made loud movements.

"You're tall and good, but a little anxious not to appear that way," Erika told her, waking back up with a drowsy voice. Then they wrapped themselves up in a hug.

Claudia washed herself in a little bathroom crammed with empty bottles stacked in the cupboard next to the mirror, and observing herself saw that her face was crumpled, her eyes swollen, her lips surrounded by a red halo.

She found Erika in a T-shirt and pants, so sleepy that she struggled to stand up against the door of her room. Now you could see that she was a girl with muscular arms, very different from when she had collapsed onto the bed. In her mouth she exhibited two black windows in the place of her upper premolars. Claudia stared without wanting to and Erika said, "I have weak teeth, but I laugh anyway." In her face a different light turned on.

That night Claudia left with the feeling of having slept at the home of an old friend or family member. Even if they'd said goodbye, she knew they would be seeing each other again very soon. She stared at the building she had emerged from to memorize it, it was all white with yellow frames around the windows. Wooden stairs and balconies, fragile doors that would give in with a good kick. A woman in a chador and two little girls had left the door open so she could go out, Claudia made a gesture to thank them.

We were two perfect solitudes, two monads. I was polite and knew how to make small talk with anyone, but on the inside the fire was gone. I liked remaining in Martina because it kept anxiety at bay, everyday life was bearable, I hid in the shadow of a mulberry tree, walked on the dark beach of Torre Canne. Domenico came back for a few days with his wife and daughter, when I heard I fled to the countryside and went to eat the violet petals of the starflower and shoots of the mallow the way Claudia had when her father died. In Martina the wind rattled the shutters and made the windows whistle almost every day of the year, I inserted the earplugs that Claudia used to put on to go dancing.

Every day Claudia's job was to explain that damn software to hopeful twenty-year-olds scattered around the world. But going to work also meant the small pleasure of filling the blue vase with flowers. Her Vietnamese florist at the Karl-Marx-Straße station wrapped begonias, hyacinths, peonies, white roses or sunflowers in paper bouquets. The darker and colder the city outside, all black and white, the more colorful the flowers in her office.

The girl whom Claudia had first met was not the same person when they spent time together during the week. On Saturdays Erika entered into an alien dimension and subsisted on protein bars, amphetamines, chocolate ice cream and tap water, a true alchemist of synthetic substances. After that first experience, Claudia avoided that world because it was so hard to come back down to earth on the Monday after dancing for twenty hours straight, and kissing dozens of strange mouths, with the illusion of fulfilling every possible desire. Better to keep her distance, she told her innate sense of discipline. On Sunday nights she would go to Berghain and wait for Erika to leave the enormous cement box that boomed up and down Friedrichshain. The whole weekend was balanced on that expectation, that precise moment toward eight o'clock at night when Erika's shadow would be cast against the sole window on the second floor, the white and blue lights flashing against the glass. The silhouette of her face, the loose hair and Wonder Woman tiara, made their appearance like the blurry outlines of a mirage. There she was, her arm raised to say, I'm here.

With her eyes bulging and her mouth distorted by a smirk, Erika devoured the noodles they would buy on Gleimstraße. She would describe what she had seen in the club, scratch her arms and her head, stroke Claudia's hand. Paul Oakenfold in the background, wild abrasive music that resembled Erika, and at times the air felt like the sizzling of an egg in a pan. To Claudia it was what Erika's brain must have sounded like.

Outside the world of Berghain Erika wore her hair tied back or gathered under a cap with a visor, loose clothes, and the shabby look of someone who dresses to keep from feeling cold. A dark windbreaker with the zipper all the way to her chin that she would pull up and down compulsively, rubbing it against her throat. Although she was younger, Erika had very specific ideas. Ligurian, family of restaurateurs, she dreamed of opening a big American-style bar. She'd been living in Berlin for three years, worked off the books at a handmade-bags shop, and received unemployment compensation thanks to two years spent behind the counter of a gelateria. Her eyes opened wide whenever Claudia spoke to her about Antonia Pozzi or Rina Durante. She would reply with the sextiles and quadrants of the great astrologer Lisa Morpurgo. She treated influenza with tisanes of plantain and helichrysum. Thanks to Erika Claudia discovered that she had Mars and Venus in the eighth house, the moon in Aries, a Virgo ascendant, and above all a sun sign that was the opposite of Erika's.

On certain days of the week she would lounge naked in the Liquidrom of Hallesches Tor, a small thermal space where she traipsed along the edges of a big pool in clouds of steam. "In Berlin you can dress however you like, or not get dressed at all." Despite the cold and the white sky, for her the city was like warm bedding in which she felt comfortable.

Claudia made progress with her German, every time she came across a new expression she would repeat it out loud hoping for her friend's approval. She wrote down the sentences she learned in a leather notebook tied shut with a string. She would dwell on long words, to her they were like playing with Legos. You could build new words by putting together four or five roots. Claudia liked the linguistic vitality by which two or more words could be combined to define a nuance. Mark Twain wrote that in Berlin one could learn everything except German. But Claudia was able to learn German precisely because she did not study it: she experienced it as an adventure, like an explorer, on a prolonged search inside a mine from which precious minerals could be extracted. One of her favorite words also regarded me and defined our attitude toward living in other worlds, imagining impossible stories, a word that doesn't exist in Italian except by paraphrasing or describing it.

"Can you teach me a new word?" she would often ask as she crossed the city with the girlfriend who could have told her where to get the best coffee, which bouncer was nicest, how often the M13 line passed, or the password to a speakeasy, but who didn't know the location of the Wall, the Cathedral, or the capitol building. They walked and walked, until the sun disappeared behind the cranes that devoured the Ostkreuz horizon. One night Erika pronounced her favorite word: "Kopfkino."

"Movie in your head?"

"Yes, I have lots of movies in my head, but I can never watch them to the end," she explained, shivering and curling into a ball with her arms. It wasn't cold, maybe it was one of those movies that was playing at that very moment.

Claudia reflected on her own Kopfkino: she spoke with the clouds, ate white mulberries, swam in the waves of the Adriatic. Then she wrapped her arms around Erika, she of the strong muscles and robust bones, who in an earlier era would have survived childbirth, plagues and famines. Claudia, instead, with her skinny prominent bones, would have died from tuberculosis. For a moment her Kopfkino turned bleak, as if she had been touched by the shadow looming over her friend.

"And you, Francesco, do you still play Kopfkino?"

"Yes, and it's always about you." But I knew that Erika wasn't like all the men that Claudia had been with, Erika was a girlfriend, and occupied the same vast luxurious field that I had occupied all my life.

One Sunday when Erika was tripping, Claudia prepared a hot bath for her. She poured a capful of jasmine bubble bath into the tub, a jet of water spattered against the foamy surface, while the trance music subdued the frenzy of Erika, who slid inside, naked. Claudia admired her small proportionate breasts, strong ankles, she wanted to caress them, although her skin had a yellowish sheen.

"Can you read me something?" asked Erika with her body hidden below the water, her shoulders rising above the foam, proud. The tips of her hair were wet, leaving the nape of her neck exposed. Claudia picked up her cell phone and looked for a poem.

"Read me a fairy tale," said Erika.

"Which one?"

"*Pippi Longstocking.*"

"But *Pippi Longstocking* isn't a fairy tale."

"I hate you when you're so fussy, read me *Pippi Longstocking*!*"

Claudia looked it up on Google and found the beginning:

"Once, way out, at the end of a tiny little town, was an old overgrown garden and in the garden was an old house, and in the house was Pippi Longstocking. She was nine years old and she lived there all alone..."

"I'm all alone, too," Erika interrupted her.

"You're not alone now."

"When I was Pippi Longstocking's age I was like her."

While Claudia was reading she felt overcome by the most senseless but profound feelings.

"Are you crying?" asked Erika.

"I don't know what's happening to me." Claudia sniffled, in self-defense.

That night they slept close to each other, half-naked. Erika turned toward Claudia and with her eyes closed placed her arm around her neck. Their mouths drew near, and the fresh breath of mint toothpaste filled Erika's nostrils. The two lips joined and then the elbows, the knees, the ankles. It was not an erotic pleasure but a bizarre joy without orgasm, like in the dreams of adolescence. It was the first time for Claudia with a woman; for Erika, it would never be clear.

When they woke up Claudia felt a pleasant languor, Erika's black hair smelled of smoke. "Do you want to live with me?" Claudia asked. An opportunity like that had never occurred to her before.

"Yes!" Erika answered, huddled on one side, her eyes closed.

Claudia was left bewildered and somewhat unsettled. It wasn't a negative feeling, but it wasn't happiness either.

Erika fell back asleep, Claudia kissed her forehead and went through her day at the office feeling effervescent.

She couldn't wait to get home to be back together, but a message from Erika was cause for alarm. "Sorry, I felt cold and put on some of your things, I left the house a mess, tomorrow I'll come back to clean it up."

When she got home, the closet looked like it had exploded, as if Erika had rummaged through her things. She worried that she had been wrong to trust her. The bathroom was a swamp and the bottle of bubble bath was empty.

Claudia swallowed her anger at the mess and focused instead on Erika's smell and the shape of her face, the words that her mouth had uttered in the moment of their pleasure. Erika vanished for a few days.

She reappeared the next Friday with three big suitcases and a guy with long hair, not terribly clean, a scruffy beard and a rotten mouth with a smirk that betrayed a willingness to attempt an unwelcome pleasure. "He helped me carry my stuff, do you mind if he sleeps here?" Her eyes twinkled unabashedly.

The two of them rutted. All night.

Claudia squeezed her pillow, biting it the way she used to as a child when she tried to sleep. She listed the German names of flowers she had learned by looking at the Vietnamese woman's window at the U-Bahn station: Sonnenblumen, Tulipane, Hyazhinthen, Rosen, then she moved on to the berries: Erdbeeren, Brombeeren, Johannisbeeren. Erika's friend was Italian and he had been hitting on Claudia, too, and for a moment she was terrified, because if Erika had wanted and insisted on it, Claudia wouldn't have known how to say no.

When at daybreak she heard her bedroom door opening she sensed a feral presence and smell. He came close enough to sniff at her, then he placed himself next to the bed. He slipped on his pants and shoes and sat down on a stool a couple of feet away from Claudia. She convinced herself to sleep, she was turning into a vegetable, praying that thorns would grow on her skin to keep that heavy breathing far away.

"You're beautiful," he said.

Turn me into a plant, oh god of gods. The man's hand caressed her head, in her heart an uproar. "Let her sleep!" Claudia remained in a fetal position, her face against the wall and eyes half-closed.

"Maybe she likes it."

"No, she doesn't," said Erika, firm and enraged.

He barked back to scare her before leaving, slamming the door to the apartment.

Claudia had turned around.

"Hug me," said Erika. Below her creased forehead her eyelids opened and closed to invite pity.

She was different, more adult, as if sex with that stranger had lasted a decade rather than a night.

"I won't hug you, I want to know what kind of trouble you're in."

Erika approached and planted a kiss on Claudia's sealed lips, looked her in the eyes. "I want to save enough money to open a bar."

"Don't get mixed up with the wrong people."

Erika raised an eyebrow. "I know how to handle myself."

"Did you use a condom?"

Erika rubbed her hand over her face as if it were a windshield wiper. "Trust me."

"I want to trust you, but you brought a creep into my home."

"He's just awkward."

"No, he's a pig and in Berlin there's a gonorrhea epidemic."

"We didn't use a rubber, but he's safe."

Claudia straightened out the improvised bed on which she'd slept, turning her back on her friend. "Just what I expected." Keeping busy allowed her to channel her fury.

"I don't go out with degenerates," was Erika's justification.

"No sex until you get tested," Claudia exclaimed, without much conviction, as she went into the bedroom, the bed was torn up, the sheets all crumpled. "You made a mess," she scolded, knowing how unbearable she sounded.

"What a temper when you're jealous."

"I'm not jealous, I'm disappointed and angry, and an asshole like that is not welcome in my house."

"Do you know what a femidom is?" Erika had changed her tone again.

"I don't know and I don't want to know."

"A condom for women, a latex sheath with two loops at the ends. We can have fun without your sacred vagina being touched by the lurid extremities of me, the plague-sower."

"You're not funny."

"Or we could use a dental dam, a latex sheet to place on your mouth before kissing a cunt completely covered by a thin layer of film."

"You're taking this lightly but I'm dead serious."

"It'll be as exciting as eating a lobster in Saran wrap." Erika clung to her and gave her a poke.

Claudia felt a mix of emotions that would stay with her in the days to come. Rage. Suspicion. Excitement mixed with terror. Worried that she would find an unwelcome guest at home. Fear that Erika would leave and never come back.

"She is certainly not ordinary," I muttered through clenched teeth, when what I really wanted to say was that I didn't like Erika at all and that Claudia was inviting in some serious trouble.

"I know what I'm doing, I'm not crazy," Claudia replied, as if she read my mind. What could we call this miracle, this relationship she and I had invented for ourselves? What could we call our shared instinct, that sympathetic power that allowed us to know what the other is thinking? It was more subtle and sophisticated than love, it was a free and independent nation, and it had no name.

Some time later Claudia called me, upset. She had run into the guy whom Erika had brought home that night. The world is much smaller than she imagined: he was staying in Gorlitzer Park with a few deviants, and belonged to the category of Italians who hung out in "Ghetto Italia," the expats who had given up on integration, lowlifes who, having not found jobs when they arrived in Berlin, succumbed to the shadowy world of resentment, located somewhere between marginalization and unvoiced bravado. They had left home with the desire for everything modern and cosmopolitan, and at the first obstacle they retreated to their lifelong habits, the worst of them ended up dealing at the clubs.

He stopped her on the street, asking whether she remembered him and saying that he had nothing against her for kicking him out, even if among Italians it's not something that you do. The same extortionate, self-pitying attitude that Claudia detested. In those few seconds he managed to tell her that Erika was both a dealer and a user.

In his words Claudia discerned a familiar stench. She turned away from him as you do from certain nightmares in the morning when you haven't slept all night. But she mulled over his words and the mysteries of Erika, and cried briefly on the U1 while its yellow cars shattered the blue of the morning sky over the columns that punctuated old Kreuzberg.

She had a mind to sit Erika down for a talk, but as she climbed the stairs she heard a clamor of footsteps and music coming from her apartment: a party at her place.

Erika opened the door in a black tank top, red shorts and a hat covering her eyes. "We're chilling with a few friends, I'll send everyone away now." She said it as if she didn't have a care in the world.

Claudia noticed more than a dozen dark figures huddled in the four corners of the room, they looked inanimate, like coats thrown haphazardly on top of each other.

"Why didn't you tell me?"

"It wasn't part of the plan," Erika laughed.

"I don't want drugs in here." Claudia placed her hands on her hips.

Erika suddenly changed tone, knitted her brows. "Who do you think you are, my mother? Have you forgotten how you stuck your face between my legs?"

"There's no need for you to say that in front of your friends."

"None of them speak Italian."

"That reminds me...I ran into your Italian friend on the street..."

Erika didn't seem surprised. "He's not my friend, and you shouldn't trust him, I'm done with him."

"And you're about to be done with me..." Claudia was on the verge of saying. Instead she hugged her.

"I'm going now. In two hours I want to find my home back the way it was," Claudia warned with a firm voice and the meanest face she could muster.

When she returned the apartment was in perfect order and smelled of detergent. Erika was waiting for her on the bed dressed like Wonder Woman, the lasso around her neck.

"Claudia, do you want my opinion?"

"Frank, you're the only person I trust."

"She sounds like an irresistible bitch."

"Even more than you can imagine."

"That's why you like her."

"I wouldn't have told you otherwise."

"You're going to get fucked over again."

"I'll take that as a blessing."

"I'll come to Berlin to save you."

"You shouldn't come here to save me, but to save yourself."

When we closed our connection, I remained in front of the computer where I'd been staring for hours at the blurry silhouette of Claudia. For the first time I wanted to go away, not to change my life, but to add myself to the things that were happening to her.

One morning in late September Erika called her, desperate, she was lost and couldn't find her way home. She'd been riding the bus back and forth for hours without remembering the right stop and claimed that a little boy was threatening her with an apple as big as his head. A few days after the giant apple episode, Claudia noticed that Erika was speaking in a confused and often incomprehensible way, as if parts of sentences remained stuck in her brain. She shivered at the thought that Erika might not recognize her anymore. During those weeks, Claudia continued to wait for her on Sunday evenings, wash her back in the bathtub and read her *Pippi Longstocking*, from Italian they'd switched to German, as if divesting of their native language was a biological molting, a phenomenon that would renew the shell of their identity.

Erika once asked her if she wanted to come with her to the Golden Gate, a club carved out of one of the former storage areas supporting a railroad bridge in the

Jannowitzbrücke area: whenever the train passed the walls shook, amplifying the music. Claudia said yes.

The club opened on Fridays and closed on Tuesday mornings. It had a tiny garden, two benches and a straggly plant. Claudia wore tight pants, hiking boots and a black V-neck T-shirt; Erika, white shorts, a black bandana on her head, and a long fake braid that reached her rear end.

After about an hour of music, Erika shouted in Claudia's ear, "I'm going to the bathroom." Claudia followed her. On the iron stairs the banister shook, their ankles vibrated.

"Are you going to do a bump?" Claudia asked.

"I can't believe you're asking me that!"

Claudia nodded, and Erika went wild.

"You act like your mother, fuck, you want to beat me like your mother, I love you and you take after your mother." She laughed as she was saying this.

"You don't know my mother," Claudia answered something along those lines.

Erika locked herself in the bathroom to do a hit of something she'd never tried before. The smoke and sweat-tainted air made her itchy. You're always a little different after trying a new drug. One part of her would be gone forever, like after your first joint or opium or hallucinogenic mushrooms.

Claudia heard Erika cough loudly in the bathroom, and then sneeze. When she came out, they went back to dancing for a few minutes, then Erika bent over, like in the videos of ancient tarantella dancers wearing white robes who used to spin around in the piazzas of Galatina on the feast day of Saints Peter and Paul. A line of drool painted a yellowish beard on her chin.

Less than twenty minutes later two nurses appeared with latex gloves and took her away. The dense musical notes intertwined with voices and shouts, you could no longer discern any one sound. Claudia shivered as the intermittent glare of the ambulance colored the square blue.

Claudia didn't want to show her face during the Skype call, but let the words tumble out.

"I'll be firm," she concluded, as if only to reassure me.

Every day for almost two weeks Claudia appeared at Urban Clinic at five o'clock sharp. In the garden, enclosed by a wrought-iron fence covered with ivy, ghosts moved about slowly in white gowns and plastic clogs: a few hours earlier they had experienced ecstasy followed by convulsions. Erika was one of those ghosts. When she left the clinic she was pale, her skin glued to the bones of her face, her head shaved, her eyeglasses as thick as the bottom of a whiskey glass.

Her convalescence was long, once she got home. Erika only ate food from the juicer, and in a catatonic state watched YouTube music clips and ethnic cuisine videos. Claudia started to look after her with a tenderness she didn't know she had: she was fine because she was looking after someone who was sick. Each act of kindness was preceded by a request for permission. "Can I prepare a tisane for you?" "Can I massage your neck?" Claudia realized that she loved that young woman assigned to her care in a way she had never loved anyone. And she told her.

Erika responded to Claudia's loving words with her own, but her tone was feeble.

Then one morning Erika woke her up with the announcement that she was going back to her parents. Her lips were white and her teeth opaque. Claudia realized that her new life was already over.

To forget her, Claudia went dancing for months. It's not true that you dance only when you're happy. There were abandoned factories, anti–air raid bunkers, warehouses on the edge of town, scrapyards, mills that had survived the war. From Thursday night to Monday morning every neighborhood had red or blue lights turned on in places that during the day looked uninhabited. In the environs, men with their collars flipped up guided the traffic, with barely a nod, of thousands of clubbers roaming the city.

She looked for a place where she could settle down for a while, she couldn't stay in her own, it reminded her of Erika. She rented a room in an apartment by the Spree river inhabited by two teachers from Hamburg. They were a couple of young vegans with a vegan Doberman that Claudia fed a can of tuna, punished by the immediate cancellation of her lease. Then she ended up at the home of a typographer married to a woman who specialized in esoterism, who on Saturdays, in the wood-and-lace living room, gathered other magic enthusiasts for mysterious and extremely long séances that ended promptly at dinnertime.

The summer sunsets in Berlin are pink streaks against a sky of different shades of blue: aquamarine, topaz, aragonite. The sunsets are not for everyone, shared only with the acolytes of a sect that the rest of the world considers a gang of naifs.

When yet another relative, friend or former classmate asked her why she didn't return to Italy, she would answer:

"I'm fine here."

"But what do you do there?"

At that Claudia the provocateur would spring to life: "I get high."

Meanwhile, instead, she meditated, practiced tai chi; on the phone she spoke to me about mantras, made me listen to them. Indistinguishable voices, male or female, repeated obsessively, "Ong namo guru dev namo," *I bow to the divine will*. And I listened to them and bowed to Claudia with all of her stories.

"I feel like walking on walls like in *The Matrix*," she once said.

"Cockroaches walk on walls," I replied.

"Francesco, what's wrong?"

"I miss you."

"Once upon a time you would have told me that ladybugs walk on walls while moths alight on them."

"I detest moths."

"But they are like me, they come out at night and fly toward the light." Then she laughed and her sudden burst of good humor was irresistible. I felt alone and would have preferred to talk about something practical, the house, work, life, but there was no time for anything, except for the two of us, the ladybugs and the moths.

One day she arrived at the office, punctual as usual, but instead of her colleagues she found two workers intent on unplugging the colored wires of the computer, and others busy removing the desks. Her blue vase was in a corner upside down sticking out of a wastebasket. A woman with eyeglasses and a tired smile came up to her, waving a sheet of paper. "Fräulein Fanelli?" That "Fräulein" transmitted a perverse electricity to Claudia, like when she was little in the countryside, running away from home, and got scratched passing between the olive trees. The woman gave her a termination letter that she could bring to an employment center to begin the paperwork for unemployment assistance.

"The company is having problems with Germany, but this is a great country. Here you can start over again."

She looked me up immediately, incredulous, babbling. "Frank, I'm out." I'd never heard her so undone. The conversation was wrenching, I could hear her rapid footsteps on the cobblestones, every now and then she would stop and laugh hysterically, then start talking again and walk, breathing heavily, saying this might be an opportunity to invent a new job, then she would self-destruct, accusing herself of being incompetent, good for nothing. "I've never been honest with myself, I've always chosen compromise, I should never have returned from London, I should have majored in literature, I should have understood a little more about who I am, I should have burned bridges much sooner." In those weeks we heard from each other a lot, I should have taken the first plane from Brindisi to be with her, but a mysterious force kept my ankles chained to the ground, the same talons that had held me back ever since I was born, and I was deathly afraid of the gashes they could give me.

She had an interview with a multinational company, and found herself sitting in front of a woman who resembled her. Not physically, because she was short and had dark black eyes, amaranth lipstick and curly jet-black hair, but in her gaze Claudia could see a restless person who was asking her the same questions she would have asked herself.

"Why did you, an Italian, choose our company?" the woman asked, in German.

Claudia was expecting it and responded with a ready-made answer. "I consider you the best and I aspire for the best."

"I understand, but we only have offices in northern Europe, and you come from a place that has sun twelve months a year, here in Berlin there are days that end at two and we have to take vitamin D pills every day for our bones."

To Claudia this consideration sounded a bit out of the ordinary. "I'm not afraid of the dark," she replied, trying to convince herself most of all.

While she was sending her resume around desultorily, her heart not in it, she met a young Argentinian psychologist whom she saw for a few sessions of psychotherapy. She lined up her triumphs and defeats, never calling the latter failures but rather crossroads or turning points. In those few sessions, she reexamined her life critically: the outrage her mother had committed shouldn't be repressed, but she had to shake it off, if only to ward off bad luck.

After the last unsuccessful interview, she realized that maybe she should stop looking for a job that matched the aspirations of what she had been until then, and the aspirations of the society that had raised her. There was a lot of talk about sustainable negative growth and in Berlin minimalism was the latest craze, small buildings with basic services, but large gardens where you could join a gardening collective or grow strawberries and tomatoes.

On the subway she read the advertisements on the walls of the cars: a specific target, people who wanted to change their lives. Language schools, financial consultants, courses for aspiring writers. The most brazen were the scientific studies looking for guinea pigs to test new medicines. She went. She found herself in the antiseptic room of a private clinic along with various kids who gave her the impression that they'd escaped from an institution or a difficult family. She noticed a pretty girl in a parka with curly hair and a ring that hung between her nostrils: she wanted to give her a hug and ask what she was doing there, getting injected with toxic substances for three hundred euros. But two men in dark suits and a woman in a white coat arrived, handing out the ethical commission's certificates, which no one seemed interested in reading, and asking the aspiring guinea pigs for their age and documents before starting. Everyone was younger than twenty-two. When it was Claudia's turn, the woman blocked her. "Not you." She was too old for the experiment. Claudia had read the general requirements but, deliberately perhaps, had forgotten them a moment later. Behind her neck she felt a chill, the breath of time.

One of the two men escorted her to the door, other aspiring guinea pigs were seated in the corridor, she strode down it draped in the shame of that rejection.

"Hey, do you remember me?" she heard someone ask. The voice had a foreign accent. The boy was wearing blue overalls and a fuchsia T-shirt, his eyes were staring at her, from a pocket a screwdriver stuck out.

Claudia's stories were like imaginary islands on the nautical maps of most people. But I clung to them like a castaway.

"It was the guy who was in Erika's lasso when we met."

"The hot guy?"

"The last man that I kissed."

"What ever happened to him?"

"He said that he liked my lipstick."

"What?"

"'Catrice Nude doesn't go with the blush you have on.' That's what he said."

"And you?"

"He looked at my lips and smiled, I only told him that Catrice was a generic, if he was that good he had to guess the brand, and he did. Nude-Tastic."

"Was he also there to donate his immune system to the cause?"

"No, he's a Hausmeister, a kind of maintenance man, he works at clinics and hostels."

"German?"

"Georgian, his name is Andria."

When she recognized him, Claudia envisioned him bare-chested in a painting by Pellizza da Volpedo, elongated on a ladder amid sparks that bounced off his welding mask, a shy and melancholic Hephaestus.

That afternoon they walked toward the bicycles attached to the racks on the sidewalk, then they went for kilometers, next to each other, walking, their bikes in their hands. He liked her, even if he would never dare to admit to himself the deep reason for that liking: she reminded him of Erika.

Exhausted by the long walk, they decided to take a tram, but they let many go by, since they continued to talk intensely, to talk about themselves, then she took a white Kleenex from her bag and unfolded it. "My father made my mother fall in love after giving her a silk handkerchief. This one is paper, but for me it counts just as much."

Andria laughed and answered that on paper you can write, if the message is beautiful it remains forever. His eyes were a color between green and hazel. He lowered his head and came close to her neck. Claudia thought he wanted to kiss her and remained still. He had a nice smell. Rather than his lips she felt his nose, for just a few seconds. After sniffing her he licked her neck, her ear, her temples.

"You're salty," he said.

"Now I'm going to taste you," she answered, sticking out her tongue, heedless of the strangers running toward the doors of the tram. She started with his eyebrows, then his eyes, descended to his cheekbones, sucked on his nose and his barely closed lips, his chin, drawing into her mouth a male smell she had never experienced: youth, stone, iron. Claudia felt it in her nostrils and in her mouth. She had an uncontrolled desire to blend into his purity, lend it her experience and be contaminated by it in turn.

She followed him to the Plattenbau on Leipziger Straβe pedaling on her red bike, the spokes making the sound of crickets at sunset, the sky was violet over the ivory of the massive apartment buildings teeming with young immigrants and students. Andria's apartment was hidden in a labyrinth; on the other side of a heavy door, a tiny twenty-meter-square cell jammed with irrational odds and ends. They made it to a small bed covered with a brown blanket. She undressed him, stopped at his member which emerged surrounded by little black curls, kissed it, it wasn't hard, his breathing quickened as if he was holding his breath. She ordered him, "Touch yourself," but he misunderstood and reached his fingers between her legs. His hesitation excited her even more, she bent over, guided it, now it was chubby and curved, but he couldn't get it up and she was horny. She helped him to enter although he wasn't ready. He buried his head in the pillow next to her, and in her ear he said, "I've never done it."

"Are you a virgin?"

"No, I've never done it with a woman."

After she returned from the trip to Vietnam, my mother chose to live at a masseria of trulli in the open countryside. My father reacted by buying a new drill and making a dozen holes in the wall of the bedroom, as if he were trying to hang imaginary paintings. In all the years that he was being betrayed by his wife he had never flinched, but when she left all he could see was a landscape with a thousand morasses, and taking care of the house was the easiest way not to drown in them. When I asked him to explain this phantom of home repair, he said that thanks to those holes the rooms would be able to breathe.

I accepted my mother's invitation to spend a few days together on the Gargano peninsula. With us came a friend of hers named Tonia, a support teacher at private schools, silent and judgmental, she had been with her in Vietnam.

Elisa Fortuna in her one-piece bathing suit, her back naked and golden from the gentle sun of July, her thick hair tamed by a barrette, stood out from the other bathers. The men cast glances at her.

We argued about a couple of their friends.

"I hope they get married soon," said my mother.

"Mamma!" I started to scratch the base of my neck, as if a column of insects had started biting my head. "But if your marriage to Papà was a failure?" and I thought of the unbridgeable gap between the two ends of the sofa when they watched TV.

"Marriage is a photograph, something remains of the person you loved for your whole life." I didn't understand whether she was talking about Enrico or my father.

Tonia started to stare at me while I scratched, awkward and furious, as if I had paws.

"He always does this when he's nervous," my mother reassured her.

Then they left me alone on the beach, I kept my eyes on them as they walked away, one ahead of the other. They were eclipsed behind the rocks as the sun fled and the sky darkened from cerulean to navy blue. They had their own harmony, Elisa slim and colored, Tonia wrapped in a white pareo, her hair short and gray. She was younger than my mother, a little chubby, and called my mother Lise, asking her not to walk so quickly because the pebbles on the beach hurt her.

I liked that handful of minutes before nightfall when I returned from walks on the Vieste pier with

Tonia and my mother, their faces moist and the smell of embers on their clothes. I liked the ritual of the last shower that washed away the sun of that day. Then I would polish the screen of the laptop on which I had worked in the afternoon because in the evening my date with Claudia awaited.

I told her that my mother sent her warmest wishes.

I noticed that Claudia had cut her hair short, and her face seemed disproportionate to the rest of her body, as if there had been a growth of that masculine part of her that had such a powerful attraction to me.

"I've got an issue at work but I'll solve it," I confided to her, hoping to hear some good advice.

"Maybe this is the right opportunity to leave everything," she said, banishing my every wish for confidences.

"My roots are here," I replied, irritated.

"Do you remember the story of the inverted tree?"

"No."

"Plato. Man is an inverted tree, his roots are in the sky."

"I feel like the lemon tree at your house, its roots are firmly planted here."

"But they're not. Between the two of us, you're the one whose roots are in the sky, all you have to do is realize that."

"And you?"

"Frank, I cut my roots, I'm a trunk ready to sprout."

For a while I'd been having problems with Dente the gangster. He had approached my father, complimenting him on the rapid advancement of his son in the real estate business. This kind of flattery through a third person usually portends a curse or a warning. "C'mon, that one's still living with me," my father answered to stay on his good side. When he was young Dente had been an altar boy and done some prison time. Nowadays he made his living as a loan shark.

A few days later—I had just finished showing an English agency a pile of rubble that I was passing off as a nineteenth-century masseria—I was approached by some thugs who when we were all younger used to shake down the kids on benches near my house. They were blackened by the sun, their arms bare, their lips swollen from brawls on the edge of town. "The owner doesn't want to sell anymore," said the oldest one.

"I don't know you," I answered, rushing in where angels fear to tread.

I looked at their shadows on the ground, which were getting shorter the closer they came. "Vele', we've known you ever since you were a little snot. Do you know who sent us?"

As if between us there was a ritual to which I adhered, I lowered myself to their threatening tone. "I don't know and I don't care." I played at being a tough guy, but I think I sounded more like someone shitting his pants.

"We're sent by Dente, who's a friend of the owner," again from the older guy, he was missing a front tooth. I focused on the hole that opened in his mouth before replying. "And I am the owner's representative." My voice trembled imperceptibly, as it always did when I stood before an authority. They noticed.

"The owner will soon be Dente."

"If that's the case, I'll see about it with him."

They left, giggling to each other, my client had fallen in with the wrong crowd, and thanks to him now I risked falling in with them, too.

I went home more annoyed than scared, I was greeted by the sight of my father in his underwear in the hallway. He was complaining in a loud voice into the telephone receiver to a woman who—after seeing me—thought I was his latest girlfriend.

Except that for a few weeks now we'd no longer had a landline and the telephone was a decoration, a souvenir of a time gone by.

One day my father went into the classroom with his customary nonchalance, but minus the tracksuit and sneakers.

"Veleno, who died today?" the janitor had joked to him. He did not deign to answer, breaking a complicit, decades-old habit between them of trading wisecracks and jokes.

The students looked at him skeptically. My father, who had always waged war against anyone who came to school without a tracksuit, was breaking the rule that he himself had imposed.

He took his place behind the desk amid the clamoring of the students, stood up and pulled out his semiautomatic Beretta M9. The shouting mutated to an ashen silence. Professor Vincenzo Veleno pointed it at his temple. A "No" shouted by someone covered up the metallic click of the trigger. Tick. Bang. Professor Veleno went limp.

The pistol was unloaded.

Professor Veleno picked his head up from the desk, smiled and took attendance.

He was summoned by the principal to clarify whether this was a joke or something awful that he didn't want to name. The explanations were vague, the extenuating circumstances nonexistent, he was forced to take a leave of absence. My father was a farcical character, and farce relies on vulgarity, every skit demands applause. At school the students no longer applauded him, were indifferent to his puns, no one even knew the dialect on which most of his humor was based.

"I'm alone, Franceschino," he admitted, speaking about his stunt. And he looked at his big hands. "I wanted to make them laugh."

"It's not funny when you pretend to shoot yourself."

"I wanted to be taken seriously, no one does around here."

"I've taken you seriously ever since I was born, even if there's a ton of things I've never understood. About you, and about my mother."

"We're two nutcases, that much you must have understood." He was being honest. "Then she found a man better than me."

"Papà..." Feeling sorry for himself wasn't his style.

"But maybe not that much better since she still lived here," he added.

"Maybe she stayed for me." I almost immediately regretted saying this.

"I've had my affairs, too."

"I believe you."

"I could have had more, but I didn't, because of you."

"Are you telling me you kept your pecker in your pocket for my sake?" His paternalism was involuntarily comical. That change of tone was a blessing in disguise. Our conversation was becoming too introspective for his tastes. "Anyway, if I hadn't fucked, you would never have been born," and he laughed. Once again I would not know the truth of Elisa and Vincenzo.

I said good night to him and made as if to withdraw to my room.

"Don't wiggle your ass when you walk," he told me, continuing to laugh.

"I don't wiggle my ass," I said, defending myself, but he threw a walnut at me. It wasn't a violent gesture, there was an element of camaraderie. But I felt dirty, and unashamed. I felt dizzy. Where am I, and who is he talking about? Dying for oxygen. Glass inserted under my nails. I went to bed wide awake, my head filled with heavy thoughts. It was a sleepless night until the day illuminated the shelf with my small collection of books and childish knickknacks. My bones were still strong enough to change my life. I gathered my strength to write her a text, a cry for help. "Do you have a spare bed?" And although the day was young the telephone confirmed that I had a soulmate on the other side of the world. "Your hour has come, Francesco."

Part Five

Sehnsucht

(Noun. Feminine. Compound word consisting of
sehnen, to desire, and *Sucht*, yearning. Nostalgia
for an unattained or unattainable desire for something indefinite in the future or for an unreachable
asset. It derives from the old German *sehsuht*, which
indicated the disease caused by the yearning for an
unreachable object, and can be translated into Italian as *struggimento*, heartache. The desire for desire,
the malaise and melancholy of every living creature
that longs for the impossible or even for the infinite.
Refers to the nineteenth-century concept of achieving a symmetrical male-female duality: "The androg-
enous flower is the only living thing that does not
experience Sehnsucht" [Johann Wolfgang Goethe,
The Metamorphosis of Plants].)

The Syrians seem to never end, a half million they say, maybe more, a long, exhausting single file crosses the border between Hungary and Slovakia, like the columns of prisoners of war; they march with their homes reduced to a small bundle, their children on their shoulders, and cross the puszta, while the Hungarian police vans survey the route—to make sure no one escapes the line.

It must have been the second or third top story on the television news in the days leading up to my goodbye, which like all goodbyes contained a small dose of finality; the TV cameras filmed the refugees, the microphones interviewed them, a cameraman tripped an old man who was running, in a panic, carrying children in his arms, he was a father but already looked like a grandfather. For us in Puglia it was déjà vu: when the *Vlora* had arrived, more than two hundred meters long and with twenty thousand Albanians holding firmly to the mast and to God, the children seemed like adults.

They were asking for bread but at the port of Bari, where they docked, soldiers were waiting for them. Some took off their belts to push them back into the sea, others instead shared their ham sandwiches to feed them. The usual history of mankind, the conflict was not between good and evil, but between the weak and the strong, and the strongest are the ones who, without being afraid, know they might lose everything.

"Take a look, you're just like them," said my father, still in disbelief at the news of my departure, as I was closing my suitcase. He continued to jiggle in his hands the keys to the car I was leaving him. While my mother had blessed me with a card, "Good luck, Uva Nera," he could not relent. "They're running away from problems just like you."

"Their problems are a war," I snapped, because he had touched a raw nerve. My father deep down was not a friendly and acrobatic cuckold, but an old and very bitter solitary wolf.

"Your problem is that you don't even know what a war is, and if there was one you'd cut and run like them," he scolded.

"You don't either." I had always been the weaker of the two of us, but with one foot out the door I felt for the first time that I had gotten the better of him.

"Don't close the agency, hand the management over to someone, listen to your father." His remarks made undeniable good sense, but I brushed him off with my truth. "I don't want anything that obliges me to return here."

Unlike the millions of emigrants who were leaving a family, I was returning to my family, returning to love, where all the most significant things of my life had been born. Claudia was waiting for me, I had even sniffed the smartphone on which her texts appeared.

In the sky that welcomed me to Berlin the violet of the Ionian Sea to which I had bid farewell reappeared. I crossed the countryside between the airport and the city, a forest of wood and stone, tall houses without balconies, the wide canopies of beach umbrellas emerged from some windows. I looked outside, and the iciness of the German language screeched in my ears. The announcements at the stations squawked, but to those incomprehensible words I was entrusting the obscure sense of my new life.

The relationship between Claudia and Andria had progressed, based on a mutual need to be looked after. As if with time they had sought to share not passion and sensuality, but tenderness.

They worked at the same place.

He had handed her an ad from a company that trained personnel for jobs in nursing homes. Claudia realized that Andria was showing her a path. While it wasn't a form of love, it still came very close.

Taking a part-time job at a rest home was not a sustainable negative growth choice but rather an opportunity: she earned enough to live on and read all the novels she wanted. At around one p.m., from Monday to Saturday, she would ask the guests of the home what they would prefer for dinner. Among the three alternative menus, one was prepared directly by her. German soups, Japanese ramen and Korean udon, she had become a specialist. She liked the dirt from the vegetables sticking to her fingertips, and tasting the vegetables while the sauce was cooking.

Her favorite patient was a sweet elderly man, Torsten; she would greet him by stroking his hand, paper-thin skin that seemed to crack when she touched it, he would turn red and smile.

"I adore him because once he told me that sooner or later we all become like floors. Soft and warm when we're young, but then we get hard and cold," she told me, amused.

They rarely slept together, Claudia and Andria, and when they did she stayed awake because on Andria's body she could smell the sex of other free-spirited men like him. A vinegary odor that left her in a daze. It acted on her like hypnosis, and her big nose became like the sensitive tip of a divining rod. Yet no one had ever made her feel so safe. "You have to feel safe with the person who loves you," she had written to me many times. One day an aggressive cashier at the REWE supermarket had made fun of her accent, and on Andria's face a bestial expression was drawn that she had never seen on him before. In Martina when they want to know who you are they ask, snapping their fingers, "Come ti metti"— Where do you fit—that "metti" encompasses ancestry, relations, marital status and goals, the way you exist in space and time, how we *fit* into life, on bended knee, ready to flee or to leap. But Andrea had never bent his knee, this is what Claudia liked.

"Your suitcase is too big," she said, pointing to the trolley I was pulling.

We didn't kiss on the lips, almost no physical contact, I toyed with my luggage and followed the snaking metal rails all the way to the tram stop.

"I'll show you my place, then I have to dash to work."

In her face I could read a hardening that I couldn't explain. She was no longer the "all skin and bones girl" that made her mother worry about her health; her cheekbones were still sharp, but her cheeks were fuller, her eyes busy deciphering thoughts that arrived from afar.

The city was boiling beneath my feet, the sidewalk shook from the subway and the crowd emitted a constant buzzing.

"How are your grandparents?" she asked.

I wasn't expecting that question, many years had gone by since I had introduced them to her.

"They're at an institution, they were no longer able to live in the countryside by themselves."

"Like where I work. In the end we'll all end up there," she remarked with a frown.

"Something like that. It was their decision, but they weren't happy to go."

"And their land?"

"We've abandoned it, one day someone set fire to the vineyard. They found the burnt body of a dog, it had been filled with gasoline."

Claudia brought her hands to her face. "What bastards."

"Everything was destroyed."

"Even the well?"

"What well?"

"The one your grandmother showed me when we went to visit her, don't you remember?"

"No."

"Your grandmother told me that she wanted to show me something, and it was the well. She told me that a woman had been thrown into that well a century ago."

"She never told me."

"You don't tell certain things to men because they can't understand them."

I was confused and also a little offended that my grandmother had revealed this secret to Claudia ten minutes after she'd met her.

"I'm afraid I know why she told me. But I didn't understand until years later."

"My grandmother is someone who used to make up grim stories to scare the shit out of us," I said to lower the tension.

"Your grandmother told me that wherever there is a well, there is always a woman who ends up getting thrown into it by...a man."

"Really!"

"If I had remained in Marina they would have thrown me into a well."

"We're not savages."

"So what would you call what Curcio did to me? Isn't that the same as throwing me into a well?"

"I don't follow."

"A few years ago I read a woman writer...Alba de Céspedes, who said that women live at the bottom of a well, and only those in the well understand compassion."

"I don't understand what you're saying."

"Your grandmother was asking me for help."

"My grandmother is fine."

"I'm happy to hear that, but I've been wanting to tell you this for many years."

When we got on the tram I had the feeling I'd been wrong to come. My father was right, I was like the millions of Syrians who arrive here without finding anyone. Our lives had grown too far apart since the time we'd loved each other openly. Claudia then took two seats and, patting her hand on the one next to her, invited me to sit down. My head leaned against the nook between her neck and her collarbone. Upon contact with her skin my forehead burned. The foreign words of the passengers on the tram were no longer the ice of a few hours earlier but a murmur in the background. I smelled the air of the new city filtered through the skin of Claudia, who had started to sing softly, "Too Much Love Will Kill You," by Queen. Three stops must have gone by, but since we had fit back together it felt like an infinite fissure in time. Claudia sang without saying anything about herself but saying all the things I wanted to know. Two guys boarded selling newspapers and holding paper cups blackened by coal, behind them a woman wrapped in a black burqa and a stroller with two babies piled one on top of the other, boys pushing a bedspring in the back of the tram, from a violin came the unmistakable Fifth of Beethoven.

We got off and followed a pack of blond children on bikes. "We're in Pankow," Claudia said, and looking around I saw streets punctuated with plane, poplar, and beech trees, with the smell of forest and fresh air. "I live over there," and she pointed to a gray building surrounded by other buildings that were also gray, like the sky. As we crossed the street she invited me to take a look at the bushes, because at night they shook with the furtive hesitation of metropolitan foxes. As always, there was much more she wanted to tell me that I would not be able to understand.

In the apartment she ordered me to take off my shoes, showed me my room and then hers, I noticed that there was nothing other than the bed, a desk, and an armoire. The rest of the house had cardboard boxes filled with stuff—books, lamps, baubles, postcards, glass jars—as if a move was imminent. She said that she would sell them at the Flohmarkt, she didn't want anything in the house that created "dark spots." She lived with little, a pale red poppy emerged from a pre-serves jar filled with wet potting soil, dry basil leaves decorated the surface of a tin bucket hanging by the window. Objects are permeated with dangerous ener-gies, possessions weigh on the soul.

Coming into the bedroom she said she had to change, but did not ask me to leave her alone. She did it as naturally as if we were brother and sister, her clothes landed on a chair, while from the armoire came the scent of lavender packets. Our bodies had changed. Her legs were a white expanse on which you could read the sky-blue filigree of her capillaries. The thinning hair over my temples was speckled with white. But our stomachs were similar, hazelnuts settled halfway down a thin stem, the swollen belly of skinny people.

"Did you know that you can learn a lot when you read the notices at City Hall?" I said. I heard the distant sound of the tram, the humming of a radio.

"Your workplace, it had turned into a funeral par-lor. That's what I always said. You were right to drop it."

Claudia had slipped into an amaranth uniform, spun around on her heels in a half pirouette, as if to say, "Look at me."

"Undertakers do respectable work."

"After I saw how they treated my father, you'll allow me a superficial generalization."

Apprehensiveness over what I was about to tell her was the cloud that had accompanied my journey from a terse sky.

"What I mean to say is that in the notices at City Hall..." On the one hand I felt like what I was about to say would hurt her, on the other I didn't want to hide anything.

"I know," she said, interrupting any other circumlocution I might have attempted.

"What do you know?"

"That my mother is getting married to Marco."

Once again she left me dumbfounded. "Don't you think it's in really bad taste?"

"If they love each other nothing is in bad taste," she added after a few moments of silence but in a harsh voice leaving no room for misunderstanding.

Something didn't add up.

"I don't understand, Claudia, are you giving her your blessing?"

"I don't bless and I don't damn anyone, you should know me better."

"They're being married by Padre Agostino, I can find out whether they've filed for joint ownership of property," I insisted.

"Ich bin fertig, Francesco!" she said firmly, although there was now a crack in her voice.

"You can't just let her walk all over you!"

"There are tons of things to do here, there's work, there's music, there's Andria."

"There's Andria," this was supposed to be a friendly acknowledgment, but it came out sounding more than a little bitter.

"Yes, there's Andria, a guy who's had a million more problems than anything you or I have experienced, a guy who taught me that sometimes you have to be like metal, and take on the shape of the blows that life delivers."

"Too philosophical for me."

"It's not philosophy, Frank, you and I were raised with the conviction that everything should be confronted head-on, as if we were fucking sledgehammers."

"With sledgehammers we built trulli, masserie, entire towns."

"Stones crumble and metals mold, I'd rather give my property to the people of my present rather than the people of my past."

I remained in silence for a moment, stung by a fit of jealousy at her last statement.

"You've never been this way."

"Which way?"

"What you just told me, about my mother and Marco, their property situation, you know, their stuff, I haven't changed anything in my life. It's as if you had told me that someone was bad-mouthing me. Why? You're not the kind of guy who traffics in catastrophes and gossip."

"Well maybe I am, or maybe I just wanted to make you see that, even if we were far apart, I have always looked after your interests."

"There are no interests to look after, all we can do is be close when we need each other, even if things went wrong sometimes and we weren't there for each other," she said with renewed calm.

"When were we not there for each other?" I should have asked, but instead I felt like a nine-year-old boy knocking at her door in desperation.

"My mother loved me in her own way and in her own way she will love Marco." She buttoned up her uniform all the way to the collar.

"I want to meet Andria," I told her.

"If he's not out cruising at some gay bar, we can go to Kitty's tonight."

"What's that?"

"It's what the Berliners call the KitKatClub."

"One of those places…"

"Much more. It's my home away from home and maybe it'll be yours, too."

"Do you want him and me to become friends?"

"I don't plan other people's lives, I just have a strong feeling that you'll like him."

"How many times have your feelings steered us wrong?"

"They might have been wrong about me, but I was never wrong about you."

Once I was alone in the house I was surprised that even though it was June, my hands and feet were frozen and my nose dripped. I felt a mixture of tenderness and estrangement.

I sat on the edge of the bed in front of the big mirror on the armoire. When she was little Claudia was afraid of mirrors because they recorded things of the past and from a mirror the grandmother she had never known might suddenly appear, or some other dead person whose image had been trapped inside there. I remained in front of that mirror, without moving, long enough for it to record my pose and the thoughts that were brewing inside. I would leave the house and wander around the city until late, seeking intimacy with the new world; I would register for a German course for aspiring workers.

I spoke with two waiters, an employee of the language school, a group of tourists, two lowlifes, in the universal language of making faces, smiling, I curled my lips, winked with my right eye, affirmed that the food was good by pressing my index finger against a cheek, tried to decipher the sign of a homeless Lithuanian who needed money to return to Vilnius.

I walked for two hours ignoring the tall poles painted green on which the yellow cars of the U2 shook, and continued down the tracks with the same obtuse precision as a locomotive that executes orders. And my orders were reduced to the bare bones, go eastward, to the border with the countryside, on the trail that the guidebook advised only for those who had already seen everything in the city. In Lichtenberg there were lots of guys in tight T-shirts, bald heads, feral eyes, I'd reverted to being little and dark, I felt their eyes on me like a blanket of needles, until the sunset filled the sky with orange and pink. I was wrong to come to Berlin, I would never have what it took to succeed in this new life, and Claudia would never go back to being the woman I used to know.

I got as far as Rummelsburg, where the tram takes a curve to enter the municipality of Friedrichshain. It was a busy intersection, next to the yellow tram stop an actor was performing a farce, ignored by the pedestrians.

When I got home Claudia opened the door, tall as can be, her eyes didn't look like they had makeup on but they sparkled.

In the living room I spotted a dark shadow as the evening struggled to fill up the space of the day. The shadow stood up, the features lightened, the square cheekbones, the thick neck, the forearms two white levers that emerged from a dark T-shirt as tight as a glove. Andria was compact, powerful, with large manicured hands. He introduced himself, amiable, a light peach fuzz around his lips, his sideburns two commas that framed a big smile.

"Francesco."

"Piacere. Andria."

"Parli italiano."

"Un pochino," he said, pressing his index finger and his thumb together till they almost touched.

"He's learned to gesticulate like us," said Claudia, and he looked at her as if to ask confirmation of what he had said.

Claudia translated patiently, Andria spoke to her in German, and she answered him without making me feel excluded: he was sorry that he couldn't speak to me in Italian.

I thought that my future months in Berlin would all be like this. The aphasia that I had fled that day by saying a few words in English would be a scourge. I wouldn't be able to convey nostalgia, anxiety and other complex emotions, every nuance would shrink to basics: "I'm hungry," "I'm thirsty."

Claudia led us to the bedroom, my cassock was laid out on the sheets, the long sleeves folded at chest level.

"You unpacked my suitcase?" I asked, surprised.

"Does it still fit?" Claudia said, as if my question were superfluous.

"I haven't grown since I last wore it twenty years ago," I said.

Claudia looked at it with an expression creased by laughter, as if she couldn't believe she'd convinced me to tag along with them that night.

"The cassock is tight around the waist, we call it a talare because it reaches your tallone, your heel," I explained in a know-it-all voice I myself found unbearable.

"This one reaches your knee," she remarked, bursting into laughter.

Andria looked at us silently through the door, he had the eyes of someone who takes the exact measure of his surroundings.

"Can I do your makeup tonight?" Claudia asked. She said I wouldn't need blush on my dark skin. "We need a brightener," and she was already rummaging through her makeup kit. "We'll apply an earth tone, with fingertips."

It was a declaration of love, we looked at ourselves in the mirror as if the reflections were not us. Claudia spoke in German and I realized that she would also be doing Andria's makeup. For a second I'd thought this would be a first with the same enthusiasm as explorers who reach an unknown place.

Andria sat on a chair next to me. Now in the mirror all three of us shone. I wished this moment could be recorded, the day that I returned to Martina I knew I would miss it. Only much later would I learn the right word to describe what I was experiencing: *Sehnsucht*. A feeling of desire mixed with nostalgia, excitement mixed with the anticipation of something mouthwatering.

Claudia's fingertips pinched my face while my color changed in the mirror. She picked up a pencil, ordered me to close my eyes. The pressure of the tip made my eyes water, when I opened them I saw her already busy drawing Andria's. With a brush Claudia spread a different color on his cheeks from the one she had used on me. The mirror recorded our chromatic harmony, we were a single person.

We walked and talked excitedly without fully understanding each other, stopping at small bars that reeked of smoke where empty beer glasses clinked while Claudia and Andria sat on top of each other, leaving me to enjoy the sight. We were fifteen, at most sixteen years old. Before getting on the last subway that would take us to the KitKat, he gave me a sharp look, he had eyes like a wolf. When I was little wolves were my favorite animals, because they were always on the dark side and they died at the end of every fairy tale, like human beings in the flesh.

At our stop dark figures exited with backpacks and trolley suitcases marching toward the same place. It seemed like any hour of the afternoon, but it was already two a.m. There were colored mohawks, a beautiful woman in a see-through tunic and a fur draped only over her shoulders, leaving her curves uncovered, a boy dressed in red rubber. A family with children descending the stairs looked at us and smiled.

The line in front of the club was a black snake, dark overcoats and long jackets hid the most outrageous outfits, other people instead were already half-naked, with see-through shirts, stilts under their feet, pants with zippers over the ass crack, a girl with two lines tattooed on the back of her legs like old-fashioned silk stockings.

Claudia and Andria held each other's hands, my blood boiled with muddled thoughts: when she and I walked I had only rarely held her hand, her soft back or her rough palms that never sweated. I was suddenly struck by a summer vision of us as teenagers: the fireworks at Locorotondo for the feast of San Rocco, cars parked next to the stone walls of the country road, people anxious to be showered with gunpowder, eyes ready to be filled with colored pinwheels, the darkness permeated by chattering, and the two of us illuminated only by the stars and the moon, waiting for the first crackle of fire in the sky. We were breathing the same climate of suspension.

We entered under a silver disco ball with the neon sign "Life Is a Circus," the expressionless face of a bouncer examined me saying something I didn't understand. Claudia spoke with him and ordered me to open my backpack. They took out my cassock, the men around us laughed. The evening's theme: "CarneBall Bizarre," a fetishist or sexual outfit was de rigueur. I found myself in a small corridor where people undressed frantically, taking wooden hangers from a metal container and handing bags and clothes to the wardrobe people. Once again Claudia had been right, the priest's habit that I hadn't worn for years didn't fit. I tried two or three times, but the buttons didn't reach the buttonholes.

The mistress at the entrance looked at me pitifully. "Either priest or naked," she uttered in English.

This had always been the fork in the road of my life, and I had always gotten mired in the useless middle way.

"Take your clothes off," Claudia said, pulling me toward her and looking me in the eyes.

"Naked?"

"Whatever, but clothes off."

She had never before seemed so grown-up. She had ordered me to strip. My dream, inside something that had seemed like a nightmare.

The liberation began with my clothes tossed into a dark bag, I was left in black boxers and shoes. Claudia gave me a hug and planted a kiss on my lips.

I reached a dark lobby where the music rocked the floor and a camouflaged humanity—police uniforms, white hospital coats, fake furs with fox tails, horse or dog muzzles, bodies tied up with rope—danced relentlessly in the colored smoke. In the pool naked men shouted, swimming between giant inflatable dragons. On the cushions that framed the pool bodies were entangled: a woman, naked and lame, dragged herself next to two guys in studded suspenders and gave a blow job to one. In any moment someone might have taken flight on long feathered wings. Maybe someone did, but after a certain point my memories are vague. In the bathrooms, Italians and Spaniards promised happiness in the form of crystals to dissolve in water or cook with a lighter, until they were scattered or kicked out by undercover bouncers. My heart was pounding, I was hot, the water I was drinking from the faucet never quenched my parched throat.

I climbed the stairs to a mysterious loft with a childish excitement, like when I was little and carefree. My hand intertwined with Claudia's, hers with Andria's. There was a pink room, permeated by a floral essence, in the middle a gynecologist's table on which a man with open legs was being sodomized by a Black guy with a shaved head, wearing red shorts with white trim and gym socks that glowed in the dark. In one corner a cage held a Viking, a Black guy and a Native American who were messing around, rutting with pleasure. We approached this sculpture of sweat and caged-in flesh, I had the temptation you get in museums to stroke the marble, the skin was taut and moist. Then a tiny girl in a black tank top appeared and started to flog the three men with a riding crop: a game I struggled to understand but that gave me a feeling of perdition and joy. She laughed when she saw us and offered us the riding crop. "Want to give it a try?"

Claudia led us to a sheltered corner that quickly became the destination of a pilgrimage of onlookers: we were the show. I wasn't afraid, I yearned for a kiss from Claudia; I had yearned for one beneath the blossoms of the chestnut tree and among the junipers of Martina, but there it would be more beautiful, with the powerful music, the staring of men and women who egged us on rather than judge us. Andria loosened his pants, extracted his dick, but, but still nowhere near an acceptable erection, lay down stomach up, and Claudia bent over, took it in her mouth, looking me in the eyes. I couldn't believe it, I wanted to cry and scream, inside I felt dikes collapsing and walls tumbling down. For a lifetime I had harbored in silence the same questions: "Do you have a boyfriend?" "Do you have a job?" "Do you have a home?" "Do you have a future?" "Do you have a plan?" "Who are you?" "Where do you *fit*?"

"Go down on him, Uva Nera," said Claudia all of a sudden. The most important person in my life with a wide-eyed gaze and a dick in her mouth, the dick of a guy I had met a few hours earlier, pulsing and covered with Claudia's saliva. For twenty years I had desired her, every night imaging what it would be like to enter her beneath the sky of our countryside, what her saliva tasted like, between the bitterness of the walnut and the sweetness of the almond. I kissed Claudia only after the pleasure of her Georgian boyfriend had passed there. Is this what happiness was? What would they have to say in the world I'd left behind? There we were, on a planet that looked with pity upon the land of the slanderers.

An intense kiss, my nerves detonated, I melted, beatitude was the absence of urges, the joy of somnolence that numbs a tired body. Yes, this was happiness. Until a strange tongue, hard and ferrous, squeezed in: Andria was kissing us, and I smelled the sea, the pleasure you get walking with cold salty feet on the broiling sand.

An older man, with a long beard, tried to press his penis into Claudia's mouth, he smiled: she smiled back, gave a pat and a kiss to the tip of his turgid member, but then shook her head in a sign of refusal, and when he stood up everyone was gone, the crowd of onlookers had had enough and was now circling around someone else. We went back to dancing and kept on kissing, Andria and Claudia, Claudia and me, me and Andria, our scents blending together.

We kissed on the subway and then on the tram, as daylight took over the sky. On the last bridge that took us home we marched one behind the other with our arms on the railing, I had Andria's breath on my neck. I lost myself once again in Claudia's gait, it had been years since I'd seen her walking from behind, she resembled a white flamingo. Only a few days later would I learn that flamingos have white feathers when they're sick or malnourished, they eat balancing on only one leg, but they don't know how to limp.

I grew fond of the chirping of blackcaps coming from the linden trees. They had ruffled crests, wild eyes, and were able to sing in the cold. I envied them on those mornings when chilblain split your hands and walking down the street was torture. As soon as I could I would seek shelter in the tram or some café. How could animals resist that cold? And human beings, in a city where starting in October the sky turned pale silver, how could we manage to survive?

My mother was parsimonious with updates on her new life, I could catch occasional glimpses of it in some of her advice, which tended to leave a frivolous aftertaste: "Dress colorfully, the cold keeps its distance from color." My father launched dour dispatches of a self-pitying and extortionate flavor: "When you return you'll find your grandparents in a nursing home and me in the morgue."

Six months had gone by since my arrival in Berlin and I still lost my way, misplaced documents, or got scammed. In German class I trudged through the quicksand of the Vorgangspassiv and the Konjunktiv II, regretting that for more than thirty years I had underestimated grammar. Bearing the features of childhood and old age, when you have to blindly trust other people, I lived in a limbo of sorts.

The German teacher was an energetic girl with red cheeks. We didn't understand a word she said, nor did she understand us. She gave us pop songs by teenage groups to memorize, the stanzas had blank spaces to be filled in after repeated listenings. Sheer torture. I bestowed perfunctory smiles, gulped Turkish coffee along with my classmates—Syrians, Kurds, Latin Americans and Koreans—and we all constantly misunderstood each other. To get their attention I would act like a silent-film actor, all gestures and faces, and then get terribly sad on the subway, while trading glances with other passengers who looked as comfortable as people in an ad for the public transportation system.

For a period I tried to get a whiff of the real estate business in Berlin, but realized immediately that it was another world, even if out of habit I subdivided the building façades into apartments, and apartments into rooms, another game of Tetris. In any small Italian province the supply was always greater than the demand; here it was the exact opposite: for every house there was a herd of aspiring leasers or buyers ready to pay cash in hand, to sell everything for the sake of a seventy-meter-square apartment. The speculative bubble had ended more than a decade ago, the occupied buildings of East Berlin and Kreuzberg had been forcibly cleared, Spanish and Russian funds resold slums and stables that they passed off as lofts for ten times their value. Real estate agents in Berlin were not salespeople at the flea market, as I had been, but headhunters. They were more like the chief of personnel at a company: they didn't have to sell houses, they had to choose buyers.

I got a job at a vegan bistro. I didn't make much, but it was enough for a decent life. Simplicity had become a necessity. The bistro had shiny doors painted white, otherwise it was dark and gloomy. The architecture of Berlin cafés gives off the impression of being bold, but on the inside reveals a neglect bordering not infrequently on filth. In that murky aquarium, I sliced cakes and served tisanes among chairs fallen off a truck and dusty love seats. My French colleague was muscular and tanned, sang to herself while arranging teapots on the burner and quiches on trays, imparting just a few basic instructions: I appreciated her sparing me yet another round of dialogue between the misunderstood.

I walked a lot, in the city I felt of sense of life and death intertwined, a destiny that belonged to me. I walked so much that I lost cognition of time. The variety of people was intoxicating: the young tourist with a bottle of Club-Mate, the middle-aged man with vodka on his breath and a loud voice, the young couple with a child on a sled, the Viking with the wooden bicycle on a U-Bahn platform. Everywhere there were stumbling blocks and the rubble of Old Berlin, a piece of the wall wrapped in cellophane or an old ruin surrounded by modern apartment buildings. A city where you're happier than anywhere in the world when you're happy, and sadder when your mood turns dark.

Claudia never did go back for a night at Kitty's. On the days that followed, dazed and joyful, I had felt a beginner's euphoria, but there is no true happiness unless you can share it with someone. And with her, despite our living together, it seemed impossible. I wondered why I stayed, since we spent so little time together. At night she was always exhausted, brushed me off with a few words and collapsed on the small sofa in the living room. Her fatigue assumed the form of a crumpled blanket that stuck to the folds of her body and took their perfect measure. "Regnava nel silenzio / alta la notte e bruna..." she would sometimes sing, taking a stab at one of the high notes of *Lucia di Lammermoor*, but it was only repertory from when we were young.

Sometimes she would tell me about her patients, grouchy or gallant, silent or talkative, alone. I saw her while she was tending to them, taking care of their meals while her nails grew black and her hair dripped with vegetable oil. It was laughable that two people like us, with such disorderly eating habits, had embarked on a new life of service to the hunger of others.

At times the silence of the night was enough to calm us, when fatigue and the smell of the cafeteria had left us numb. Beyond the roofs you could glimpse a long line of illuminated windows, the sign of a city that was still awake, while the noise of the tram heading toward the center of town at every hour of the day and night was there to reassure us. It seemed to be saying that despite everything Berlin was still the right place for us. A city where every illusion of freedom, integration, solidarity and democracy seemed possible.

When she could, Claudia went running at Weißensee, a nearby city lake a stone's throw from the center, where a few brave mothers dove naked on limpid mornings in mid-season. We had grown up in a town filled with bell towers that announced the mass, and a little road that would take us to the sea shortly before spring ended or winter began. Without a dip in the water we were lost, dirty, and undone. Getting wet was a kind of purification before every new and promising chapter of our lives, the start of the school, academic, professional or sentimental year. Although we were far from the sea, I would have renamed that period of my life with Claudia the "aquatic period."

One Saturday night I came upon her awake in bed, reading her Kindle and listening to music. She was in the dark.

"Can I lie down next to you?"

Claudia couldn't hear me through her headphones, but seeing me in the doorway with the palm of her hand she patted twice on the empty space in her bed. She removed her headphones. "Lie down," she said.

"Why don't we ever talk about what happened at Kitty's?"

"Because it's better that way."

"Are you never going to kiss me again?"

"I wasn't kissing you."

"Who, then?"

"I was kissing everything that we used to be and no longer are."

I had the feeling that this thought had slipped from her head, as if she was pursuing a line of reasoning all her own. Our desires were changing, but not their intensity.

"Andria is an important person for me, you know," she said in a voice that was suddenly maternal.

I was afraid that Claudia had noticed every time I got excited imagining them together. "I know," I mumbled.

"Which is why now that it's over I wouldn't want you to be pissed at him."

"Did you break up?"

"We were never together, but the relationship that we used to have is over."

Claudia was setting my future before me in a new configuration, those energies that some call demons contain the same substance as aspirations and fears: they should be embraced wholeheartedly.

"Can I go out with him?" I asked.

"Why not ask him?" Her intelligent eyes scrutinized me, she brought her cheek close to mine for a kiss. "Don't get upset if you don't understand what he says to you."

She was the one to write my text to Andria. An innocent, neutral request: to see a movie or watch a TV show together.

The first time that we met at his house, we spent the afternoon watching *Orange Is the New Black*. That afternoon was followed by others. I found it exciting to pass the time on the soft narrow bed of Andria, it was the achievement of a goal after decades of wandering. There was something symbolic in the obstacles I had to overcome to reach him: walk alongside immense buildings populated by students and immigrants, make my way down endless corridors. Andria spoke to me in English while I tried to practice the first rudiments of the German I was learning. We spoke about ourselves without understanding each other, "Ich liebe dich" was a threat and "Ich habe dich lieb" a compromise. They were clumsy but sincere exchanges, he did my makeup with a steady hand, as if we were teenagers, and maybe this is what kept us so lighthearted. Andria wore makeup when he went clubbing, it was an innocuous ritual that allowed him to pass through a magic door. When you return home the music is a persistent buzzing in the ears and the eyeliner marks the remains of dark tears. In his face, flashes of an archaic masculinity, on his bedside table a knife tucked into a leather sheath, a silver box with tobacco, and the instructions for his—soon to be our—anal lube. Edible, tasteless, odorless.

At the age of thirteen he had already joined the protests with his older sister and parents during the Rose Revolution in Tbilisi. At eighteen he was called to arms. Until a few months earlier many of the draftees had still been in school, and never thought they would end up with a machine gun in their hands walking kilometer after kilometer in heavy leather boots with mud up to their ankles. Andria had befriended some boys from the provinces, and the one who stood out the most was Cristiano with his smile, a talkative strawberry blond who one morning, while they were washing up in the shower, pulled Andria to him by the wrist and tried to kiss him. Andria broke away in a panic. He was angry. That night he couldn't sleep; thinking back on what had happened, in his semiconscious state, he could still feel the grip of Cristiano around his wrist. He was afraid to admit it, but he had enjoyed that rash gesture. He wondered whether Cristiano's back was as smooth as his hand. Almost without thinking, he started to touch himself.

As I listened to his story I relived the summer when I had confided in Claudia about Domenico. Like me, Andria had also come to Berlin in search of a place where he could love, in pursuit of a yearning that had lived inside him for decades. During the early days here he had hooked up with young gay tourists at the Nollendorfplatz hostels. In the eyes of Westerners, with their perfumed beards drawn with a compass, a guy like Andria, who had fought in a war, was irresistible. Yet he felt uncomfortable when they remarked on this, since the war had not lasted long, he hadn't fired a shot, hadn't killed anyone to defend his homeland, a homeland where, moreover, certain inclinations had to be hidden. When he talked about how cruel the torture of gays was in the army, his heart would burst. Claudia was the first person to pay him any real attention. After meeting her, Andria knew that there was someone to whom he could tell everything, who loved him without judgment.

Our first kiss without Claudia happened on a night that felt like New Year's Eve. It was still summer, thousands of Turks were on the streets honking their horns like mad, tossing confetti and firecrackers from the car windows. The uprising against Erdoğan had failed and his supporters were celebrating, trying to convey their joy to all the other Turks in Berlin—hiding behind their windows, in pain—who had favored the attempted coup. In the confusion Andria brought his lips to my neck, I reciprocated with a caress, like the reflex of an averted blow. Then he took my head and kissed me. His beard scorched my cheeks, the touch of a freshly lit match. "Kurze Pause," I said, breathing, as if coming up for air. I swallowed air and saliva. Someone in a car threw a beer bottle at us and missed, Andria yelled at him in Georgian, then he embraced me from behind, saying that with him at my side nothing would ever happen to me. I had never seen the world from that perspective.

Andria was always repeating that he was free, as if that "Ich bin frei" were a sort of exorcism. He was constantly cruising, one afternoon I followed him like a blind man holding on to his guide dog, our destination was Lab.oratory on Friedrichshain, a basement where a hundred horny men—all perfectly dressed from the waist up and naked from the ass down—were dancing, mixing their humors in an aluminum tub. The music was a mirror of water in which to swim. I sucked Andria's cock, his strong fingers pressed against the back of my neck.

Later I asked him, "Why were you with Claudia?"

"Because with her I wasn't masculine and I wasn't feminine, I was Andria, just Andria."

We wandered around the city kissing without fear. In a park in Prenzlau, surrounded by poplar trees and Ping-Pong tables, we leaned against the damp bark of a tree, the music of Lab.oratory still in our ears.

I noticed a man staring. "Is he looking at us?" I asked Andria. It was a mistake. Andria looked up toward the man with the bushy eyebrows. The man walked away to a corner of the park, then turned around and shouted something.

"He had to go as far away as he could to say what he thought of us," Andria said with a ferocious expression. "He lost control. We didn't."

I didn't reply, the germ of a dark heavy awkwardness had fallen between us. A fly walked on Andria's neck, I grabbed it instinctively; I had never succeeded in grabbing one as a child but in Berlin, evidently, the flies were more stupid and naive, and they trusted human beings.

I don't like childhood stories, but Andria's were special. For example, the harvest days in Georgia. Every Georgian is familiar with that world, and has listened to the must turning into wine inside clay urns or terracotta vats buried in the ground. There was something epic about his harvests, unlike mine—confined to a small subsidiary plot, with a grandfather who shows you how to cut a bunch of grapes without harming the plant, from vines as short as us five-year-old children. For him every harvest was a siege of heaven, the vines were oaks and wine the nectar of the gods. At any moment I half expected him to pull out a pair of scissors like my grandfather had, I would have shown him how I severed the bunches of verdeca grapes, which are as tiny as fish eyes. His grandparents' generation had also met their future wives or husbands on summer nights, amid the plaintive notes of a musical instrument. He and I were much closer than we thought. He looked like an angel, with his arms wrapped around a foam rubber pillow, I kissed him while he slept, then I put on wool turtleneck sweaters to cover the bruises from the kisses that turned into bites.

One night he made a date with me to meet him at the Mariendorf subway station, the streets covered with leaves, coat lapels turned up, a few flecks of snow that portended a storm. We entered an apartment building with aluminum doors and window frames, no elevator, and on the top floor, in the doorway, a Turkish boy with thick black eyebrows and waxed pectorals, in his underwear, asked us if we had ever been there. Andria answered for both of us. The boy then launched into a long sermon, from his bored air I understood that it was a speech he must have given a million times. In a small room we got undressed and a hardworking woman in a white nurse's uniform—except for the magenta borders on the epaulettes—handed us two towels to wrap around our waists. We ended up in a room where a dozen bearded men were smoking a hookah. They were naked and the aromatic smoke in the air tickled the nose. Andria stroked me between my legs. One of the men approached from the back of the room, fat, with a messy beard and droopy eyelids. "Can I suck you off?" he asked me.

This was the first time I had received such an explicit request, until then a little music, a hint, a look, or a smile had always mediated. I answered no, because even rejection needs to be fully exercised. Saying no was completely new to me. The bubbling of scented water in the hookahs was hypnotic. Shisha, flowers and tobacco. Andria passed the hookah to me, made three smoke rings. I wrapped my lips around the mouthpiece to inhale, the filter was hard as a bone, closed my eyes partway with one of his hands on my head and the other resting on my knee. I traveled to a place from thirty, maybe forty years earlier: I found myself in Martina, the fall had begun a few weeks earlier and in a little while we would decant into bottles the fermented must from the large terra-cotta capasoni. My mother was seated on a low stool with her skirt pulled up to her knees, replacing the empty bottles with the ones that were full. My father inserted a twenty-centimeter-long rubber tube into the recipient that held the freshly fermented wine, inhaling with his lips from the opposite end, the wine ran through the tube, reinforcing the effect of rarefication. When the wine reached his lips, my father inserted the tube into the bottle or into the demijohn placed lower down, in compliance with the principle of communicating vessels. He lifted the bottle and showed me the flow that slowed down until it stopped and started to flow back; the effect created small and suggestive air bubbles in the tube. "Come, Francesco, breathe in," he said, and after placing my mouth on the rubber tube, I breathed in and felt the flow hit my teeth, strong and tart. I could never avoid accidentally drinking that gulp of pungent wine. The whole Veleno family took part in the harvest ritual.

When we were back on the street, where the sleet had turned into snow, a gang of human shadows gathered on the opposite side of the street and whistled at us the way shepherds call to their herd. All afternoon Andria had inhaled the smoke with a look of joyful bliss, but at that derisive whistle he became humorless and his eyes turned beady. An object cleaved the curtain of snow in a glint that ended against the chassis of a car parked on our side of the street. It was a cigarette lighter. Right after that they started throwing beer cans, stones, and then ran off yelling "Schwuuuul," still whistling like a cloud of blackbirds.

Andria crossed the street and chased them. He reappeared shortly after with a cloth bag and a wool beret, spoils from the fight. He smiled at me sadly. "Go back to Claudia tonight, I want to be alone." It was an order. I replied automatically. "Okay."

The car headlights became rarer, the only vehicle around was a yellow bus headed for the outskirts of town, rumbling in low gear on the bumpy road. Andria vanished amid that noise, and I stood there, motionless, without feeling cold or afraid, but with the suspicion that I could not really count on him.

I texted Claudia, called her, but she didn't answer. I was seized by an irrational jealousy.

"What happened?" She called me back at one point, while I was taking shelter in the lobby of an infamous club, the first one I'd found, filled with junkies and trashy punks.

"Andria told me to go back to your place, he doesn't want me tonight."

"What did you do to him?"

"Nothing."

"Maybe that's the problem."

God how I hated her when she acted like that. Her pocket wisdom had always solicited my blind acquiescence, but this time I knew she was wrong although I said nothing.

"Frank, I'm about to fuck this guy I met two hours ago on Tinder."

"Are you telling me not to come?"

"No, come, but I want you to know what you might find."

"Is he cute?"

"He's half my age."

"You didn't answer my question."

"Let's just say that I'm about to enter unknown territory. It's more ethnographic research than a fuck."

"So has Andria dumped me?"

"Why didn't you follow him and ask him? Why don't you confront him?"

"It's cold here and I don't understand anything that people say to me."

"I've got to go now." She was teaching me a lesson and I was perfectly aware of it, which is why I didn't call her back.

A few minutes later I had unprotected sex with a stranger inside that infamous club, I experienced it in the worst possible way, with shame. Depressing thoughts gnawed at me. A part of me still desired the pleasure of priests, whom I imagined concealed beneath a mysterious blanket of masturbation and nocturnal emissions, but ascetic, without smell, without sweat, without contact, obsessively onanistic. Like my love for Claudia all these years.

We Europeans were free to travel within an enclave, but outside that enclave was the world to which Andria belonged. Our free Europe, without walls, was not the same as Andria's. Georgia is not an EU country and Andria was forced to leave Germany when his visa expired. I felt my back being caressed by a cold sharp stone, someone was making the decision for us. I'm sorry, Claudia, but we are not allowed to go beyond the horizon that we can see, and people who come from there stay with us just long enough to realize that they will always have borders to honor.

There were no tears of farewell. The first man with whom I was about to fall in love departed after an abrupt goodbye in the middle of a snowstorm with his skin still smelling of hookah and shisha. In one of his last texts he wrote that what he always liked about me was my linguistic chaos, the way I had invented a language, our language, the one that only he and I understood. I would have to make those words suffice during his absence. His words to Claudia were more nuanced. He had decided to depart without useless farewells because he nurtured the hope of returning. Neither Claudia nor I believed he would, which is why one afternoon under a clay-colored sky we got into an argument. We were leaning against the window that looked out on the courtyard, she was sipping a tisane from a mug that she held with both hands to absorb the warmth that it emanated. These long long winters made us assume the same posture, giant moths with our stomachs against the glass that irradiated the last pale light of day. The cold froze the branches of the elm tree in the courtyard.

"You should have married him," she burst out, breathing into her tisane.

"Marry him?" They said that the elm was the tree of the Witch's Sabbath.

"Yes, you should have married him since you were the last person he was with." She had a neutral tone of voice.

I turned around to seek in her eyes the meaning of what she was saying. "I only have experience with unhappy marriages, as you know."

"It would have been the first happy marriage in our lives," she said, disconsolate.

"Only if you had gotten married with us."

A shadow darkened her face.

"My mother remarried."

"She never stops being wrong."

After months Claudia was talking to me about her mother.

"I never told you how I found out about their wedding. She sent me the invitation, I don't know how. But she managed to find and humiliate me."

"It's not a humiliation."

"But she thinks she's humiliated me because she got married twice and I'm still the spinster of Ceglie, that's how things are in her world."

"Exactly, in her world."

"I feel humiliated because she found me and anywhere I go she will always find me. Our origins stick to us like a giant birthmark on the skin: you can hide it with as much clothing as you want, but it's still under there and when you get undressed you see it."

We had left our families behind, bearing deep wounds, but our families had not left us.

We couldn't let Etta and our demons get the better of us. So I said something provocative, as if her mother were there listening. In a senseless monologue, I told her about one of my most extreme adventures with Andria, in the most infernal *men only* club that we'd been to. A place where you ended up clinging together in a single body, where modesty crumbled into dust and you ended up crying because the height of pain verges on the height of pleasure. I told her that there I had stopped being afraid of disease. Anyone who entered that place was freed of the sickness he had inside by experiencing another type of sickness. I saw with my own eyes the limits of the human body being overcome, the journey toward the extreme.

"You see too much death in sex, Frank," she said in a whisper, then she added, "I don't understand why Andria didn't fight..." I was left speechless. As if out of everything I had told her, the only thing that mattered was the fact that she missed Andria.

"All the people that I love go away, Erika, Andria, while my mother..."

"I'm still here."

"You'll go away, too."

"I promise you I won't." And I repeated it with all the solemnity I could muster.

According to a Nordic legend, the woman who gave origin to humankind was a tree, an elm tree to be specific. I spent every sunset in the days that followed watching the tree in the courtyard reflecting the light of the buildings in its crystals of ice.

The U-Bahn, although we didn't dare admit it, was a little like country life. On board you scanned an infinite variety of humans, masks, voids or excesses, but in the end we all seemed to recognize each other. On her Instagram account, Claudia started writing little vignettes to accompany the pictures she took with her cell phone on her walks around the city. The hatchet of a man screaming at mysterious presences, a fake hand barely visible from a fur muff, a boat, enormous plants whose leaves hid people, baby carriages filled with military bric-a-brac, plaster violins and colorful costumes. She liked the navy-blue palette of the subway with the letter *U* and the squawking recorded voice, "Aufsteigen, bitte," "Zurückbleiben, bitte." She was fascinated by that alienating invitation to get in and stand back, maybe there was a way to learn something about a people through the loudspeakers of a subway. In Milano the obsession was to not go past the yellow line, in Berlin, to quickly do what you're there to do.

The only time she didn't was when she ran into the recruiter from one of her job interviews. She remembered their surreal conversation about the sun and vitamin D. Claudia recognized her on the U-7, she was in a black full-length down jacket and a wool cap, without the tense, anxious expression of their first meeting. She said hello and smiled, as the yellow cars rustled with travelers grabbing hold of the straps.

"Was für ein Zufall!" Claudia said to her.

"Sì," the woman interrupted, leaving Claudia with her mouth open. She was Calabrian, and about to return to the south. "I've had it with vitamin D tablets, I want the sun."

"Do you have a job?"

"No, my mother is dying."

Claudia stopped to stare at the black down coat leaving the yellow car, walking quickly toward a destination as far away as the origin of her breath.

Claudia spent less and less time at the nursing home. For a while now she had been preparing the menu using a program linked to an outside catering service. She was tired of wearing the uniform and acting perpetually nice. She said that she would soon be able to work from home and create an application that would connect the caterer to other nursing homes.

"Let's go swimming," she proposed one day.

The building smelled of plaster and paint, piles of frozen leaves were scattered in the courtyard: one part was still under construction, like many other things in a city where at certain moments the cranes filled the sky like a flock in migration. At the entrance a man in a felt beret apologized for the terrible appearance of the structure, and added that within a week the works would be completed. He handed us soft towels, accompanied us down a pebble walkway to the pool, the air warm and the wind whistling outside. The sliding door closed behind us, there were benches covered by naked bodies, only one man was wearing a bathrobe and in that community of nudists he appeared to be the most scandalous of all.

The towel did not drop, Claudia slipped out of it. I reached her free of clothing in the warm pool.

"Everyone could use an hour of nudism," her voice amplified by the high ceiling made the place more like a church than a pool.

I grew conscious of her white flesh, the elastic of her underwear had left a mark on the rectangle of hair between her pubis and her belly.

"Go down," she ordered me.

"Yes, sir," I replied, with ironic zeal.

Submerged in the green and white water I listened to the music that came from the underwater speakers, an iridescent foam followed Claudia's body as she moved toward the middle of the pool. I reemerged and saw her with her small pink nipples and wide elbows leaning against the side of the pool.

"Come here."

"Yes, sir," I said once again.

She gave me a look with a challenge. "Would you do it with me now?"

"Always."

"Even if it was the last time?"

"I don't know if I'll be up to it."

Inside that warm water I felt her hand travel the small space that divided us, she stroked me between my legs, gave a short strangled sob, we were far from the other visitors to the baths. Pleasure has a color and ours was white, like the marble against which I pressed her limbs; it was snow, milk, quicklime. I thought of the stones in my town, so blinding in the summer. Quicklime disinfects the millstones and purifies the cellars and the cones of the trulli. We were a single body. No one there could know that we came from a town where painting with quicklime was called "allattare"—nursing—because whitewashers nourished the stones to strengthen them, gave them milk like mothers to their children. Our love was the quicklime we had used to nourish our hope for happiness, the most illusory and deceitful form of human dependence.

A cramp, a damn pain in my calf forced me to detach from her. It was the wake-up call. She disappeared under the water.

"Claudia, wait for me..." I implored, and turning toward those who were watching us from the side of the pool, hardly surprised by what they had seen, I said, in Italian, "It's not what it looks like."

"It's much worse," came the voice, sharp, of Claudia, who was slapping the water and hugging me.

"Will it never happen again?" I asked her as we were returning home, arm in arm like two ex-lovers who loved each other so much and no longer share sex but only a great, infinite affection.

"You do understand me, don't you?"

We remained that way for the rest of the trip, Claudia huddled against me, then the metallic voice announcing Antonplatz, our stop. In the tiny lane that led to the main door, a young woman smiled at us. Claudia extended her hand, as if to push away a wall or an invisible curtain between us and the stranger. Out of the corner of her mouth she said, in disbelief, "What are you doing here?" The stranger planted a kiss and breathed on the palm of her open hand. "I'm back." Opening her down jacket, she then pointed to her belly. "Or rather, we're back." Behind her was a suitcase as big as a steamer trunk.

Erika was in the city again.

Part Six

Torschlußpanik

(Noun. Feminine. The fear of not achieving a goal because one does not have a child, a family, or a specific professional status. It is also used in politics: when the Berlin Wall was built, an article in the August 18, 1961, issue of *Time* magazine said, "A disease has struck all the inhabitants of the eastern sector of the city, and this disease is called *Torschlußpanik*. Its origins date back to the nineteenth century, when the gates [*Tore*] of the cities, which were circled by walls, closed [*Schluß*] at sunset. Once, in Hamburg, when a beautiful day had brought many citizens out of their houses, the closing of the gates caused a riot and scenes of panic [*Panik*]. *Ausbrugische Ordinari Postzeitung* 104, May 2, 1808.)

The sun radiated a cheerful light, like a golden gong, on the terse Sunday landscape. The street was covered with a carpet of yellow flowers scattered by the wind the night before. Not much time was left till the baby's birth and Claudia convinced Erika and me to visit the neighborhood's open-air market, a long row of tables with trinkets and toys, used shoes, and dog-eared books. The children behind the stands were all radiant, but disciplined in their self-set goal: to sell as many things as possible. They might trade something, the blond boy would buy the blue hairnet from the dark-haired boy, who would buy a wooden gnome from the boy with the gigantic feet, and the boy with the gigantic feet would in turn buy a fan from the girl with the boyish haircut. There was probably a terrible rivalry among them, even if none of the adults would admit it.

At the entrance to a building, I noticed a solitary child with the richest table. He looked incredibly sad. His stand was about fifty meters away from the others'. He was husky and seemed to have a jaw like a bulldog; next to him, in the shadow of the lobby, was his mother, who also had a bulldog jaw. I observed the scene for several minutes: no one stopped to buy anything because no one passed by there, not a single child of the many riding down the bike lane on colored bicycles with helmets on their heads bothered to even look at him. I was distracted by Erika, who called out to me with three short, rhythmic, sharp whistles. "Stop wasting time, Francis."

The past few weeks had given me the opportunity to appreciate her animal magnetism. She was smart and enterprising, a person not easily contented. Her eyes sparkled with the expression of someone who, ultimately, doesn't take anyone seriously. From the start she had treated me like a child or, worse, a pet to torment, since, having lost my job, I stayed home playing the part of Hausmann (as here they call the men who take care of household chores), while Claudia was busy starting up the catering business.

They both stopped in front of a stand piled high with clothing, Claudia showed Erika a blue onesie with red buttons; a little boy with a puffy face and his parents stared at her in expectation. They couldn't know that the two women were actually talking about something completely different.

"Are you on Tinder?" Erika had asked in an innocent voice, but with the look of someone perfectly aware that she's made the other person uncomfortable.

"I browse around a little is all."

"It's a place for sex maniacs and losers." She knew how to infuriate Claudia (that, too, is a talent).

"Who says that I'm not a sex maniac and loser, too."

"You're a goddess, I won't let some creep set a finger on you." Erika had looked up with a jerk, her black ponytail swung back and forth, slapped by the sudden movement.

"I hooked up with a young guy, for fun," Claudia admitted.

On her Tinder profile she had written, "No One-Night Stands, 5'9". Multitasking. I can walk and breathe at the same time." More than one person had replied, "What do you mean, *walk and breathe at the same time*?"

Claudia had also noticed the stand in front of the doorway, with one finger she adjusted her sunglasses on her nose, shrugged her shoulders, and crossed the street to approach the child with the bulldog jaw. He didn't move, although his obtuse expression started to relax. Claudia smiled and asked him something. The child replied, serious, on his toes, and showed her a colored ball. Claudia pushed her sunglasses up on her head, there was a polite exchange between her and the mother, then a twenty-euro bill appeared between her long knotty fingers. The child lit up while the mother, from the shadows, dug in her pockets for change. Claudia shook her head no, she didn't want anything.

She came back to us with the pink and lilac ball,

uninflated, printed with the face of the princess from *Frozen*.

"You gave him twenty euros!" Erika admonished her.

"A child would never sell a ball, and if he does he deserves a little extra."

"Then why did you take it from him?" she continued.

"Because it's his sister's."

"He sells his sister's things?" I asked with a hint of scandal.

"His sister is no longer with us."

"You bought the ball of a dead girl," said Erika, outraged.

"We've lightened the burden on that child."

"I don't want it."

"We'll give it to Francesco and he'll take care of it." She handed me the smooth clean ball, it smelled like rubber. In that moment I thought it was the most precious thing in the world. It had a story to tell.

When we got home Erika came into my room and stood there staring at my hands holding the ball.

"She really did, she gave you that child's ball." Her pale face colored. "If you ask me, Claudia made up that story about the dead girl." Then, in a whisper, "Keep the ball, Francis!"

Ever since we had become three, we had developed the habit of whispering. Complicit alliances were woven between me and Erika, Erika and Claudia, me and Claudia; we spoke smelling each other's breath and sensing the heat that our bodies transmitted; we were so close that we could eavesdrop on each other.

I kept the ball because that's what they both wanted, although neither would ever admit it. Their relationship pivoted on occupying space. Claudia had gotten rid of superfluous things: shoeboxes, pots and pans, shoes. Everything had been packed up and left in the lobby of the building with a sign, "Geschenk zu mitnehmen." The house had been reorganized with a practical sense and diplomacy because of Erika. Claudia had given her room to her, and in mine—now ours—put a futon. She had also identified the clinic where Erika would give birth, getting the contact information of the gynecologist known at the nursing home.

She and Erika cooked together, slept in an embrace as they once had, and sometimes meditated facing each other, listening to a melody that every ten seconds was interrupted by a gong; while an energetic field grew between them the interior worlds migrated from one body to the other, and they exhaled recriminations and regrets. Claudia said that she could feel the transformation of her pain into a light burden, while Erika confided that she meditated on her own breathing until she could hear the child inside speaking with the voice of an adult.

Three weeks seemed like three years. We had diligently prepared the bed on which Erika spent her days awaiting the birth of the child. She took up half of the sofa with her legs outstretched and her ankles on a pouf, her hair in a tangle, her face turned toward the window, as if the elm tree were a powerful magnet that attracted the attention of our metallic hearts. Taking care of Erika required a tacit understanding between Claudia and me, so deep that we no longer needed words to communicate to each other. Sometimes Claudia spoke in dialect, as if the daily confrontation with the new language summoned from her depths some expressions of our grandparents. She would call me sciulisciato (messy) and Erika scecuscitata (lazy and airheaded), although the word reminded me of the term *scucito*, unstitched, and all three of us were a little unstitched, as if the thread that tied us together didn't really hold the fabric of which we were made.

With Erika I experienced highs and lows, we were too neurotic, and two neurotics together are like ions with an equal charge: they repel each other. Erika was escaping from a bad situation. Mario, the father of her child, was portrayed as a mediocre guy happily proud of his mediocrity, a guy who in front of the *Mona Lisa* said, "To me this Gioconda looks like a bitch, and she's ugly," expecting the full approval of others. Erika had met him on a cruise ship with her parents after her return from Berlin. He worked on the ship, wore a white uniform that made him look taller, and because of the brown color of his skin he looked older, but they were the same age. They had sex one hour after they'd met, he was wild, rushed. Erika branded him an *airhead*, and in that moment she needed to be carefree. He didn't realize how lucky he was to be always living on the sea, which is what Erika liked about him. *The emptiness and the sea.* They were together for a year. He cheated on her a lot, and she knew it, but she didn't care, she wasn't in love, and felt that soon she would be looking for fullness after all the emptiness. And instead, despite precautions, she ended up pregnant. And he made the worst decision of all: no decision. Months went by. Who knows why, but when I listened to her story it all sounded so damn familiar, as if he were an exemplar of the men I had grown up with as well as a very small undefined part of me. Erika told us, scandalized, that when she wanted to have sex with him he would say, "My son is there, we can't," and of course it was a daughter, although he always said "my son." Erika had written an email to Claudia: "I'm coming back to you, I want to give birth to my daughter next to the only person who understands me." But she never sent it, saving it in the draft folder, a vault filled with postponed actions, insults and regrets, wild declarations and requests for compassion. Erika consisted entirely of her omissions. And the only possible action that had led her to our house.

Erika was proudly independent, once she even put me on trial because she claimed that I looked at her belly too much, and one time I caressed it, giving her the impression that it was a distinct part of her body. "It's not a dog, it's my belly!"

I helped her to get up from the sofa and together we reached the bed. I asked her if everything was alright and she reassured me: "I'm just very tired, we walked too much."

She lay down on the side of the bed, in a fetal position; in the dark I could feel the presence of Claudia, but I could not tell where she was. Until the mattress gave a thud, now she was in the bed, too.

"Tonight I'm staying here with you," she said, in a whisper.

I went back to my movie. I heard coughing and did not even try to imagine which of the two it might be, but I did have an outrageous thought and acted on it. I went into the room where Claudia and Erika were resting, fitted together like dessert spoons, one inside the other, their breathing regular. Claudia's was barely perceptible while Erika's was fuller. I stretched my hand out over the bed, it was warm, both were on top of the blanket, as if they had been waiting to feel tired before getting undressed and slipping between the sheets. I stretched out behind Claudia like the third spoon, between my stomach and her back was the encumbrance of the ball she had bought from the child, the smooth clean rubber kept us divided and at the same time inextricably united. I could feel her warm wrist caress my face. I was missing Andria and evoked him with all my power as I sniffed at Claudia's hair. There are moments in life like the conch shells that as children they told us had the sound of the sea. For at least an hour I could hear the splashing of the sea, then the faint night-light on the bedside table turned on like the flutter of a moth, Erika sat up in the dark, spectral, her face disfigured by a grimace of fear. By reflex I squeezed the ball against my stomach. Claudia's head rose up and through a slightly drowsy mouth she whispered a sentence that struck me in the chest like an ice pick: "Did it break?" The pronoun, to me, an avid reader of the Holy Scriptures as a child, reminded me of the Red Sea of Moses.

Claudia slipped on her jacket, called a taxi and accompanied Erika down three flights of stairs supporting her by the forearm. They crossed a long garden, bolts of lightning illuminating the black sky as if it were day. The first drops of rain were heavy and cold. I followed Claudia and Erika, hauling a suitcase that had been placed in my hands. A few minutes later I was looking through the windshield at the city turned gray by water, the Turkish driver spoke only his own language, the puddles exploded beneath the tires.

Erika and Claudia disappeared into the blue light of an elevator. I stopped in the lobby to shake off the dampness in my hair, around me were women with veils and men with turbans, in a rigid distinction between genders and nationalities. I waited an empty indefinite time until the silver sheath of the elevator returned Claudia to me with a face filled with tension.

She had been crying. On the edges of her eyes tiny white residue gleamed, like the skin after the sea has been dried from it. I caressed her hair.

"Let's go home, it's stopped raining," Claudia said as she zipped up her jacket with an abrupt gesture.

"What about Erika?" I asked.

"She doesn't want me with her. She told me she wants to be alone with Mario."

"But he's not here."

"Exactly. She'd rather have no one than me."

"We can't leave," I protested, with a disconsolate sigh of opposition.

"Of course we can't, but I took on all of her problems, kept her from falling apart, tried to convey love to her, the only power that I have. I was loyal." Her eyes were bright, the salt on the edges was gone, they had melted any further tears. She put on a shiny beret, a bluish reflection shimmered on her head. I could sense the break, that moment when we are no longer ourselves, just fragments.

"You can count on me." It was the only thing I managed to say, small talk I had used when closing a deal during the period of my life as a real estate agent.

"I have always counted on you." Her lips settled on mine innocently, then she pulled away to assure herself that I had understood: that kiss was the seal of a love that was special and chaste.

"Shall we go?"

"Let's go," I echoed.

Then after walking toward the exit she suddenly stopped. "Are we doing something stupid?" She had changed expression, as if the tension had been swept away by the wind.

"In my opinion, we are."

She giggled. "I'm as nervous as if I were the one having the baby."

A pale ray of light illuminated the waiting room. I had fallen asleep on a bench, unknown or unrecognizable voices spoke softly; then came the clear voice of Claudia.

"She weighs almost three kilos, Elfo is a healthy baby."

We waited until the last drops of Advent for our first outing as a family. The early weeks with Elfo had been frenetic, and sleepless. Dressed in white, all lace and embroidery—a Polish woman's trousseau hidden in a trunk that Claudia had bought at a flea market—she looked like someone out of a grainy photo inside a wooden frame, a rural village daguerreotype; nothing in common with the colored sashes with which Claudia tied her to her chest.

We called her Elfo, but made an effort not to. At the age of forty good intentions are hindered by habits, we made mistakes that we promised not to repeat. We counted on the fact that her childhood would be better than ours, no one would prevent her from reading *Pippi Longstocking*. On the birth certificate her name appeared as "Elisa Fortuna": Claudia had proposed it, Erika had accepted. My ancestors would have been proud of such a conservative choice for the least conservative person

I knew, yet it gave me an uneasy feeling, as if it threatened a dark mystery about the relationship between my mother and Claudia that I was not allowed to understand.

The baby girl was healthy and showed no signs of laziness, contrary to the pediatricians' suspicions in the early days when she attached to Erika's breast and wouldn't suck. Her nursing problems disappeared when her natural father renounced his paternal rights. None of us thought it was a coincidence.

We considered Mario small-minded, macho, and referred to him by the nickname Erika had given him: *the emptiness and the sea*. But I did not detect symptoms of cowardice in his decision not to recognize the baby, but rather a glimmer of caution. For Erika, instead, it left an open wound, a resentment.

"He'll reappear when she's grown up," Claudia assured her.

"Yes, but only to check to see if she's turned into a boy," was Erika's sarcastic reply.

"Have you eaten, Elfo, you little rascal?" Claudia asked in a languid voice.

"She can't answer, right now there's no difference between a dog and my daughter!" said Erika, but Claudia, setting her knees on the ground, the palms of her two hands open, started to bark with her tongue out, pretending to wag her tail, breathing heavily like an excited dog.

"Finally a woman has you on all fours," Erika teased. The baby had softened her sharp irony, made her less stinging, sarcasm was no longer the blanket she pulled up to hide how frightened she was. That daughter that happened by accident was shaping her new identity, and only Claudia could fully understand it.

Christmas lights, a joyful inventory of trinkets and delicacies, earthenware mugs, torrone, wool caps, hot glühwein in paper cups, smoked herring, caramelized nuts. I pushed the baby carriage with a slight sense of panic that I masked behind festive smiles. In the darkness sprinkled with Christmas lights, I kept checking my cell phone with the obsessive desire to find a text from Andria. By now his disappearance had the bitter taste of a betrayal as well as the confirmation of a prejudice: in love, the winner is the one who flees. But what do you win? And above all: what a miserable life it must be to think love is a duel from which to flee.

Claudia couldn't bear it when I became so melancholic, she'd point her index finger at the sky as if to say: listen. "Here is a church," she said, "want to go to mass together?"

"I feel out of practice," I replied.

"As a seminarian or a believer?"

"I'm a lost soul."

Claudia laughed. Erika left us alone, disappearing into the fog with the baby. We were squeezed in, as tight on the pinewood pew as a button and a buttonhole, between the notes of the organ and the lilting voice of the Latin American priest. The church smelled of a resinous incense that was not as harsh as the kind I was used to, the arches of the naves were narrow. I was hypnotized by the shiny monstrance, and tapped out the beat of every German word to the Italian verses that I knew by heart. The Credo, the responsorial psalm, the Padre Nostro and "exchange a sign of peace" had different sounds, but the rhythm was the same. And what was the celebration if not the precise, inalterable repetition of a rhythm? A rhythm that joined us, Claudia and me: two bodies, two languages, two brains, two hearts, and a single merciful God to whom I prayed: "Keep her beside me forever."

We shook our hands for the sign of peace with the energy of a farewell. Her skin felt cold and dry. At Communion, the pews emptied, the people swarmed into three orderly lines at the heads of which the ministers of the Eucharist rose in white.

To attend mass was to seek the heart of our childhood, since the religion we learn as children affects the spirituality of our whole life. Claudia and I let our vocal cords vibrate within the melody of the German songs and prayers.

"Did you know we are the same age our parents were when you and I first met?" she said at the end of mass.

As we were leaving the church and the first snow-flakes began to fall, I realized that what she had just said corresponded to the confused thoughts I was unable to articulate. Maybe when two people meditate or pray together they lend their spirits to each other.

"Age is just a number," I flipped up my lapel, breathing ice.

"The best age to change everything," she replied.

A few days after the birth of Elfo, before a city official, a document was sealed with the signature of Claudia: in the event of Erika's death, she would become the child's guardian until the girl was of legal age. A sheet of letterhead paper with the gravity of a marriage certificate, and thus for Claudia Elfo would be like a daughter. In this sense Claudia was already asking herself the questions of a prudent educator, on the strength of the experience she had gained from past mistakes. Would her Italian classmates agree to call her Elfo, a girl with a name that ended in the masculine *o*? Behind that name lay the hope that the girl would be raised in Berlin, where our expectations were shaped by events.

Claudia finally signed for the first deliveries to her business. She personally prepared some of the vegan quiches that were distributed to her former nursing home, and I helped her, in an exception to her bureaucratic rigor, since I was not listed in the Italian consulate's official registry of Italians abroad and I did not have an Anmeldung, the required certificate for foreigners who work in Germany.

Elfo was crying that morning, Claudia and Erika tried everything, even the dog act, seeing as it had worked the last time. Claudia on her knees yelped and barked to placate the child's tears. "I hate dogs and children," she had said centuries ago when she went on dates with boys who dreamed of having a family with her. They would have appreciated the irony in her little performance.

Erika passed Elfo to her, throwing in the towel. "I'm so tired. This little monster is sucking the life out of me." That's what she'd call her, either that or mutant, alien, burden, E.T., but the more dismissive the words, the more you could sense the protective wall that Erika was building around the child against the threat of anxiety. In that attempt I could detect a form of love toward Claudia, who had been raised in the cursed brew of an anxious mother. Claudia and Erika had an exceptional understanding, undeniable, reinforced by the baby's tyranny: none of this had been foreseen when I left for Berlin. My future idyl with the city and Claudia had been transformed into a sort of commune filled with chores.

Claudia took the little one in her arms, bending her knees just a little, then she curled up in my bed softly singing "Ninnananna" by Modena City Ramblers. There were no violins or accordion, but the melody was sooth-ing. Her voice became fainter as the baby's breathing grew heavier with sleep. Shortly after, she and Claudia fell asleep in the same bed.

Erika and I were left alone, facing each other, our eyes on our phones leaning against the edge of the table, both of us scrolling through our messages, only slightly inhibited by the embarrassment of not speak-ing to each other. We were interrupted by a ringing at the door. We looked at it suspiciously. Erika wrapped her neck in a wool scarf so big you could hardly see the upper part of her face and she went to the door, ask-ing who was there: a voice muffled by the door replied something that seemed to satisfy her. She opened with-out further questions, a boy appeared in a jean jacket, with black curls, a thick mustache, and the kind expres-sion of someone who has studied a part and is about to perform it: between his arms, tight against his chest, he held a cardboard box.

"My name is Shorsh and I am a friend of Andria, I have a package from him."

He said in English that he was in a hurry, extended the package to me and left.

It wasn't as heavy as its size might have suggested. I shook it gently, as if Andria himself were inside, shrunken into a crystal globe; soft thumps announced that nothing fragile was inside.

"Before opening it I'd like to wake Claudia," I said.

"Open it, c'mon."

Claudia appeared with her face still creased by her short nap and asked, "What's this?"

"It was sent by your friend," Erika explained. Out of Claudia's sight, she showed me her tongue wagging between her index and middle fingers.

"Who?" Claudia seemed in a daze.

"Andria," I said.

Claudia bent down and pushed it with her hands toward the middle of the room. "Not much in there," she commented, "I'll open it. If it's a bomb save your skin while I go down in flames."

"Hurry up, otherwise I'll open it," said Erika.

I hemmed and hawed but Claudia was already holding the scissors, she pushed me to the side with a slight shove and cut the adhesive tape. Our curiosity was mixed with excitement to which some tension was added. Inside the wrapping paper what immediately stood out was the blue plastic of a camera: a Polaroid that Claudia had given to Andria. There was also a photo in a transparent envelope: a selfie of Andria with his lips puckered in a kiss, and on the white border at the bottom was written: "Ich liebe euch." *I love you both.* The box contained a hair dryer, two T-shirts, an edition of *Pippi Longstocking* in Georgian, a picture holder with a photo of Andria and me on the Warschauer bridge, dark circles under our eyes and our faces pale, post-clubbing, when the only salvation was the black coffee of Hakan the Turk.

"I didn't remember him being so hot," Erika commented.

"He also had a huge dick," Claudia said.

"Ah, my little expert has spoken."

"It wasn't just that," I specified, irked.

"But a big dick is always a nice beginning," Claudia retorted.

"Almost as nice as two big tits," concluded Erika, loosening her shirt and displaying her large white breasts and the purple seal of her nipples.

"Mine are better because I am *lactose free*," added Claudia, joining her nudity.

Certain sights at home were always on the agenda, and with time I realized that their purpose was to drive me away.

Claudia rummaged around in the plastic packing material until she came across a brown cloth tied with three blue rubber bands. Her forehead creased. She pondered the mysterious package. I had a strange sensation, as if that cloth held the answer to Andria's disappearance. I immediately asked Claudia to go slow, as if we needed to stop the clock to prepare us for the truth. In just a few words, Andria had bid us farewell, announcing his second or third life. He had written to us as if we were a single person, "Claudia and Francesco": in his handwriting, we seemed to have been made to be written together. Inside the cloth were a cell phone and his expired visa. Andria had been illegal for much longer

than we had known. I thought back to when Claudia said I should have married him: in that moment I
had thought she was joking, but if we had both taken
each other more seriously—I told myself now—maybe
Andria wouldn't have had to leave.

Two months passed and the days started to become less cold, the time box had remained where we discarded it, almost afraid to go near it. Claudia paid her first two major invoices, her little company was underway. Her menu was based on extra-virgin olive oil from Puglia, now, of all times, that the olives from my region were dying, poisoned by a parasite. From her I learned that chaos always wins, but if you take the time to give it a shape, chaos produces something we can look upon with pride at the age of almost forty: a child or a planted tree, a book, a trip, a photograph, a fitting burial for someone you loved. Yet that box of things from Andria sat there by the door. It held the things we had failed to do, from the most important (not marrying Andria) to the most superfluous (not learning a single word of Georgian). In our relationships with him, we had, in the end, assumed that he was transient, and would go back to where he was born, as perhaps, deep down, we actually wanted him to. That impasse was finally broken when Claudia went downstairs with a shovel to bury the box in the garden, on top of which she would plant a gardenia. Bent over with a hood on her head and a scarf over her face, she choked back her tears. We cried because we hadn't had the consolation of saying goodbye.

"I have the feeling I know you less now that I live with you than when we were far apart," I confessed to her.

Her lips contracted into a frown, she had a little dirt on her scarf and nose.

"I don't have nearly as many secrets as you think."

"Maybe it's because of Elfo, but I'm becoming tyrannical and infantile, too."

"So you want to know everything."

"Yes."

Her eyes when severe looked like pennies turned green by the sea.

"Francesco, did you know that because of Aphrodite's curse, Psyche could only love Eros in the dark?"

In these months occupied by Erika and her daughter, I had missed her little lectures, which epitomized our intimacy.

"I know nothing, I always learn too late."

"Despite the evil omens and although she did not lay eyes on Eros, they loved each other deeply, remaining joyfully in the dark." Claudia's skin was turning blue from the cold, her pink lips emitted clouds of condensation. She continued to speak.

"Her sisters were envious of her love and told Psyche to light a lamp so she could find out who her mysterious lover was. After endless pressure Psyche gave in. When she discovered that her lover was none other than the god of love, trouble began for everyone."

"Is there a moral?"

"Let's leave morals to bad teachers."

"Are you telling me that you kept something hidden for my sake?"

"I'm only saying that I accept the darkness of the person I love because it is a part of him."

Then she bent over the plant again, patting the soil that covered the roots. Claudia's hands had changed over the years, as had she; they were longer and knottier than before. I held them, they felt rough.

"Is there something inside the box you buried that I should have seen?" I asked her, pressing her hand to my chest.

She didn't answer. And it was as if she had.

I looked at the wall separating the building complex from the street, where herbs were growing that no one had planted: starflowers, which the residents tolerated, and then the first violet sprouts of hyssop, which Turkish women picked to make tisanes against stomachaches. I loved the flowers and plants of this city, they were a truth I could cling to. The new order of my life had the reassuring borders of a continent self-consciously old, but where a good number of people were not afraid of the freedom of others. Claudia belonged to the first circle of integrated Europeans with their papers in order, duly registered at the local municipality, listed in the register of Italians abroad, and with health insurance. I was like the hyssop and starflower, grown from random seeds: temporary documents, no registration, working off the books; I was a wild weed, robust and stubborn, but I could still be uprooted at any moment without protest. There were tens of thousands like me, we yearned for the randomness of the damp and the rain, with the joy of people who find themselves in their only possible homeland, the one where they don't have to answer to anyone for who they are.

The buried box, more fertile than a seed in a plowed furrow, bore fruit. One evening Claudia announced that an email had arrived. Andria wrote that "all things considered" he was okay, he had gone to his Kakheti for the harvest and at night seen a starry sky that was the most "holy" and "grandiose" thing he had ever admired. Those two adjectives appeared to us like a photograph of the black cupola bordered in light of our childhood.

That same night we challenged our ancestral fear; equipped with a beach blanket and our cell phone flashlights, we went to the lake, without telling each other why but knowing perfectly well. We felt our way down the pebble path that from Indira-Gandhi-Straße leads to the mirror of water. It was blacker than the black surroundings. Without being able to see an arm's length in front of us, we went up the slate steps and climbed over the wooden railing, with the linden trees rustling and water lapping quietly. In the pitch black the lake was invisible, we could hear it only by cupping our hands to our ears. We laid the blanket down on the wet sand, raised our chins to the sky, and saw the same starry vault that had filled Andria with emotion when he wrote to us.

"When I was a little girl I got dizzy when I looked at the stars from the roof. They seemed so far away, now instead I feel Andria here." Her wrinkled jacket made a sound, she had pounded her hand against her chest or against her stomach, to give more emphasis to what she had said.

"Me, too." It was all I could manage, the cold took away my breath and my sentences.

I heard the lake whisper and my memory felt as sharp as a knife. Our time box was below a gardenia and if in twenty years someone found it they would learn very little about Andria and very much about us. In the best of cases they would think we had been two friends who had gone home to dip their ankles in the Adriatic Sea, with no more memories of the long northern winters. In a passage from the Gospel according to Luke, a man asks if he can bury his father before following Jesus, but Jesus responds, "Let the dead bury their dead." While the law of borders had separated us from Andria, the law of hope made us believe that sooner or later we would meet again in a new world.

I had promised Claudia to get over my funk, to not let myself go to seed. So I took charge of keeping order in the house. The kitchen was a realm of airtight compartments: salt shakers, pepper shakers, spice jars, sugar bowls, thermoses, tin, wood, and glass containers lined up according to criteria that pleased the eye rather than utility. I was the enemy of utility, a quality I associated with the worst men of my childhood. Only one quadrant of the house was spared my maniacal orderliness: the territory of the baby's toys, a duty-free zone between the sink and the refrigerator, which I approached only to put back inside a piece that had escaped into the world of adults.

In appearance I started to look like one of those crazy old men who ride the U-Bahn with a carton of wine in their hands, talking to themselves: a tonsure on my head, a beard with lots of white hairs. It was my way of showing solidarity with Claudia, since she had stopped dying her hair, and now it was drained of color, as if the paucity of light had silver-plated the red.

I had no idea who I might meet in the airport on that Sunday in spring. ("I need you to go pick up a couple of guests.") I went out of respect for the arrangement of our cohabitation, which entailed running errands without asking too many questions.

At the Tegel airport (the flight from Milano I was waiting for was late), I wandered back and forth, munching energy bars and sipping protein drinks from glass and plastic bottles, rubbing the beads of a rosary I wore around my wrist in those days to pray the decades. One Our Father, ten Hail Marys, one Glory to the Father and, when I remembered it, the Hail, Holy Queen. The mysterious guests I had been asked to welcome were coming for a party that Claudia had organized for that afternoon: the inauguration of her new catering company.

The party was planned for one of those built-up areas that they call "Kolonien"—little wooden houses similar to the chocolate confections made for children—on the outskirts of old East Berlin, where once upon a time the locals spent their brief mid-season vacations without having to leave the city, and sometimes not even the neighborhood where they lived.

Finally I saw the automatic door open, the flow of passengers emptying into the waiting area, a handful of Middle Eastern families arguing loudly and their relatives waving to get their attention. I envied the vitality and happiness of reunions. Immediately behind them I spotted two women in big sunglasses lugging their trolleys. Wrapped in similar trench coats but of different colors—the shorter one in blue pastel and the taller in red damask —as comfortable as can be with identical shamrock-green bouffant hairdos. The taller one, in the red trench coat, came toward me smiling, lifted her eyeglasses to her forehead, and said, "My child, you won't have any hair left!"

Petrified by surprise, I stammered some small talk, my mind fogged up, my mother's hand grabbed my wrist. "Breathe." When she saw that I had turned my frown into a smile, she said, "Do you remember Tonia?" indicating her old friend, who was already laughing at me.

Right behind the colony where our party was taking place there were huge abandoned chemical factories and the former Tempelhof airport now turned into an expansive grass field over which hot-air balloons and kites flew. Small campsites with the barbecues of families who clinked glasses while the children's shrieks rose to the sky. Our colony was inside a labyrinth of blind walls, tall boxwood hedges, pitched roofs on low houses—like the marzipan desserts we have for Easter—behind a tangle of small cranes, winches, water pumps and floral wreaths.

On one side of the lawn a couple dozen kids were dancing with green wigs and berets on their heads, paying tribute to Claudia, who had squeezed into a tight pea-green T-shirt and wore a lime-green wig on her head. Upon our arrival the hostess broke away from the guests and, wiggling her hips, came toward us with a cup filled with Aperol. She and my mother greeted each other as if it were an old habit. I relived the morning on a distant day when upon awakening I found them busying themselves in the kitchen, after having talked all night about Enrico. Back then I had envied, loved and hated them, I would have bitten and then kissed them with the fury of the betrayed, begging to be admitted, to be able to listen without opening my mouth.

The music grew louder, we heard voices singing a Balkan song, then Celentano and Cutugno: the DJ loved mixing electronic music with the Italian singers whom everyone in Germany knew. Two women slipped off their shoes and started to do pirouettes on the grass. Claudia took the microphone, welcomed everyone in Italian and in German. She said she was happy about this day that we were spending together and how founding the new company was really just an excuse to throw a wild party. A much younger man went up to her and whispered something into her ear. Claudia smiled and then, sending a shout-out to her old colleagues at the nursing home, shared a memory of her elderly patients, whom she said had taught her a lot of jokes about Italians. She told one of them while looking my way, as if she were addressing me alone: "How do we know that Jesus was Italian? He works at his father's company, thinks his mother is a virgin, and his mother thinks he's God!" Everyone laughed, except for Tonia and my mother, who didn't understand the language.

The music started again, Claudia went over to Erika and planted a kiss on her mouth, people clapped their hands, waving glasses of red wine in the pink afternoon air. A part of me was dying to show my mother what would have happened if rather than a family park we had been in the men's room of Berghain or on the mezzanine at Kitty's; but another part was terrified by the idea of showing her how low I could stoop in places like that. At one point, however, I vented the ill humor I'd been repressing. "You came for Claudia and not for me."

She seemed to have been expecting my recriminations, and shook her head, looking at the young DJ. "You never invited me, I would have come running."

"You're my mother, you don't need an invitation." I refused to drop the issue.

"Mother, son . . . now I'm just Elisa, that's all, and you're just Francesco. As Elisa I came here to see my friend Claudia." In two gulps she emptied half the glass. "She invited me, or rather, invited *us*," she added. Tonia, from the other side of the meadow, returned a loyal smile.

My mother placed her lips on the rim of the glass again, sat down and placing a hand on my leg invited me to do the same. "I have something to tell you," she said, clearing her voice and going close to my ear, as if she didn't want anyone to hear. "Twenty years ago Enrico gave me a masseria."

"A masseria?"

"I know what you're thinking." She knew perfectly well that I had already turned her news into a missed real estate opportunity.

"In which area? How much work does it need?" I asked her.

"I sold it."

"You sold it? Who sold it for you?"

"Don't worry, I did well."

I felt violated, I had been one of the best salesmen of masserie, they had even threated to kill me when Dente was still around, it was a fact and I demanded that my mother recognize it.

"With that money we can do a little traveling," she added, ice-cold.

I looked at the hint of down on her temples, a groove that disappeared into the green bush of her hair.

"Was it important to you?" I asked.

"Now it is even more important since it allowed me to help Claudia, before it was only a place where I buried my memories."

I thought back to the night when I had run into her and Enrico at the train station, I thought of her legs, her messy hair, her naked ankles, her shoes dangling from her fingers.

Then she drank the last sip from her glass, looked me in the eye, pointed to a guy who was dancing with Claudia with an expression that left nothing to the imagination.

"He's twenty years old," I told her.

"Am I not allowed to look?"

Erika interrupted us. "Claudia has told me so much about you, we're both crazy!"

The compliment seemed sincere, and my mother accepted it with a smile. "When it cools down we were thinking about going for a ride on the hot-air balloon."

"Don't even think about it," I said.

"In fact, you'll take care of the baby," said Erika.

"She's a savage beauty," my mother commented when Erika walked away.

"No, she's just a savage."

The meadow shook from the music, I observed the concentrated look on the DJ's face and the backs of everyone else.

"What was Andria like?" asked my mother, point-blank, while I was watching the amorous skirmishes of Erika and Claudia.

"What do you know?"

"I don't know anything, just the name. Claudia told me you had a story with a person and this person's name was Andria. I never asked anything more and she never added anything."

"Did you know that he's a man?"

"No, I didn't." For the first time that afternoon my mother was less sure of herself. "But I'm not surprised."

"He was here illegally, now he's back in Georgia," was all I said, with a shrug of my shoulders.

"He won't be back."

I observed her hands covered with freckles and wrinkles, the time gone by, when those hands picked me up from the cradle.

"Were you happy together?"

"We had lots of fun." As if she hadn't heard, I repeated that word: "Lots."

"Start to have fun again, without him."

Tonia came up to us, as if she had understood the difficult moment we were having, and handed us a sprig of mint. "Smell it, it's different from Italian mint," she said.

"Everything here is different," I replied, "even you two seem different."

"In what way are we different?" Tonia didn't look happy.

"You look a lot younger."

Tonia's round face melted into a smile. My mother hugged me tight.

The music stopped, Claudia said something in German and in almost a trance we left the small enclosure of the colonies and went to the green expanse of Tempelhof. The music came with us, imprisoned inside a Bluetooth speaker that followed the parade of friends. We strolled down the broad avenue in single file, giant elms on either side. I put Elfo in a baby carrier, and turned around to look at the long figure of Claudia near the silhouette of my mother. One, leaning slightly, listened to what the shorter one had to say. I went up to them.

"Here he is, we were talking about you," said Claudia, "you're the only one who's not wearing anything green." It was the theme of the picnic.

"I don't like green," I replied, but she and my mother had gone back to speaking intensely to each other.

"I'm convincing your mother to come live here." Claudia placed my elbow on her shoulder, said that life was too short to worry about convention, we would spend a thousand Sundays like this, waiting for the right moment to return to Martina and look at the sea from the plane, and then dip our ankles in the light blue sand of Lido Bizzarro before coming back to the long twilights of Brandenburg.

Children in shorts and party hats pedaled between the adults, raising their arms toward the sun: yellow, red and green rumblings filled the air.

The hot-air balloon flew over us, covered with colored hexagons, a line of people waited their turn to climb on board, fanning themselves with blue pieces of paper. Claudia laid a towel on the ground and plopped down on it with her legs crossed. We all followed her with the docile obedience of children when they imitate their teacher's movements. She took from her bag a timeworn book, its pages yellowed, *Racconto d'amore*, by Biagia Marniti. She cleared her throat and opened to a page that had been tortured by a fold. "Riposare vorrei / Dove gli alberi sono quieti"—I wish to rest / where the trees are still. This was the beginning of a poem on how the shapes of clouds evoke the persons dearest to us. I would never stop admiring someone who has infinite faith in humanity, so much faith that she will sit down in the middle of an abandoned airport and read verses by a poet from Puglia.

Claudia, you never did anything wrong precisely because you did everything wrong, you always failed and the times that I followed you were the only times that I was truly happy.

My mother gave a pinch to my neck. "So, are you going up with us?"

"No, I'll watch you while you go up, it'll still be nice."

At least an hour went by, yet time seemed to pass very quickly, I held little Elfo close to my chest as she sucked on a rattle. A pleasant smell of skin and apple rebounded to my hot nostrils. My mother, Erika, Claudia, Tonia and other familiar faces took their places in a gondola under the burner, which had begun to shoot tongues of fire into the open mouth of the balloon.

Sunset was near, the best hour for hot-air balloons, people crowded around filling up space, in the distance they played violins and beat on drums. Claudia and Elisa smiled at me with their elbows on the edge, my mother was a little afraid and smiled through gritted teeth.

From my pant pocket, a telephone call insinuated itself, I answered while continuing to look at Claudia and my mother, they had become two dark and green silhouettes in a bluish sky dotted with tiny sparks, I interpreted their arm movements as a farewell to me and the world, from which they were taking a break. They could never have interpreted the chill that paralyzed my smile. I had answered the phone with a mechanical inertia, a voice from the other part of Europe communicated to me that the hammer had been pulled back manually, the trigger pressed, and the barrel had expelled a bullet. This time my father's pistol had fired a shot.

Epilogue

Amore

(Singular. Masculine. Said of foods, flavor.)

The saints always come from the sea, with their hands empty but abounding with miracles. When they arrive their bodies are dead but their spirits are holy, they lie in reliquaries, are awaited on the shore to prevent famines, droughts, or the unrelenting plague. Saint Nicholas and Saint Theodore arrived in humble urns on wooden galleys that docked at the ports of Bari and Brindisi. Saint Martin also came to Maramaldo from the sea. When it doesn't rain for months our peasants pray to Saint Comasia with their chins facing the Adriatic, because it is from there that the mistral wind brings clouds filled with rain.

At sunset, before the procession, I, too, take a look at the sea beyond the hills of the valley: it is a lead plate framed by thick groves of olive trees that for years have been fighting their own war, rusting like barbed wire. The gray sky is drawn by orange nimbus clouds that fade toward the horizon; Holy Thursday is always cold, no matter when it falls. The statues are assigned at the

San Rocco sacristy, after a frugal meal in the corridor of the old insane asylum attached to the rectory; the howls of the mad are still trapped in the darkness; in one of the cells they say you find the braids of women who were tied to the bunk beds and the dentures of the last madmen to be locked up there.

We are about eighty men, we all know each other, and for many of them I know "where they fit," and many believe that they know "where I fit." My period in Berlin has branded me forever in their eyes as "il tedesco," the German, a word they pronounce with sarcasm. I am well aware that for most of them I'm a guy who didn't make it, who had to come back. But they are the same ones who thought I had fled, an emigrant will always have to wear the label of cowardice.

"Returned but still spatriato," they say, alluding to the fact that I do not have a wife, a child, a steady job, but only a suitcase that is always packed. I am lost at sea. Someone "interrupted," according to their idea of the world. There are rare friends who are more careful, and call me *scapulèta*, which is a little better than *spatrièta* and is used for oxen that free themselves of the yoke.

I haven't been in a place so full of men since my days at Lab, when I hung out at hookah bars to beg for the gram of the happiness I had felt with Andria on our wild nights.

I can't go near the table where the satraps of the procession assign the mysteries for Holy Friday and the positions for the procession of Our Lady of Sorrows that crosses the city all night long. On a pew, lined up, are demijohns of red wine and trays of capocollo snacks that will help replenish our energy. A man with a mustache and sunburnt skin breaks two eggs inside one of the demijohns, then he shakes it, a foam forms on the rim. "Wine with eggs will give us fuel," he says, reassuring us about the magic potion that no one dares to taste.

We will walk for kilometers bearing the plaster statues on our shoulders, reciting the rosary and singing hymns to Our Lady of Sorrows. No one dares to say it, but the statue that leads the procession has a bold earthly appeal in her shiny face, with her eyes turned upward and not downward, unlike anyone who experiences sorrow; her slender hands hold a white lace handkerchief, the clothing in which she has been adorned, piece by piece, is scented with lavender. The dozens of men in the procession, bare-chested, spread talcum powder on their shoulders and necks, interlock their fingers and stretch the muscles of their forearms, lengthen their tendons, bend their elbows. The older men have hairy ruddy skin, while the younger have tribal tattoos and waxed skin, tiny beads of sweat slide down their necks, as if they had already made a huge effort. The temperature is hot, the air is foul. People speak in loud voices, waiting for the assignments to arrive. Finally the old priest appears, accompanied by a young cleric in a white suit and eyeglasses with invisible frames, in his hands he has the sheet with the list.

"That one's illegitimate," says a shirtless guy, his six-pack covered by the face of a dragon. "Illegitimate," in his language, stands for "faggot": if one of my old buddies from the Berghain were to come in, they'd see everyone here as *illegitimate* except for the little priest with glasses.

"Here comes the pistolero," shouts another man. With a scarf around his neck and a folder under his arm, behind the priest and his "illegitimate" deacon, my father arrives. They hug him and give him pats on the back that indicate long-standing complicity.

"What a son you raised," says one guy pointing at me, while from my corner I observe him, amused. I know what he's thinking, I know how disgusting he finds all those who, like me, go to the processions; but now he has to get on their good side, because he has started to get into politics, to wear ties, to say that "first comes Martina and then comes Locorotondo," the town nearest to and much richer than ours. He doesn't know, but I came back to sabotage him, my presence in the city is the source of annoying rumors that he shoos away like a stray dog with fleas. They say that I closed the agency and went to Berlin to marry the daughter of Dr. Fanelli, and that she rejected me at the altar because I owed money to Dente. "He made money," "He must be a spy," "Lost his mind," "Scapulètə," "Spatriato!" Few people—maybe none—are capable of suspecting what I did, what I saw, and who I love.

Months have gone by since my father shot at the thief who had stolen the car (my car). He had surprised him at a traffic light, grabbed his pistol from its holster, loaded, aimed and fired: not at him, but at the tire. While everyone in the immediate vicinity looked the other way, the curious started to appear at their windows, and the car kept going with the flat tire for two hundred meters, until it stopped near City Hall. A short scuffle broke out, the two men were surrounded by shouts of incitement from a bunch of deadbeats. My father called everyone in his phone book to tell them what had happened—embellishing the story with invented details—and to hear himself commended. The honorable Renna in person had invited him to be a candidate on the ballot for the upcoming local elections. He accepted, giving the news to relatives and friends during a dinner, brandishing a bottle of Primitivo like a cudgel, thereby setting into motion his move toward a new life.

My mother, after stopping in Berlin, had taken the opportunity to fly to Tenerife for a long vacation with Tonia and avoid having to witness the political reincarnation of her ex-husband as a new hero of the people. At her age I want to be like that, wake up with nature, be sought by the people who love me.

During the procession I prayed with an intensity I had learned through the meditation exercises of Claudia, I am not cold. The silent crowd casts somber glances at the faces of us statue bearers, we wobble when the march stops, and stamp our heels when we start to walk again. We're dressed in black, with a button that holds our velvet cloaks in place, our heads are uncovered so we can be looked at in the face by Christ on the cross, who follows us until the end of the long procession, and also by our great Lady.

The procession with all these statues surrenders to this evidence that a single god is not enough for everyone. But the Gospel taught us that love is infinite, all you have to do is recognize it, it's a fluid that crosses the continents. On this wave I let myself be transported to the Tigris and Euphrates, where the stars shine much brighter than here; there will be a round white moon that watches over the place where everything was born. I start to pray, through the corners of my mouth, I pray that Andria really is alright in Georgia. I pray even though one of the bearers next to me gives me a puzzled look. I know what he's thinking, I heard him confide in his pal: praying is for girls, rosaries are for the sanctimonious, the only thing men are supposed to do is carry the statues and remove their hats. But under the statue of Judas for which I happened to be picked, and to whom they assign less expert bearers—in the past they would have been risking their skin, because people used to throw rocks at

Judas, while today they only give him dirty looks—we are all equal, "all in the bosom of Christ," as they say in the old part of town when you're safe.

Then, there she is, I see her. A tiny spectral creature, curved in a white tentlike wrap, a wool cap on her head. Etta Bianchi. The sharp angry gaze that shifts right and left, like the periscope on a submarine that has surfaced on the water. She scrutinizes me, then looks away. I should leave the statue and go after her, quit the procession just to tell her that time does not return; but her eyes have already slid down to my shoulders. She thinks she is more important to other people than she actually is.

I continue into the haze, the distant chants of the procession, going toward the break of day. When morning arrives I will need a quiet place where I can be alone. Night cleanses the mind, says a poem by Mario Luzi that Claudia loved.

We descend from the stairs of the collegiate church where the procession ended, we advance as if someone were pulling us with a rope. Some stay in town, some go to the outskirts of town or the countryside, everyone pulls a blanket over their head, their shoulders aching. Sleepiness competes with the desire for a hot shower, the smell of freshly burnt coffee in the coffeemaker of my father, who is already awake and waiting for me.

"I'm proud of you," he tells me. He's up, dressed the same way he was the night before, his face smaller than

I remembered. "You shouldn't have had to carry the statue of Judas, not you," he scolded.

"Do you really believe?" he then asked me as I was heading toward the bathroom.

I have to at least fool my shivering into not thinking it's cold through the sound of hot water running, the caress of hot steam on goose bumps is like a razor.

"I believe more and more each day," I reply without looking at him, but he has already left. I heard the door slam.

I've started to tend a very young olive grove. It's an impulse that many people have followed since the *Xyella* bacterium infected acres and acres of ancient olive trees.

I am growing a dozen plants, I feel like an alchemist because I mix potassium, phosphorous and nitrite salts. And like all alchemists I am seeking a mystery to unveil while I sow on the soil these reddish granules that will nourish the young roots. This new life resembles in its way the life I had in Berlin with Claudia when we tended to the food of others. Today I whitewash the stones with lime and nourish the earth with fertilizer.

Since that time I've dedicated myself to the property in the countryside left by my grandparents, I chose the ancient Ogliarola trees that do not start to produce fruit for twenty years. I did it against everyone's advice. The nurseries propose genetically modified olive trees that in three years produce fruit. But I am keeping the old ones, which will adapt more slowly to a changing nature. Trees can also take the long view. The first olives will be picked by the adult Elfo, during one of her vacations in Italy. It's madness to plant trees that will bear fruit when I'm old. Or maybe patience is just a form of humanity, the same humanity my ancestors had when they planted Ogliarolas between the Ionian and the Adriatic. Now I've finally understood.

When the nice weather began I moved to my grandparents' trulli, which are damp and silent, even if this patch of land is little more than a construction site filled with promise. At the election my father received three votes, he came to the countryside to bring me the news with a face full of wrinkles that hadn't been there before.

"Between you and your grandparents there's one vote missing, one of you threw me overboard." He has the eyes of a madman, he's come to the wrong place to settle a score.

I don't have the courage to tell him that I didn't vote. To make up for it, every Saturday I go to see my grandparents at the white villa where they spend their days sleeping in two wheelchairs; they ask me about the grapes, although it is still too early to harvest them, and this surprises me more than their age. We say the rosary even if Grandfather is not a believer; I pray with them and for them, but this they must not know.

At night I hear the chirping of the crickets, rustling from inside the walls, the squeaking of the bed, and all around the noise from the rada, the natural harbor, I open my eyes, the dawn emerges through a glint in the embrasure. I have a bad connection and to read my texts I go to the heart of the vineyard, where the signal is also weak. The workers in charge of restructuring the countryside always arrive very late, find me in the vineyard and think that I am already at work, while instead I am waiting: every Monday I send a text to Andria's old number, which turns out to be nonexistent. Every text is transformed into bits before being codified in a binary digital signal. o e I, o e I. Good and Evil, Cause and Effect, Black and White, Land and Sea. No one will probably intercept this fragmented message of love slipped into the neck of an imaginary bottle: "Do you remember when we were at the Gleisdreieck Park, sitting on the grass, the warmth of the air mixed with the smell of the meadow, as if it were sweating..."

I need to give substance to love. The dialect of my city teaches that love does not exist. When two people love each other, the most they will say is that they wish each other "bbun," that is to say, "well." Yet the word *amore* does appear in the old dictionary of the priest dialectician Giuseppe Grassi, as a synonym of *flavor*. If a fruit does not have *love*, this means that it is insipid, unripe. Back in the day when the psychologist for the military checkup asked me if I had had a childhood without love, I always answered no: my grandparents and parents gave me food that was filled with "amore."

Andria returns through a copper-colored sunset, or by smelling the rosemary that our ancestors called the herb of memory. We bit each other many times when we were at certain parties, in moments of ecstasy he dried my sweat with a handkerchief and bit it when I was far away. I was the one who gave it to him: there were always white handkerchiefs with embroidered hems at the Ostbahnhof flea market, which we passed by on Sunday mornings on our way home from nights of adventure.

In the predawn hours I wake up at four o'clock with an interrupted dream, a premonition: I see Andria floating on the heads of souls dancing inside a cellar or abandoned factory, torches are being lit all around while the sky turns indigo. My heart beats faster, the sense of guilt creeps in, a void occupies the black space between wakefulness and sleep, I am incapable of taking care of the people I love.

When the dune-colored hood of the rental car appears before the front door, my heart starts beating like mad. Through the car window I immediately recognize her carmine head of hair gleaming under the noontime sun. I'm more startled to see her without Erika than behind the wheel in a bathing suit.

"Did you two have a fight?"

"You know how she is." She shakes her head. We embrace sliding our cheeks against each other.

"What did you do to your face?" I ask her.

"I discovered that I'm allergic to the land, to my land."

Her body has recently begun to speak to her. At first the allergy introduced itself very discreetly on her forehead, then her legs were covered with red blotches and on her face a rash appeared in the shape of a butterfly with wings spread up to her eyes.

She is finally in Italy on a beautiful June day, but it is as if her body has grown unaccustomed to that air and that sun.

"When I came back I was full of infections, too, and my hair is falling out." Maturity turns the skin into a map of roads that are more and more crowded. "Anyway, I like your new cut," I say, softly touching the side of the head that she shaved.

She walks away and steps between the stones. The locusts sing from deep inside the marjoram bushes, Claudia echoes them: cri cri cra cra.

But she's not carefree, it's as if she wants to entertain me and keep me far away from the shadow hanging over her. Under the pergola she does a pirouette. The table is set with a sky-blue tablecloth and carafes of water and wine.

I prepare her for the worst with the wine. I found it in a demijohn, it belongs to a past harvest and by now it's the color of rust. Maybe the grapes were crushed by me when I was a boy.

Claudia rushes from one corner to the next of the tiny farmyard in front of the casedde. "Today I'm going to do something that might make you angry."

"Dein Wunsch mein Befehl." *Your wish is my command.*

"I'm hungry," she says.

I go into the palmento, the water is boiling and I lower the spaghetti into it, the smell of the fresh tomato puree is amazing.

Five minutes, the time it takes to cook the spaghetti al dente, and then a couple of minutes to garnish the plate with three leaves of basil.

We sit across from each other, I hold her hand. "I want to say grace," I say. Claudia nods, placing her palm over mine. "Lord, bless this food and remember those who have none."

The shadow of the pergola draws scribbles on her face.

"It was a mistake to come back to Puglia, even for only a few days."

I feel tears welling. Very few people have the gift of knowing what it means to cry over a love that remains rather than a love that's lost. The crisis averted, rescued from the brink. Only the chosen few will know what it means to cry together: after an orgasm, after pages of novels read out loud, after listening to the Intermezzo of *Cavalleria Rusticana*. I am not one of the chosen ones, in Claudia's presence an unhappy listlessness always triumphs.

"I don't recognize anything, I only see old men everywhere, roads in disrepair, cars going crazy, people bent over their cell phones, burnt olive trees, trash, aggressiveness all over the place, a putrid sea. There are people here who hate everything they are not and never can be: foreigners, liberated people, people who have studied, young women and those of us who left. These last few days have been awful, I thought they would never end."

Claudia is showing her weakness, she would never admit that she has just let loose a "lament of the expats," as she and I have always called it.

"You're being unfair."

"The only place in the world where I can allow myself to be unfair is where I was born, right? It's a place that I used to love."

She twists her fork in the plate, forming a ball of pasta so big that no one could ever ingest it.

"It's not so bad here in the countryside," I tell her.

"I spent an afternoon inside a bagnarola just to get reacquainted with the sea."

A bagnarola is an octagonal stone turret, on the shore, where the noblewomen from the pink villas on the seaside used to spend their days shielded from male eyes (or to have clandestine sex with young fishermen). I was startled by the image of Claudia hiding in the stone turret on the Leuca beach.

"You needed for no one to see you." I caress the knuckles of her hand, the bones are rock spikes, I want to grab on to them like a rope, because soon we will be separated again.

"Francesco, can you do me a favor?" Her tone has turned solemn, she's stopped eating.

"Whatever you want." I'm a soldier standing at attention.

"Don't get upset with me when you don't understand the things I do."

"That's the reason I love you, and have from the start."

"I'm afraid of losing Erika, she's full of life, rich, she acts like she loves me, but then she makes certain remarks..." She stops, doesn't want to tell me, I insist, I want to know. Claudia gives in.

"I'm going to give you one example that gives you the whole picture. She says that when I read poetry to the baby I turn gloomy."

"You're not at all gloomy."

"I read nursery rhymes, Erika says I should hear myself, that I read poems filled with dead people and ghosts. She says that I'll turn Elfo into a *broken girl*."

"What do you answer?"

"I told her that the poems have flavor, they have smells, they have life. Sometimes she doesn't seem to understand the most basic things about me."

"You've always been fanatical about poetry."

"Erika is a little like the times in which we live, she doesn't appreciate the fertility of poetry, she doesn't understand the value of our roots, the value of her interior life and our daughter's."

Claudia is drowning in bitterness, she lowers her eyes, curves her neck.

"I'll always be here," I promise.

"Me, too, even if I'll never come back to Martina, I will always be waiting for you up there."

"Up there is our happiness." Up there is Berlin, but maybe we just like the vagueness of the word.

"Do you have ice?" she asks me, with the glimmer of a smile.

I go away for a few seconds, empty four cubes of ice into a clay bowl, then go back outside with the sun in my eyes. Claudia is gone. I turn around looking for her at the door, in the vineyard, on the roof. Her cell phone is leaning against a leg of her chair, as if she had dropped it. My voice calling out to her vanishes into the mugginess of the day.

I venture into the vineyard, between the weeds, the vegetable plots and the orchard of almond, black cherry and fig trees. The workers have left behind some rusty iron poles that they'll use to build the scaffolding for the last part of the job. I call out to her, but the only response is the echo of the plains. The woods are not too far away; a warm and gentle Grecale wind shakes the hibiscus.

"Claudia…"

Then a foreboding: I retrace my steps, down to where the workers have started to enclose the well. It's a gulch from which a chipped stone cylinder emerges with a wrought-iron cover from which a chain for the bucket used to hang. The mouth of the well is sealed with a wire mesh, the small gravel clearing is an arsenal of construction equipment; with my heart in my throat I cross it and discover that the mesh has been removed. I stick my face down in the pitch-black: nothing appears except the black abyss of any country well. *Claudia. Claudia. Are you there?*

In that moment a black snake slithers through the oregano and sagebrush that have grown between the stone wall and the vineyard, it seems to have lost its way, moving its head right and left, like an eel, seeking the damp shade of the stone wall.

"Do you think I'm so desperate that I would throw myself down a well in Martina Franca?"

Here she is, Claudia.

"No, I wanted to warn you about the snake," I lie.

"You know it's not a snake."

"No? What is it then, a dragon?"

"A harmless grass snake."

"How do you know?"

"I could tell from its eyes, a snake has vertical pupils, a grass snake horizontal."

"Your eyes are really sharp," I tease her, but it's the first thing they teach you in the countryside: when a slithering animal comes toward you, you can only understand the danger you are in by looking into its eyes.

Claudia walks through the vineyard, I follow her as far as the orchard, she climbs a tree, her legs dangle in the air.

"I wanted to be alone with you and him," she says.

"Him?"

"The cherry tree? It's here that you told me about your first kiss with a man."

"It was an almond tree."

"It doesn't matter." Once again she is right. Then she arches her back, her knees bend, she wraps herself around the big branch and, drawing on the force of gravity, falls on her feet in a pink cloud of dirt.

"I've always wanted to bite you," she says.

"What?"

"Bite you," she repeats, and asks me to stand still while she approaches my neck. Her teeth sink into my flesh producing a brief pleasure followed by an intense pain.

I shout, "Stupida!"

Claudia laughs, a thread of saliva hangs from her lips. My life is in that sparkling string, the inextricable bond that keeps us together.

Claudia is behind me again, I try to wriggle out but she is stronger, she overpowers me, and behold, another bite: I manage to free myself and run toward the pergola, but she wraps an arm around my throat. I fall to the ground, my face is in the dust, she's on top of me, with her knees in my back. It's a game for just the two of us and the rest of the world is excluded. A perfect silence descends upon the countryside, but the peace lasts for only a sigh. From the districts of Farinata and Finimondo, to the northwest, a rumble suddenly arrives. After a long time the Tornados and F14s are lifting off from the military base of Gioia del Colle, and it's not a good sign when they fly low and race toward the east. Claudia and I look at each other, annoyed, as if that noise has broken an enchantment.

For the rest of the afternoon we remain seated in the shade of the pergola reading poetry, with the secret aspiration that every verse in which we see ourselves was written for us.

We look at the woods, at the sides of the road, and at the foot of the low stone wall, where tufts of cyclamen decorate our barrier with pink. Out of season, only we can see and comment on them, but this is our secret.

We sing songs and recite verses that are older than us, we are outside of time and have the illusion that we are safe.

Berlin, Weißensee, July 31, 2019

Notes from My Desk
or Room of the Spirits

The events and characters in *Spatriati* are, of course, products of the imagination, and any reference to things that actually happened or people who really exist should be considered accidental. Small changes in the topography of the places described and in the chronology of historical events, news items, or customs have been made in places for dramatic purposes.

Spatriato is the past participle of the verb *spatriare*, which means to go away, or as the Treccani dictionary says, to be expelled from one's homeland. In some southern dialects, including Martinese, it has other nuances, such as uncertain, disoriented, vagabond, scatterbrained, with neither art nor part, in some cases even an orphan: the word *patria* derives from Latin and means the land of one's fathers, therefore a spatriato can also be a person who has lost their father or never had one.

For the titles of some parts in Martinese dialect, I referred for sentimental reasons to the old *Dizionario martinese-italiano* by Giuseppe Grassi (Schena, 1984), since it was the first dictionary in which I learned the smattering of dialect that I can speak today. For the term *spatrièta*, which appears in its correct phonetic form in the opening of Part Two, I consulted the dictionary *La parlata dei martinesi e altri ricordi* by Giuseppe Gaetano Marangi (Nuova Editrice Apulia, 2010).

In the novel there are quotations, homages and references to literary works, places and historical events. In the following section I will list some information and some debts to what Robert Walser in *The Walk* called the desk or room of the spirits. References to the published English translations have been provided by the translator.

The first quote after the title page is from a letter that Giacomo Leopardi wrote in 1827 to his friend Pietro Giordani after one of his many flights from Recanati, in which he floats the theory of remembrance for restless and unstable people like himself: "Since I was often changing my place of residence, and stopping in one place or another, for months or years, I realized that I never felt content, never centered, never naturalized in any place, no matter how excellent, until I had memories to attach to that place." I found this passage in *Letteratura italiana*, edited by Enzo Sicliano (Mondadori, 1986).

Part One *Crestiene*

The quoted definition of *Crestiene* is from page 3 of *Christ Stopped at Eboli*, by Carlo Levi, first published in 1945, and in English translation in 1947 (Farrar, Straus and Company).

Games without Frontiers, also called JSF, the initials of Jeux sans frontières, was a public event promoted by Charles de Gaulle in the mid-1960s to foster friendship between Germany and France. The Games quickly became a major summer occasion during which young people from many European cities competed. Martina Franca represented Italy, and was the host of the event on July 11, 1980, which was won by the local team. In the film *Fantozzi subisce ancora* (1983), there is a shot of this event.

In this part of the novel, Claudia is reading Banana Yoshimoto, a best-selling Japanese writer who in the 1990s became very successful, starting with the novel *Kitchen*, which was published in 1988. Osamu Tezuka is a manga writer and the creator of many cartoons, while Rumiko Takashi is universally considered the queen of manga. In the 1990s Granata Press published the Italian edition of *Mermaid Saga*.

Street Fighter is a video game that came out in 1987, but Francesco's schoolmates play the second edition, which started to be sold in Italy in 1991. The player chooses one of eight fighters trained by different combat schools in the world and has the goal of defeating the other seven.

"Come as You Are" is a song by Nirvana from the album *Nevermind* (1991). "Starman" is a song by David Bowie that came out as a 45 in April 1972. "Sentimiento nuevo," written and performed by Franco Battiato, is the final track on the album *La voce del padrone* (1981). "Vacanze romane" is a song by Matia Bazar, an Italian pop group, included on the album *Tango* (1983).

Domenico Carella was a painter, a student of Franceso Solimena, and an imitator of Luca Giordano. His most significant works are in the Palazzo Ducale of Martina Franca and in the Basilica of San Martino. His *Last Supper* was painted in 1804.

The quotations from the Bible in the novel, from Exodus and the Gospel, are from the New King James edition found on the website BibleGateway.com.

The correspondence of Sibilla Aleramo and Dino Campana was collected in the volume *Un viaggio chiamato amore* (Feltrinelli, 2000). In 2002 a film adaptation came out, directed by Michele Placido, inspired by their correspondence.

Caro Michele is a novel by Natalia Ginzburg, first published in 1976, and translated into English by Minna Proctor as *Happiness, as Such* (New Directions, 2019).

Although Elsa Morante is one of Italy's top writers, very few people read her during their high school years. Dario Bellezza was a well-known poet in the 1980s and '90s: after his death some of his poems came out in the I Miti imprint of Mondadori, which distributed his books of poetry at newsstands for 3,900 liras.

The passage from Lucian of Samosata (120–180 C.E.), quoted in the last section of this part, is from *Bis accusatus*. This is the passage that appeared on the esame di maturità for the classical Liceo in 1999.

Part Two *Spatriètə*

Martina Franca is a municipality of 47,000 inhabitants in the province of Taranto, halfway between Salento and the Bari area. It borders on Ostuni, Ceglie Messapica, Cisternino, Locorotondo, Noci and Albertobello. This group of towns forms the Valle d'Itria, which con artists have recently nicknamed "Trullishire."

All construction in Martina is done using a hard red stone painted white with quicklime. The stone is extracted from the ground rather than caves and is often used by the peasants to make dry walls that are low enough for people to step over them. A *trullo* (plural, *trulli*) is a cone-shaped structure built without cement or mortar, the same technique used for dry stone walls. Trulli have an elongated shape and are pointed at the top. Some people believe they once served as places of worship, but in reality, since they were built without mortar, they could be raised and demolished in two days, and were therefore a way for the owner to avoid paying property taxes. In Martinese dialect, a small complex of trulli is called *casedde*. *Pajare* instead are much simpler structures, found only in the Salento area of Puglia.

A *masseria* (plural *masserie*) is a complex of buildings on a farming estate, some dating from the sixteenth century, with a main house for the owner, smaller dwellings for the peasants, stables, and barns. Today many have become luxury holiday accommodations renowned for the authenticity of their meals.

The Gessyca Gelati refrain was a big hit from a popular commercial with Andy Luotto in the late 1980s.

Artificial Intelligence is an electronic music album put out by Warp Records in 1992. It includes tracks by some of the main precursors of modern techno. Spiral Tribe was a group formed in the United Kingdom in 1992 and one of the main inspirations of rave culture.

The Taranto steel mill was inaugurated in 1965 and in its period of maximum growth employed sixty thousand workers. It was first called Italsider, then Nuova Italsider, and after privatization it became Ilva and today ArcelorMittal. From the big Pianelle forest of Martina Franca, about five hundred meters high, you can see the giant plant, which occupies three-quarters of the metropolitan territory of Taranto, with its rust-colored clouds and the sea at its back. For anyone who wishes to study the history of this industry, I would advise them to read *Fumo sulla città*, by Alessandro Leogrande (Fandango, 2013). I would like to quote an excerpt from the last page, because it is a splendid counterpoint to the view of Claudia and Francesco: "From the roof of the house where I grew up, I gaze at the chimneys of Ilva which loom before me, the motionless cranes at the harbor, the ships anchored while waiting to unload the mineral or load the sheets of steel, the gulf that opens to the horizon, the islands of San Pietro and San Paolo, and then the old city again, the traffic jams at night, the big buildings that follow one another, neighborhood to neighborhood, often identical to each other, the beginning of the countryside and the road that runs straight toward the hill of Martina Franca."

For a period during the 1980s, Martina Franca appeared in the news in relation to the plane crash near Ustica, because it was the location of a giant NATO radar station whose enormous antennae could be seen from dozens of kilometers away. All that remain today are some small mushroom-shaped cabins where the American soldiers used to live.

The scene where Claudia is imprisoned inside a square drawn with chalk by Etta is something I borrowed from Primo Levi. In his beautiful short story "Titanium," from *The Periodic Table*, a grouchy factory worker closes a little girl inside a painted circle.

The image of the skies of Puglia leaving scratches was inspired by a letter that Franz Kafka wrote to Oskar Pollak in 1902, in which Prague was compared to a stepmother with claws.

Gli Oesais, a Barese parody of Oasis, were played by Emilio Solfrizzi and Antonio Stornaiolo, two actors still very popular today who in their youth performed on the local scene with the stage name Toti and Tata. Together with their writer Gennaro Nunziante they made fun of the vices and virtues of show business with clever parodies, such as the parody of the playwright Carmelo Bene as Carmelo Meglio, and mocked the hermetic political verses of Italian poets through the character of Mino Pausa, an aspiring poète maudit—*maudit*, or cursed, mainly by the others.

"La Cura" is a song by Franco Battiato from his album *L'imboscata* (1996).

Il pensiero meridian by the sociologist Franco Cassano is an essay that was published in 1996 by Laterza and shaped the identities of many Pugliese scholars or simply readers on the value of time, of slowness, in the provinces. Considered one of the key texts of the Nuovo Meridionalismo movement. It was published in the United States as *Southern Thought and Other Essays on the Mediterranean*, translated by Norma Bouchard (Fordham University Press, 2012).

In 1998, the leader of the Workers' Party of Kurdistan (PKK), Abdullah Öcalan, was wanted by the Turkish government and stayed in Italy for sixty-five days in the hope that he would receive a political asylum that was never granted, despite the many protests in his favor organized mainly by university students. Giuseppe Tatarella was a center-right politician highly respected for his diplomatic qualities, which earned him the nickname Minister of Harmony.

Part Three *Malenvirne*

Vittorio Bodini is probably the best-known and -loved poet of Puglia. The poem that Claudia is reading under the lemon tree is from his collection *La luna dei Borboni*, first published in 1952 and currently published, like all of Bodini's work, by Besa.

Claudia's books constitute an essential library for anyone who wishes to study twentieth-century Pugliese narrative. The novels mentioned are *L'ora di tutti* by Maria Corti, published in 1962 and reissued by Bompiani; *Analisi in famiglia* by Maria Marcone, published by Feltrinelli in 1977; *Passaggio in ombra* by Mariateresa Di Lascia, published in 1995 and reissued by Feltrinelli; and *La malapianta* by Rina Durante, published in 1964 and reissued by AnimaMundi Edizioni. From Marcone's novel I borrowed the concept of "grow forest," and from Durante the idea of "collapsing while standing still."

Nichi Vendola was the governor of Puglia from 2005 to 2015. His policies were focused, especially during his first two terms, on the promotion of tourism to the region and youthful entrepreneurship, to such an extent that it led to talk of a "Pugliese Spring." His slogan was "La Puglia migliore," a better Puglia. *Perché la Puglia non è la California* (Baldini+Castoldi, 2000) is a nonfiction work in which the manager Franco Tatò presented solutions and proposals to improve tourism potential and social innovation in the region.

The Martina Franca donkey is the most majestic species of the Italian donkey: a black mane, gray muzzle, broad back, and withers that exceed one meter sixty. From childhood we are raised with the biblical story of Balaam's donkey, through which God spoke, the only animal in the Bible conferred this privilege (Numbers, 22:23). People from neighboring villages call the Martinesi "Ciucci," donkeys, because they are so stubborn: it is no accident that many of us are convinced that the donkey who carried Jesus into Jerusalem, who according to some legends later came to Italy, also passed through Martina.

Camere separate by Pier Vittorio Tondelli is a novel from 1989 (Bompiani), published in English as *Separate Rooms* (Serpent's Tail, 1992), in a translation by Simon Pleasance.

"Screen women" refers to the *Vita nuova* of Dante, in which the "donna dello schermo" distracts his attention from his beloved Beatrice.

Gustav Janouch's interview with Franz Kafka was published by New Directions in 2012 as *Conversations with Kafka*.

Part Four *Ruinenlust*

In Berlin club culture was a great laboratory for cutting-edge music, especially electronic music. It brought into harmony the two souls of the city after the collapse of the Wall and made many foreigners who had come running there in the past thirty years feel at home. Berghain is the most famous techno music club in the world, established in 2004 at a huge abandoned power plant in the Friedrichshain neighborhood. It's known by all fans as one of the most exclusive techno clubs because of its strict access policy, managed by the bouncer and photographer Sven Marquardt, who allows in only a small percentage of the thousands of people who every weekend try to enter the "Temple." Golden Gate is a small Berlin club founded in 2000 in an old warehouse belonging to the subway system. Behind it there is usually a big amusement park with a panoramic Ferris wheel that disappears into the clouds, running even when the thermometer dips well below freezing: when the clubbers step out for a breath of fresh air, they get on the Ferris wheel and come steps away from the sky; then they return back to earth completely covered in snow.

"O Superman" by Laurie Anderson is a song that came out as a single in 1981. It is often played at the Panorama Bar of Berghain at eight o'clock sharp on Sunday nights. Paul Oakenfold is a world-famous DJ, forerunner of trance music, and prominent figure in the rave music scene.

The Eric Ries book on start-ups that Claudia reads is *The Lean Startup: How Today's Entrepreneurs Use Continuous Innovation to Create Radically Successful Businesses* (Crown Currency, 2011), published in Italian translation as *Partire leggeri*.

The East Side Gallery is a 1,300-meter stretch of the old Berlin Wall painted over by international artists, and today considered the longest art gallery in the world.

The poetry collection *Il verme e il frutto* by Raffaele Carrieri can be heard online, read by the actor Riccardo Cucciolla in a video from at least thirty years ago. Anyone who wishes to own it will have to place their trust in fate since *Poesie scelte* (Mondadori, 1976) is practically introuvable.

During his stay in Berlin, Mark Twain tried to study German, but with poor results. He exacted his revenge by writing a short pamphlet titled *The Awful German Language* (1880).

Lisa Morpurgo (1923–1998) was an Italian writer and one of the first and most authoritative scholars of astrology. Her *Lezioni di astologia* (1983) is published by Tea today.

Wonder Woman was the first female hero of DC Comics, created by William Moulton Marston, a psychologist and feminist, and a practitioner of polyamory. With her lasso of truth she forces villains to confess their crimes.

Part Five *Sehnsucht*

The definition of *Sehnsucht* is a quote from Johann Wolfgang Goethe, *The Metamorphosis of Plants*, translated by Douglas Miller (The MIT Press, 2024).

The *Vlora* is the Albanian ship that docked at the port of Bari on August 8, 1991, with more than twenty thousand people on board. They were looking for a new life in Italy after the fall of the Communist regime. For us in Puglia those summer days were a powerful reminder of the fall days in 1989 in Berlin when the East and the West embraced each other again: with the *Vlora*, the people of Puglia and of Albania reconnected the threads of their history.

In the magazine *Mercurio*, there was a debate in 1948 between the writers Natalia Ginzburg and Alba de Céspedes. Ginzburg wrote: "[Women are] really crying because they've fallen into the well and they understand that they will often fall into it all their lives and this will make it hard for them to accomplish anything worthwhile." De Céspedes replied:

I, too, like you and like all women, have a great and ancient experience with wells: I often fall in and I fall in with a crash, precisely because everyone thinks I'm a strong woman—as do I, the moment I'm back out of the well. But—unlike you—I think that these wells are our strength. Because every time we fall in the well we descend to the deepest roots of our being human, and in returning to the surface we carry inside us the kinds of experiences that allow us to understand everything that men—who never fall into the well—will never understand. ("On Women: An Exchange," translated by Alessandra Bastagli, *New York Review of Books*, December 22, 2022.)

"Too Much Love Will Kill You," written by Brian May, is a song by Queen that came out in 1992, after Freddie Mercury had died, but was recorded in 1988 at the time of the album *The Miracle*.

The KitKatClub is the most extreme and transgressive club in Berlin, established by Kirsten Krüger and Simon Thaur in 1994. Every Saturday night it hosts the "CarneBall Bizarre," a fetish-themed circuit party that lasts until the morning, to which one gains entrance only by respecting a very strict dress code. A cosmopolitan place where free spirits from all over the world meet, the KitKat is also known for the picturesque and extreme performances of some of its artists, acrobats, rope masters and hypnotists. In the long line of people waiting their turn outside the building, many transform themselves, stripping naked or putting on feathers. One night two men chased each other with hatchets, but without provoking any feelings of terror or causing the people in line to flee. The Lab.oratory is a club only for very extreme men, in the same vein as Berghain. Various evenings at the gay clubs of the city have names that refer to laboratory activity, perhaps because of the proximity of the concept of chemical experiments and sexual experimentation. The shisha clubs like the one to which Andria and Francesco go are secret places, quite different from the shisha bars that are open to everyone. You can only get in by having the password, an invitation or the secret word. Inside they smoke special noncommercial mu'assels and practice nudism.

Club-Mate is the official drink of Berlin, recognizable by its label featuring a man in a sombrero. A carbonated soft drink with the taste of yerba mate and caffeine, it is sold everywhere, even at newspaper kiosks.

Lucia di Lammermoor is an opera in three acts of 1835 by Gaetano Donizetti, with a libretto by Salvadore Cammarano and based on *The Bride of Lammermoor* by Walter Scott.

In Berlin one-third of the population is of Turkish origin, and on the night between July 15 and 16, 2016, the city was shaken by protests for and against President Erdoğan.

"La zita di Ceglie, nessuno la sceglie"—Ceglie the spinster, no one will choose her, is a Pugliese saying coined in the past century for women who did not marry.

The original meaning of *palmento* (millstone) indicates the vat where the must is fermented, but at the Pugliese casedde this name is often given to the room where the wine is made, a kind of large living room.

Part Six *Torschlußpanik*

"Ninnananna" of the Modena City Ramblers is a song on the 1994 album *Riportando tutto a casa.*

Glühwein is a mulled wine drink with sugar and spices, similar to Italy's vin brûlé, served during the Advent period at the stalls in the German Christmas markets.

Kakheti is a region in eastern Georgia well-known for its wine tradition and excellent climate. Hundreds of varieties of autochthonous grapes are cultivated there. Many experts claim that it was the cradle of the first vine growers in history.

Torre Canne is the seaside locality closest to Martina Franca, in the municipality of Fasano. Most of the young people of Martina, however, prefer the southern beaches, such as Lido Bizzarro and Lido Buzzone.

Italians, like Poles and Turks, are the subject of many German jokes based on clichés verging on common prejudices. In the more lighthearted stories, the Italian is represented as a mamma's boy, while in the heavier ones as a mafioso or a slacker. "If a house is on fire, who gets saved, the Italian or the German? The German, because he's at work."

The Berlin Kolonien are small plots of land in the heart of the city occupied by wooden cottages with small gardens. They are full of life on sunny days and Sundays, ideal as small metropolitan vacation spots for those who don't have the time or the wish to leave the city. Tempelhof was the Berlin airport until October 2008. After a referendum with a big turnout, the large airport area became a city park.

Racconto d'amore (Greco e Greco, 1994) is a collection of poems by the Pugliese poet Biagia Marniti.

Epilogue *Amore*

On the walls of Marina Franca, the depictions of the story of Saint Martin with a mighty cavalry defending the city from the siege of the Cappelletti of Fabrizio Marramaldo in 1529—a local episode in the war between the Spanish and the French in the kingdom of Naples—was told by Cito de' Citi in 1596 in *Vita di San Martino*. According to legend, the gate at which he appeared faces the Adriatic. In recent years, some local historians, including Giovanni Liuzzi, have preferred to separate popular belief from the historical context of the era, characterized by war, plague and famine.

In Martina Franca on the night between Holy Thursday and Good Friday a traditional procession is held dedicated to Our Lady of the Sorrows. The offense to the statue of Judah during the procession is a story that was told to me; what I have written is entirely the product of my imagination, although I was inspired by the spectacular auction in Taranto, where the decision is made who gets to carry the statue in the procession of the Mysteries, an event that I have followed dozens of times and on which in 2008 I wrote a news story for the Bari edition of the national newspaper *La Repubblica*. The mystery surrounding the Taranto rites has produced many publications: in 1984 a book came out with a memorable cover and catchy title, *L'anima incappucciata* (the Hooded Soul), written by Nicola Caputo for the Mandese publishing house. This volume is still essential reading for anyone who wishes to learn about the rumors and arcana of Holy Week. The statute of Our Lady of Sorrows, unlike the papier-mâché statues of the Mysteries, is made of wood. It is conserved at the church of the same name in the historic center of Martina, where it can be disassembled and reassembled, undressed and dressed, only by the most devout brothers.

"La notte lava la mente" (Night Washes the Mind) is one of the best-known poems by Mario Luzi, found in the collection *Onore del vero* (1957) and included today in his *Poesie* (Garzanti).

Cavalleria rusticana is an opera composed by Pietro Mascagni (with a libretto by Giovanni Targioni-Tozzetti and Guido Menasci, inspired by the short story of the same title by Giovanni Verga), first performed in 1890. It is best known for its sublime Intermezzo, in which the music sounds like the undertow of a wave when the sun sets on the sea, and the caress of the violins conveys a sense of serene solitude before the beauty of things.

Martina Franca, February 17, 2021

This novel is dedicated to the memory of the writers of my region, since without them my imagination would not exist. Some of them are quoted in the book and cited in the room of the spirits, others hover in silence, like the poet Claudia Ruggeri, while still others are implicit in my life as a writer and reader and emerge over the course of time. As a joke of destiny would have it, the thinker and sociologist Franco Cassano passed away just as I was finishing the revisions to my proofs. I had hoped that he would read this book and the short paragraph where I quote him. From him I learned to go slow in giving names to trees, as he wrote in *Southern Thought*. This novel ultimately talks about people like him, whom he had already described almost thirty years ago. I bow to the ground before him.

Rome, February 25, 2021

About the Author

Mario Desiati, originally from Martina, Italy, is the author of eleven novels, including his English debut, *Spatriati*, which received Italy's most prestigious literary award, the Strega Prize. His novel *Il paese delle spose infelici* is the basis of Pippo Mezzapesa's film of the same name; his novel *Ternitti* (Mondadori, 2011) was a finalist for the Strega Prize. His books have been translated into six languages. He lives in Puglia, Italy.

About the Translator

Michael F. Moore is the award-winning translator, most recently, of *The Betrothed*, by Alessandro Manzoni. His translations range from twentieth-century classics—*Agostino* by Alberto Moravia and *The Drowned and the Saved* by Primo Levi—to contemporary novels. In 2024 Moore was awarded the Thornton Wilder Prize for Translation by the American Academy of Arts and Letters. He is the former chair of the PEN/Heim Translation Fund and has a PhD in Italian from New York University. For many years he was also an interpreter at the United Nations and a full-time staff member of the Permanent Mission of Italy to the United Nations.